# PYRAMIDION

## About the Author

G. E. Newbegin is married with two children and lives in Melbourne, Australia. He has a keen interest in technology, and as such, works in business-to-business IT sales for a day job, focusing primarily on Enterprise Cybersecurity.

When not working, he enjoys spending time with his family, reading (including comics and manga), writing, playing video games, and seeing just how deep the YouTube rabbit hole really is…

www.genewbegin.com<br>
facebook.com/GENewbegin<br>
Twitter: @madcapsules

# PYRAMIDION

G.E. Newbegin

www.genewbegin.com

Copyright © 2021 G.E. Newbegin
Print Edition

G.E. Newbegin asserts the moral right to be identified as the author of this work

ISBN eBook: 978-0-6451882-0-2
ISBN Print (paperback): 978-0-6451882-1-9
ISBN Print (hardcover): 978-0-6451882-2-6

Written by G.E. Newbegin
Cover Illustration and Design by Simon Sherry

This novel is a work of fiction. The names, characters and incidents portrayed in it are the work of the author's imagination. Any resemblance to actual persons, living or dead, events or localities is entirely coincidental.

All rights reserved. No part of this publication may be reproduced, distributed or transmitted in any form or by any means, or stored in a database or retrieval system, without the prior written permission of the publisher.

*Dedicated to my father, Ian Newbegin; my inspiration for everything. May he rest in peace.*

# PROLOGUE

Dion Wexler smiled grimly as he regarded the cage, finally able to look upon what he had summoned. Or perhaps summoned was the wrong word – kidnapped or abducted were likely more appropriate. It had taken years of study, hard work, and more than a modicum of treachery to get to where he was today... the beginning of the end. But it wasn't the apocalypse he was chasing – he wasn't that trite, nor was he self-loathing. He simply craved truth. And, like many men before him, he craved power. Absolute, unrelenting power.

He'd known for a long while that the world wasn't quite as it seemed. There was something missing in the "now" that hadn't been missing in the past. At first, he had thought it was faith – the Egyptians believed in the gods and the power of the almighty Pharaoh, and so they built glorious monuments to them. The people of Easter Island had thought their land to be so special that it needed to be guarded by great stone golems, eternally looking inward. The Greeks lived in fear and awe of the Olympians.

In his younger years, Dion had studied these religions, and always came to the same conclusion: humanity had spent eons living side-by-side with the divine… and then it all ended. The gods had abandoned humankind. Everywhere he looked, every culture, every continent, everywhere, without fail – the gods were no longer present… but people still had faith. The Bible, the Talmud, the Quran, the Bhagavad Gita – regardless of personal persuasion, faith told the stories of the gods that once lived among us.

He racked his brain for years, travelled to the ends of the Earth and back, spoken with scores of scholars, investigated thousands of tombs, examined many a dusty book of forgotten lore. Over years, via some secret organisations with which he'd come to be associated, he'd discovered the truth. But he didn't want to just understand it – he wanted to see it and live it for himself. But more than that – he wanted it *for* himself.

And now, he stood in a cold, dark room, empty but for a large, oppressively heavy-looking cage in its centre, tables stacked with books lining the walls.

The thing in the cage was difficult to see – the room was dark, and inside the cage was darker, but there was clearly movement there. And breathing… The loud, laboured breathing of something very large.

He struck at the cage with the black cane he held in his left hand, and the subsequent clanging echoed throughout the room. Yet strangely, the creature trapped in the cage did not strike out. In fact, it barely moved, and remained silent.

"It seems to be intelligent, as well it should be," said Dion, motioning to another man standing in the shadows to the right of the cage. "It knows it's trapped for now – evaluating its options. Do you know what language they speak?"

The other man shook his head. "I've never actually seen one before," he replied. His voice had a heavy South Asian accent. "I should recognise the language if you could make it talk. That is… if they still speak the same language, of course. These ancient languages haven't been spoken on Earth in thousands of years; who's to say things aren't the same… where he comes from?"

Dion sighed. In truth, he had been wondering the same thing. Supposedly, thousands of years had passed since these creatures had walked the Earth. Why would he expect that their language had not evolved, mutated… changed? Even his own mother tongue, English, had changed dramatically in just the last few hundred years. He was no linguist. That was why he had brought his colleague.

And how could he make it talk? Just walk up to the cage and say "Hi"? The idea seemed ridiculous.

He lit a cigarette, drawing deeply through the filter, and leaned back on the heavy desk behind him. He watched the end of the cigarette as the embers quickly burned the tobacco and the paper that surrounded it, leaving a red and black stump. Exhaling, he flicked the cigarette away and stood up. It was now or never.

He walked up to the cage and raised his right hand in

greeting. "Hi," he said, then cringed. He shook his head at his own stupidity.

The caged creature didn.t react. It just stood and looked at him. Dion stared back. He really didn't know what he expected – deep inside he had been hoping it spoke English, and that it would simply greet him in return, but of course he knew that was impossible.

As he turned away, a deep voice rang out behind him.

*"Ma-inim ensi-nata este. Enlil-ropur simsala-et es."*

The voice was guttural and choral, like a group of people speaking at once, a disharmony. It almost sounded as if the throat that uttered the words had more than one voice box – and perhaps it did? Regardless, it was not a voice that Dion would soon forget.

The room fell deathly silent as Dion turned to face his colleague.

"Well?"

"It sounds like Sumerian," the man replied.

"Can you talk to it?"

"I think so." He walked up to the cage, and spoke timidly to the entity in the cage, in a language that sounded not dissimilar.

And it spoke to him in return.

The man turned towards Dion. "It wants to know why it's here."

"Good," he replied. "Tell it why, then. And make sure it knows that I'm the one that holds its sigil, and *I'm* in charge."

# CHAPTER ONE

"Why is it that when I want to go on holiday, every idiot and his dog gets on the freeway?" Luke cursed at the traffic, annoyed that it had once again come to a standstill. He'd been weaving between cars in an attempt to find that magical lane that was faster than the others, but now he was trapped, and he was frustrated and annoyed. He watched as the cars in the lane he had just abandoned passed him by.

"Calm down. Don't drive like a maniac." His wife, Danielle, looked at him from the front passenger seat. "Whichever way you look at it, we're on holiday, so there's no need to stress."

"I know," Luke replied with a sigh. "I just want to get there!"

They'd only been driving for an hour, heading down to the beach for a well-deserved family getaway. It was their first for several years – the first since the birth of their daughter, Ellen, who was sleeping peacefully in her booster chair in the back seat. Usually this road was clear – it was a freeway, after all, and it led away from the city – but today roadworks were slowing things down considerably. It wouldn't be so bad if he didn't drive so much for his day job.

Driving was anathema to Luke. He used to enjoy it, when he was in his twenties and only had to drive locally, but he was older now, with larger responsibilities and a well-paid job that he needed to keep to pay the bills. Except that job was on the other side of the city, and the commute took him up to two hours… each way. Sure, he could take a train, but as a salesperson, he needed access to his car, so… every day, he bit the bullet. Every day, he braved the freeway carpark in order to get to the office on time.

It wasn't so bad at first, but it had eventually begun to wear him down, especially because the company didn't allow for flexibility with regards to remote working. Even with the ubiquity of smartphones, tablets and notebook PCs, and widespread Wi-Fi, there still existed companies that expected its employees to be tethered to their desks when not in front of customers. This was further compounded by the fact that Luke had a minor disability – retinitis pigmentosa – a deformation of the retina that made it hard for him to see in low light, so he needed to get home early. This was, of course, a good thing, because it meant he would miss rush hour. You take the good with the bad.

He was lucky, though. Many that suffered from the same affliction had it much worse. Retinitis pigmentosa could severely reduce peripheral vision, eventually resulting in tunnel vision and, later, total blindness. In many cases, vision would simply decay over the years, but for Luke, who'd had the condition his whole life, it had never gotten any worse… at least, not yet.

It was still early afternoon, but he'd had enough of driving, and given this was his holiday, he really hadn't wanted to drive in the first place, so he continued to swear at the situation as he rolled the car slowly forward.

Things cleared up once they passed the roadworks, and they continued on their way at a speed more appropriate to freeway travel. Luke let out the breath he had been holding and pushed back into his chair, relaxing his grip on the steering wheel. The tension caused by the traffic was behind him for the moment.

He looked at his wife. "That's better. Hopefully it stays like this the rest of the way."

He'd met Dani at university some fifteen years prior. They had both been studying psychology and had hit it off immediately. Given psychology was less popular among males than females, he was actually the only male in his group of friends – not that it really mattered. His wasn't the "traditional" university experience you saw in movies – he simply went to school, met with his friends, went to class, and went home. Kind of boring, really. He'd never been a party guy. He preferred the quiet home life.

At the time, he'd never thought of dating Dani. Not at first. He was somewhat insecure, and had low self-esteem, and felt she was well beyond his reach. Half Japanese and half Australian, he felt he looked too awkward to be attractive to an Italian-Australian beauty like Dani. He went the whole three years without asking her out once. He was content just to be her friend.

After graduation, Luke and his friends went their separate ways, and he hadn't expected to see Dani again, having learned over the years that some friendships were transient. Even so, he was still sad to see her go on that last day. In the months that passed, he kicked himself for never having let her know how he felt. But when the whole group was reunited for their formal graduation ceremony just under a year later, he was still too shy to ask her out.

It turned out he never had to summon the courage, because she did the work for him, asking him out to see the latest *Avengers* movie the following week. He said yes, they went on a date, and the rest, as they say, was history.

Looking at her now, he realised maturity had sharpened her features, and without the round softness of youth, she was strikingly beautiful. While Luke felt lame to use the cliche that Dani "completed him", he really believed it. She kept him on the straight and narrow. Even when they had arguments, he couldn't bear to go a day without speaking with her. More than that, he couldn't go a day without telling her he loved her. It was his thing.

"I love you, Dani," he said now, wistfully. He was

soft-hearted, and every time he said it, he truly meant it. "You're so sweet," she replied, smiling, flipping through the pages of a *Woman's Weekly* magazine.

Ellen started whimpering in the backseat.

"Oh, what's wrong Ellie, my little pumpkin?" asked Luke, looking in the rear-view mirror. Ellie was wriggling in her chair, crying out and screwing up her face. She was a little over four years old, and her personality was starting to come out. She was probably just annoyed that she had been woken up, and it wouldn't be too long before she would drift off to sleep again. Her eyes were still droopy, and her head was lolling. Luke could see the shine of drool at the edge of her mouth.

"Oh, sweetheart – I love you too!" Luke beamed.

Dani laughed.

All was well with the world. Becoming a father had taught Luke that not only did children change your life in significant ways, but they really changed the way you experienced emotions. He realised that prior to having Ellie – a child of his own creation – it had been impossible to understand the feeling of love that a parent has for their child. He'd often heard his friends saying this as they became parents, one by one, and he had laughed it off. But they were right. His heart was full. He couldn't imagine life without her. Without either of them.

In fact, two weeks after bringing Ellen home from the hospital, Luke had called his mother to tell her he loved her and to apologise "for being such a little shit as a child", as he put it. This memory was now tinged with pain, as he had lost his mother three short months later. She had been young, only in her sixties, but she'd had a stroke, and it had taken its toll. It also didn't help that the stroke had been not long after Luke's father passed from cancer. She probably didn't see much reason to hold on once she'd lost the love of her life, and she just slowly deteriorated... It had been painful to watch, and Luke was ashamed to admit that he had been relieved when she had finally passed – the stress of a family member requiring constant care is often overlooked, but it's immense. Yet to lose both parents within such a short span of time? It was agony. Afterwards, he put all of his love and energy into his own little family. They were all he had left.

And yet the truth was, after his mother had passed, life just... went on. The world kept turning regardless of the interests of the multitudes that scurried across its surface. His pain was his to bear, but he wasn't alone.

Things were in a good place now. Luke was an only child, so he received virtually everything by way of his parents' wills, and as a result he was secure financially. Plus, of course, he had a loving wife, a gorgeous little daughter, and now – finally – he was heading off on holiday.

He cursed again as he slowed to approach another traffic jam, the result of further roadworks. He checked the rear-view mirror once more. Ellen had settled into sleep again. He smiled.

What he *didn't* notice was the 18-wheeler that was bearing down on their car at speed, flashing its headlights.

# CHAPTER TWO

As a child, Luke's affliction had taken its toll. There aren't many children that aren't afraid of the dark, but for a child that can't see much of anything when the lights go out, it's even worse. In low-light situations, the eyes slowly adapt, but there's still a distinct lack in clarity that comes with night vision. As a result, the brain tries to fill in the gaps, and it's the child's own active imagination that creates the "monsters under the bed".

For Luke, and many others like him, any kind of night time clarity would be a bonus. Where most people can make out most their surroundings in the dark, Luke could effectively only detect the presence of light. All he'd been able to see at night since he was a child was essentially a blotchy field of light and dark greys against a black backdrop. To deal with this, he had always needed a night light in his room, as well as a bright portable light source – not a flashlight, as the tight beam would only exacerbate the tunnel vision effect. These days, he would often carry an LED lantern to navigate his surroundings when he needed to go to the bathroom at night.

However, this method had its own problems. He'd

effectively find himself walking through a bubble of light, surrounded by deep blackness – a complete loss of peripheral vision in low-light situations. It was frightening for him as a child. In fact, he was still somewhat uncomfortable at night even as an adult, although after years of experience he could generally navigate his way to the bathroom in the dark. But as a child it had meant a lot of sleepless nights with a sheet over his head, afraid to peer out into the unknown, more content surrounded by the unambiguous blackness that covering his head would provide. At least he knew it was only him under the sheet.

In addition, he was short-sighted, and had needed glasses from a young age. He received the usual ribbing from his peers, being called "four-eyes" and "nerd" and all manner of unfriendly things. Kids could be so damned mean. That said, through later experience he'd learned that people in general can be mean, not just kids. However, this childhood bullying left him shy and insecure, and as such he liked to keep to himself. He didn't make a lot of friends, but this wasn't really a problem, it was more of a choice – he preferred quality over quantity, choosing to make strong connections with just a few people.

He'd befriended one of these people, Oscar Baldwin, late in his high school years. Oscar – or Oz, as he preferred to be called – was never an A-grade student (and neither was Luke, for that matter), and when he finally finished high school and was given the option to go on to higher education, he had chosen to forge his own path.

Oz was a short, wiry teenager, full of life and loved by all – very much the opposite of Luke, who was tall, a little on the chubby side, and broody. They'd been at the same school for years, but never really got to talking – until after school one stormy day, on the bus.

It was one of those incredibly oppressive storms, with dark, heavy clouds that almost blotted out the sun. This caused some issues for Luke, who was struggling to navigate the seats on the bus in the low light. Unknowingly, he was about to plonk himself down beside Tony Carlisle, captain of the football team and all-round prick. To be clear, he wasn't about to sit on the seat, but on the sports bag that Tony had put on that seat, of which Luke wasn't aware. Tony looked at him with a wry grimace. The air chilled and the kids around them stiffened with the promise of confrontation… and an arm shot out to grab Luke and guide him into a seat in the next row. Oz's hand.

"Wrong seat, Luke my boy," Oz said matter-of-factly. "Come sit over here with me."

They got to talking, and the people on the bus returned to their usual hustle and bustle, while Tony returned to scowling at passers-by out the window.

It turned out that Luke and Oz had a lot in common – music, initially, then video games, books, their sense of humour, and so much more besides. Luke had simply respected the fact that this well-liked member of the "cool clique" had chosen not to be an asshole like the rest of them, and simply wanted to be friends with everyone – including him. At first, they nodded to each other when they passed in the school grounds and chatted on the bus trip home, but over time, they gravitated towards each other more frequently.

After high school, Luke went on to university, while Oz became an apprentice electrician, but they remained friends, and grew closer. So much closer, in fact, that now, twelve years later, Oz was the only friend that Luke still had from his high school days – and, more accurately, the only true friend that Luke had at all. They didn't see each other as frequently, of course (particularly because Luke was now married with a child), but they still hung out most Friday nights over a beer and some video games, each knowing much more about the other than any person had any right to know.

Apart from his friendship with Oz, school was fairly uneventful for Luke. He was a solid student, but never really excelled at anything. He loved history and science in particular, but he wasn't dedicated enough to study either of these subjects as much as he perhaps should have.

He was terrible at sports, mostly due to his eyesight. Of course, he needed to wear glasses in order to participate in ball sports, but more than that, most sports were outdoor affairs. A further complication of his affliction was that he was highly susceptible to light, which often hurt his eyes. As an adult, he almost never went outside without his prescription sunglasses, but his parents couldn't afford these when he was younger, so he preferred to sit on the sidelines during PE classes, squinting as other children played sports.

Again, this led to the children labelling him with all sorts of terrible names, and he often felt left out, but try as he might, there was nothing he could do – it was better to watch from the sidelines than be hit in the face with a basketball over and over again.

Instead of study and sports, Luke invested his time in reading and video games, preferring to live in someone else's world than his own. His parents always saw these activities as positive, helping to expand his imagination and vocabulary, and as he grew older he made online friends, so at least he had access to some form of social activity. Besides, he had few other options.

When the time came to choose what he wanted to do with his life, Luke was unsure. Perhaps modern society gave young people too many options – certainly, Luke found the range of choice overwhelming. He had a job at a local movie theatre, which he loved because he could watch most new movies, and it really wasn't difficult work, but he didn't see any future there.

However, he was at a loss for career options. He wasn't exceptional at anything, really, and had no desire to do anything in particular, though he did like people watching. He liked to try to understand what made them tick. So, he chose psychology – a science that didn't require exceptional grades, but which seemed to fit with his interests. Not that he really knew what he would do with it when the time came – that was *future* Luke's problem.

It was an interesting course, but certainly not too taxing. Sadly, he didn't really see where he could take it – while he enjoyed the concepts that were presented, he felt that most of what was being taught was simply the current zeitgeist in the industry, soon to be overtaken by the next big idea. Nobody could really be defined by any specific psychological concept – in his opinion – and his classes were simply full of people arguing the merits of the latest research they'd uncovered in their studies. It really felt like a contest of egos, which wasn't something he enjoyed.

However, he'd also chosen human biology as a minor, and that was something he could really enjoy – there were really no maybes when it came to biology; it was pretty cut-and-dried. I guess he was a man of facts and figures – he didn't like speculation.

By the time his course came to an end, though, Luke still had no idea what to do next. He definitely didn't want to continue his studies, but neither did he want to pursue any kind of social support role.

His university years came and went, and Luke still found himself working at the same old movie theatre he'd been working at for years. There still wasn't much future potential – not that "theatre manager" didn't have its own kind of allure; it just wasn't something he wanted to pursue.

Somehow, through a series of trial and error, he found himself in a sales role. While still not a job that made him happy, it kept him flush with cash, which was a good alternative to real happiness. The problem is, it was also exceedingly stressful. Sales was a rollercoaster – Luke might hit his target one month, but as soon as the new month ticked over, he was back at zero, and chasing a new number. He hated it. There was always a target on his back, and there was always someone out there that could replace him at the drop of a hat. It was horrendous. Worse than that, though, it was full of giant egos, most of them in positions of power. It wasn't easy taking orders from people he didn't respect.

Of course, all that cash lining his pockets could be traded for bottles of stress-release potions – he preferred single malt whisky and red wine, himself. It wasn't a healthy trade, but it worked for him, for a while. The years came and went. The bottles stacked up.

Eventually, he came to notice that his drinking was more than just a casual tipple. It came to the point that he felt he needed to drink every night after work "just to take the edge off". Without the drink in his blood, he felt tense… on edge. He needed it for release.

Eventually, as his relationship with Dani grew stronger, it also inevitably became more serious. From the perspective of their relationship, it was time to make a commitment, and soon they were married. With regards to his job, he needed security and consistency.

As a result, he put his nose down and concentrated on his work, setting his ambitions higher than his personal desires for fun and freedom, and he set about progressing along his career path... but that only created more stress, which led to more drinking. It was a vicious cycle of work–drink–work harder–drink harder.

And then his father was diagnosed with stage 4 prostate cancer, and the world stopped.

Luke had grown up in a very stable family – his parents hadn't separated and he was never abused or treated poorly. Yes, he was an only child, but he hadn't been overly spoiled and he had always felt loved. So, when his father's cancer progressed from stage 2 to stage 4 virtually overnight and he was given less than six months to live, suddenly everything changed perspective. Work wasn't so important anymore.

Luckily, Luke's customers liked him, and while he shifted his focus from work to family, the sales continued to come in and he never felt at risk. He did feel somewhat guilty at times, due to his solid work ethic, but he always knew his position was safe. However, the stress of losing his father took a toll on him, and his drinking increased.

Dani did her best to support him during this time, but she knew it was weighing heavily on him. They had argued from time to time in the past, but it had never been serious. Now, Luke would lose his temper without warning, which would often be so extreme he was afraid of what he might be capable of.

Then one day, while sitting in his office working on a complex tender, Luke received a phone call that he'd been dreading. His father's condition had worsened. He was still alive, and awake, but unresponsive. Luke was advised to drop everything and go straight to the hospital.

So it was, two days later, that his father passed away peacefully in a hospital bed, with Luke holding his father's left hand, and his mother sitting across from him, holding her husband's right hand.

There was no ECG beeping. No flatline. Luke's father wasn't using a respirator. But it was clear when he passed. He'd been lying motionless in his bed for the last two days, but his breathing had been loud and consistent. In those last few minutes, his breathing slowed, becoming more laboured, and louder. The sounds of the mucous that had collected in the back of his throat gave each breath a desperate rasping sound – the death rattle that many refer to when they talk of a loved one passing away slowly.

And then it stopped… and his father was no more.

Grief was sudden and severe, and Luke wept openly while his mother wailed at her loss. But the world kept turning, and outside the window, people continued to scurry about, oblivious to what was happening within this hospital room, unaware that, for Luke and his mother, the world was suddenly a different place…

Time marched on. The funeral was held, the house was cleaned and Luke's father's belongings were redistributed, and after a short period of stunned vertigo, everything seemed to fall into place. Even his mother found a new love in cross-stitch, which kept her busy and her mind distracted from the silence at home.

For a while, things could have even have been considered "good". Luke settled back into work, and soon enough, Dani fell pregnant. This, in itself, stirred new feelings of responsibility within Luke, and he resolved to quit alcohol. How could he be a responsible father if he wasn't even responsible for his own health?

Not long after, though, he received another phone call – this time, his mother was the one in a hospital bed. When he arrived, she was sitting up and talking, but he knew something was wrong. Every movement was laboured, every word slurred.

The previous night, while she had been entertaining a friend for dinner, she had suffered a stroke, and was taken by ambulance to the hospital. While the stroke was serious, it could be treated, thankfully, but the damage had been done. The doctors weren't sure she would ever return to the way she was, and she was transferred to a respite home.

This caused enough problems of its own – for one, it was prohibitively expensive. In order to keep her room,

Luke needed to sell the family home – the very house in which he had grown up, and which contained more than twenty years of memories – as well as most of his mother's belongings. There were legal ramifications, plus he was the primary contact for any and all issues that the nurses encountered. Months of his time were taken up with paperwork and admin, and all the while, Dani's belly expanded as their child grew within her.

Eventually, Ellen was born, and the world changed even further. Suddenly, Luke was a father, and the light that emanated from his daughter was invigorating. Luke was an atheist in principle, although he'd been raised Catholic, but he tended to appreciate the spiritual and the divine, and his daughter was clearly an angel.

His daughter taught him the value of real love and concern – most new parents would admit to waking up panicking at night, rushing over to the cot just to make sure the baby was still alive. Nobody is prepared for parenthood, but most people would do anything they could to protect their children once they enter their lives.

This experience opened his eyes to his own childhood, and made him go visit his mother one day shortly after Ellie was born. He just wanted to thank her for everything she had done for him, and to apologise for never having really appreciated it all until now. It was the first time he had seen his mother smile – truly smile – since the stroke.

Since she had been living in the home, his mother

wasn't the same woman he remembered. Now she just looked like an elderly Japanese woman. She'd lost her spark; she looked like an empty husk. It broke his heart to watch her struggle to speak, and strained it even further when all she could say was "if only I jusss didn wake up t'morrow…" He could see she was ashamed that the words came out wrong, but there was nothing she could do. The words were slurred and forced, and much slower than her usual cadence.

To top all this off, she was now regularly restricted to a wheelchair, her legs failing her more often than not. Day after day, her health would slowly decline… And then one day, three months or so later, she just didn't wake up one morning. Luke was forlorn that he hadn't been there when she passed, but he also felt some relief. It had been hard enough to watch his father's final moments – once was enough for a lifetime.

After the funeral, and after all the administrative work had been completed, there was nothing much left for Luke but his wife and child. For the next few months, he often found himself sitting alone, contemplating the past and what he had lost. He tried to apply his mind back to his work, but he had no love for that anymore – for the most part, he just felt it wasn't worth it. For all he knew, these may have been his final few months on the planet – or maybe they weren't. Either way, there was much more to life than working hard to line someone else's pockets, particularly if it didn't make him happy.

Thankfully, as the sole beneficiary of his parents' last will and testament, he was now financially very stable – far from rich, but he certainly didn't need to worry about work anymore. Day to day, he continued to do his job, more out of habit than anything else, but in his mind he envisioned an early retirement. He'd give it a few more years, and then he'd take a look at how he could structure his finances without a stable job, and still manage to pay the bills and put his daughter through school.

And now, several years later, Ellie was a toddler, and she was beginning to settle, and Luke was still yet to make the decision to retire. However, with things more settled, he realised this was the perfect opportunity to finally get out and do something for themselves, so he began to plan a short trip to the beach. They'd spent too long being insular and withdrawn. In fact, they'd never taken a trip as a family. It was time to get out and do something. Nothing too far away, but more than a day trip. The family deserved it, and Dani also needed the rest. She was the only thing holding him together.

# CHAPTER THREE

Luke woke from a deep sleep, his eyelids heavy, his mind a cloudy mess. He found himself on a large bed in an open white room, mostly plain except for a window to his right. It smelled at once chemically clean and horrible.

A hospital room.

There was nobody else present, and the light streaming in through the window suggested it was a gorgeous, bright day outside.

For some reason, he couldn't see what was on the left side of the room – something obscured the vision of his left eye, but he was too groggy to understand.

Despite his confusion about his location, he didn't have the energy to move to investigate – his eyelids kept drooping uncontrollably. He felt the proverbial walls closing in. Soon enough, he drifted back into unconsciousness.

He woke like this on several occasions, at distinctly different times of the day, judging by the angle of the light coming through the window. Then again, given his uncertainly about the amount of time that elapsed, he may have been waking up on different days... but it didn't matter much. Nothing really mattered. Each time he woke, he barely had enough time to take in his surroundings before passing out again, and no opportunity to gather his thoughts.

On one occasion, he saw a nurse in the room going about her business. She didn't notice that he was awake, and soon he was out again.

Another time, he saw a young man in a blue hospital uniform enter his room pushing a large metal trolley, but Luke couldn't see the items on top.

Eventually, he woke for longer periods that spanned minutes as opposed to seconds. During this time, he was able to make more sense of his surroundings and his situation.

The last thing he could remember was being in the car with Dani and Ellie, on their way to the beach… and then he remembered the truck with its flashing headlights. Loud noises had filled his head, but he couldn't remember anything beyond that point. Had the truck hit them? Where were Dani and Ellie – were they OK?

As these thoughts rushed into his mind, his head began to throb. The pain was excruciating, like a blade pushing through his eye socket and scraping at the back of his skull. Dizzy, he put a hand to his head, only to note that it was heavily bandaged.

He raised his other hand, and began to investigate the bandage with both hands, noting that it covered most of the back his head, and was also wrapped around his left eye and ear, which explained why he was unable to see the left side of the room. He poked at the bandages there. They were softly padded, and he felt no pain.

Slowly, he turned his head to the left, but it wasn't much help – he still couldn't see anything past his nose and the bandages. Plus, his neck hurt. The stress of movement and his concern caught up with him, and he fell once again into unconsciousness.

When he woke again, someone was standing over him. He was shocked, and he noticed that she was shocked as well – perhaps she'd stood over him on other occasions with no response.

He didn't know this woman, but based on her white uniform he assumed she was a nurse.

"Oh, you're awake," she exclaimed. She had a thick African accent. "Great timing."

Luke struggled to raise himself up so that he could get a better look at her, but she placed her hand on his chest.

"Don't strain yourself on my account. Just relax. I can't be here long, but let me tell you this. Not all is as it seems."

She was a strikingly attractive woman. Her skin was dark and unblemished, and her hair was a thick mop of dusty blonde. Not natural, Luke assumed, but it suited her perfectly. Her hair was also quite curly, and the only thing he could think was *that must be a hell of a lot of work*.

"My hair? Oh, it's no big deal," she laughed, raising

her right hand to touch it.

Luke cringed. He must have spoken out loud.

"Anyway, I must be going before the nurses come back. I guess I'll see you 'round."

With that, she turned and walked out of the room.

Not long after, someone else entered the room. Luke could tell they were there, because he heard footsteps as they entered, but they stood to his left so were blocked by the bandage. He still lacked the energy to turn and look.

"Sorry mate, I guess you can't see me here." It was his old friend Oz. He moved around to the other side of the bed and smiled down at his friend. "Glad to see you're awake, finally."

Luke beamed back at his friend, glad to see a familiar face. "How... how long have I been here?"

"It's... been a while, Luke. Probably... four or five weeks since the accident."

Luke's mind swam with confusion. He stared up at the ceiling. Four or five weeks? How could that be? Where were Dani and Ellie? The edges of his vision began to darken.

And he blacked out again.

The next time he awoke, it was later in the afternoon. The sun was going down, and the light from the window barely lit the room, but the nurses had yet to turn on the overhead lights. This made it very difficult for Luke to see – most of the room was a dark shade of brown or grey.

However, there was a silhouette in the window. It was the shape of a man, looking out at the view... whatever view it was. Realising that Luke was awake, the man turned, but remained close to the window.

"Awake again, I see." He was very well spoken, and his tenor demanded respect. "You don't know me, but I know you – I have kept an eye on you and... your family... for a long time."

He walked towards the bed, standing over Luke, looking down on him. Luke could make out some of his features, but he couldn't quite see his face clearly. Given the amount of light in the room, it was a struggle for Luke to see much of anything, and the man's face remained in shadow. All he could tell was that he was a tall man with a solid build, but Luke did notice that he was exceptionally well dressed, with a button-up shirt and tie, and a black overcoat.

"I did not expect you to survive that crash, but survive you did... and good for you." He patted Luke on the chest, which seemed somewhat condescending.

"What are you doing here?" Luke asked, his voice hoarse. He didn't think this man was a friend – perhaps he was from the company that owned the truck, scoping out the damage. "Who are you?"

"Oh, that doesn't matter anymore," the man replied curtly. "Given the circumstances now, it probably never mattered – although I'm sure, given time, you'll disagree."

He turned and walked back to the window.

"None of *this* really matters, anyway," he said, gesturing to the window. "We created a world of distraction to keep our minds off the real truth – why are we here? Everyone outside this window thinks they have somewhere to be, something to do. Maybe a customer is yelling at them to find their stock, perhaps their wife is cheating on them – but viewed at a grand scale… From a *universal* scale… none of it matters. There's no power here… no *real* power, at least. Not anymore."

He sighed, and approached the door.

"Goodbye, Luke. You're not likely to see me again. I guess I just wanted to close the book as I open another."

Luke heard his footsteps fade as he walked away. He scratched his head. The man made no sense.

Soon, a beaming, heavyset nurse entered his vision.

"Who was that, love?" She asked, still smiling. "You had a visitor?"

She began to inspect his bandages without waiting for, or perhaps even expecting, an answer. "These have been on long enough. Time they came off, I think."

Luke reached up and grabbed her wrists. He wasn't being forceful; he just wanted her attention. "Where is my wife? Dani – and our daughter. Where are they?" he asked, straining to raise his head off the pillow.

The nurse's smile faltered for a moment, but then returned bigger than ever. "Oh, don't fuss yourself right now – you've been through enough," she replied.

"I'm *fine*," Luke asserted. "Where is my wife?"

"Mr Nixon." The nurse fussed with her hands as she backed away from the bed. "You really must rest."

"*Where are they?*" Luke demanded, wincing as he raised himself from the bed with his elbows.

At that, someone new rushed in front of him from the left side of the room – a man wearing a shirt and tie, with a white coat over the top. A doctor, Luke guessed. He moved to Luke's right-hand side, bypassing the nurse, and looked down at him.

"OK, Mr Nixon," he said, smiling gently. "It's time. Lie back and I'll explain."

The doctor waited until Luke was reclining once again, then took the next ten minutes to explain what had happened. The truck had hit Luke's car at high speed, its brakes having failed. Astronomically poor timing – not that that kind of failure ever has *good* timing. Given the congestion on the freeway at the time, it was a disaster of massive proportions. Ten cars had been destroyed by the time the truck came to rest. Twelve people lost their lives. Another eight were hospitalised.

Luke took some time to process this initial information. It didn't sound good. Luke's car was the first to be hit by the truck, and although the impact pushed the car over the barrier as the truck ploughed through, it had rolled several times into oncoming traffic, coming to rest on its side.

The doctor continued. Ellie had not survived the

initial impact. It was too much trauma for a child her size, but the doctor assured Luke that she had suffered very little.

Dani, on the other hand, had survived, and had been brought to the hospital along with Luke. But while Luke's condition had improved over the weeks, hers had not. The damage her brain had sustained required surgery, but during surgery complications had been encountered, and Dani had passed away in the second week after the accident – that was, three weeks ago.

"I'm very sorry," the doctor said. "I know this is a lot to take in. We are here for you, whatever you need." He turned to the nurse. "Let's give him some time to grieve."

Luke's head spun. After everything he'd been through, he knew he would never be whole again. In an instant, he'd lost everything. His grief was immense. He wailed and wept openly, crying out to the void as if he were the only person in the hospital.

LATER THAT DAY, after the tears had subsided, Luke stared numbly at the window. No thoughts entered his mind – he was drugged and damaged, and he simply stared at the light coming through the curtains. The contents of his skull felt like a ball of cotton wool.

The nurse who had visited him earlier crept nervously into view.

"I'm sorry, love," she said, "but do you mind if I take off those bandages now?" She smiled broadly – a maternal smile.

Luke sighed and lay back. It really didn't matter. He waved his hand in her direction. A gesture of submission. A white flag without the white flag.

The nurse pressed buttons beside the bed, and Luke felt the bed rising. Soon, he was almost sitting upright, and his head began to throb, though more gently, this time. He was awake now, no longer at risk of sudden unconsciousness.

Gingerly, the nurse began to pick at the bandage wrapped around his head, looking for the point at which it could be peeled away. She asked if Luke could raise his head off the pillow, and he obliged. Slowly, the nurse unwrapped the bandage, and Luke experienced both a release of pressure, and a drop in temperature.

With the bandage off, Luke was shocked to note that he still couldn't see from his left eye, but he soon realised that the eye was still covered by a thick, soft patch, which the nurse soon removed. He tested the eyelid, felt the gunk pull apart as it opened, and then bright light from the window filtered in, blinding him. He assumed the eye had been covered for five weeks now, so it understandably took a while to adjust.

Soon enough, though, he could see again, blurry at first, but clearer as time progressed. The left side of the room came into view for the first time. Unsurprisingly, it was similar to the rest of the room – plain, white, and dull. There was a door there, of course, and an armchair for the few visitors that may have come along while he was asleep, watching him as he slept. There was also a side table with a glass of water placed on top. He wondered if that had been sitting there for five weeks, untouched, or if it had been placed there recently for the great unveiling of the eye. He had a feeling the nurses replaced the glass daily, perhaps wondering why it was always full.

His head, now exposed for the first time in weeks, felt wrong. The skin felt soft and sensitive, and he knew some of it was regrowth. He asked the nurse to show him.

"No worries, love," she responded cheerfully. "It's healed up nicely. You'll see."

She walked to the back of the room, rifled through a drawer, and returned with a small mirror. Holding it up to his face, she asked, "So – what do you think?"

Luke wasn't sure what to think. Where his face had been unblemished in the past, he now had a deep, jagged scar that went from the middle of his forehead, across his left eye, and down to the rear of the left-hand side of his jaw. The skin was pink, but the repair was fairly clean – the hospital had done a fine job stitching his face back together. With time, he assumed it might heal to little more than a crease. With time.

There was also a U-shaped scar that circled his left ear. Hair was already growing back around it, but clearly his head had been shaved at some point. In fact, his face was clean shaven, so the nurses had clearly been tending to him.

"You needed surgery," came a voice from the door. It was the doctor who had spoken to him earlier in the day. "You were bleeding internally, which is never a good thing, but even worse in the brain. We put you in an induced coma so you could heal."

Luke looked away, tears welling in his eyes.

"And Dani? Why did I survive and she... didn't?"

"Well," the doctor replied, with a deep sigh, "you both needed surgery for the same reason, actually. However, her bleeding was much more profound, and required more time. We did what we could, but the damage was too severe... We couldn't stop the bleeding. She'd been in an induced coma as well, since she came to the hospital, so I can tell you that she felt no pain. She passed quietly during the night."

He watched Luke for a while silently. After a few moments, Luke looked away, staring toward the window. Nothing mattered anyway. Not anymore.

Luke spent the next few days in much the same way – staring at the light from the window, thinking back on the last ten years or so with Dani, and the short amount of time he had had with Ellie.

He didn't cry much, to his surprise. Not because he wasn't entirely defeated, but simply because he felt no desire to. It wasn't going to change his situation. Crying wouldn't bring them back. His heart could hurt no more than it already did.

Still, perhaps he ought to cry more than he did. It made him feel a little guilty.

His despair, though, was pervasive. He didn't want to eat, he didn't want to drink, and he didn't want visitors. This last stance was most beneficial, because no visitors came. Day after day, he sat in his bed, staring out the window, very much alone.

Sometimes, one of the nurses would ask if he wanted to watch TV. He'd simply respond with a terse "no" and continue staring out the window. That was as much of a response as they could ask for – he rarely spoke otherwise. The only other time he roused was when the night nurse came offering spirits. Luke was only supposed to have small drink, but the nurse knew his story and occasionally left him a large glass of whisky, from which he drank slowly. Sadly, this didn't happen every night.

One day, the big smiley nurse came to tell him that he would be withdrawing from his meds over the next couple of days, and would be going home soon. She seemed to think this would brighten his spirits, but there was nothing he wanted less. To be honest, he would have preferred to stay at the hospital indefinitely – and he certainly would have preferred to maintain his regimen of extremely strong painkillers.

Still, he had known this day would come. He hadn't really needed his meds for a while now. The pain had faded, replaced by grief. Truth be told, he hadn't really felt like he needed to still be in the hospital for a while, either, but he didn't want to go home. He wasn't quite ready for that.

On the same day, Oz came to visit. He carried a plastic bag at his side and a backpack slung over his shoulder.

"Luke, how you doing?" he asked excitedly as he entered the room. "I hear you're off home soon – you gotta be stoked about that! Here, I brought you something to celebrate."

He handed Luke the plastic bag. It was heavier than Luke had expected, and he lowered it onto the bed, glowering at Oz. His scowl faded when he looked into the bag. It contained a six-pack of pre-mixed whisky and cola, one of Luke's favourite cheap drinks.

"Oh wow – do the nurses know you brought these?"

"No," Oz replied with a cheeky wink. "Do they need to? Besides, you go home soon anyway."

Luke cracked open one of the cans and took a long draught from it. The flavour relaxed him instantly, probably because it reminded him of old times. Simpler times. Times when his wife and child were still alive.

At that thought – and perhaps because it was the first time he'd seen a familiar face since he'd found out the truth – Luke felt his heart flutter, followed by a wave of intense emotion, and he wept uncontrollably once again.

Later, having finished the six-pack between them, Oz apologised for not visiting as much as he would have liked – his work was too busy right now.

"So what are your plans, Luke?" he asked. "Are you going back to work... or are you going to take more time?"

Work. Luke hadn't even thought about it. In fact, he'd completely forgotten about it. How could he go back to work now, given that his life had completely changed?

"I don't know," he replied with a sigh. "I don't think I'll go back. Maybe ever. I just don't know yet."

The logistics company that owned the truck that caused the accident had recently offered Luke a payout, and although he hadn't yet accepted it, he was considering it. The amount on offer was substantial – more than enough for him to retire on, in addition to the money he'd received after his parents had passed. He no longer really needed a job, but he had no idea what he might do with his time. He wasn't ready to think about it.

"Alright, man, that's fair enough," Oz replied, his face taut with concern. "And... what about when you go home? Do you... do you wanna stay with us for a while?"

Oz had recently moved in with Tammy, his girlfriend of two years. She was nice enough, but Luke didn't want to get in the way. In truth, he wanted to be alone. For one thing, he didn't want to be in the way, or to feel like some kind of invalid to be bubble-wrapped and tiptoed around.

But even more than that… he definitely didn't want to live with a happy couple. He didn't want to watch them still have what he had lost. Part of him wanted to wallow in his sorrow. A *big* part of him, if he was honest.

"No… but thanks for the offer." He sighed. "I guess I'll go home."

Oz took his backpack off his shoulder and put it on the bed. It was clearly brand new.

"I, uh… got you some things," he said in a low voice. "I wasn't sure if the clothes you had were… you know… still OK to wear."

He opened the bag and pulled out clothes, underwear, and some socks and shoes, all of which had Kmart tags hanging off them.

"It's all cheap stuff, nothing fancy. Just to get you home."

"Thanks, Oz." Luke was almost moved to tears. "You're a good friend. I really don't know what I'd do without you right now."

# CHAPTER FOUR

THE DISCHARGE PROCESS was simple, but Luke barely noticed. He was handed a bunch of documents, some of which needed to be signed immediately, others he could hold onto and return at a later date. These related to Dani and Ellie. He certainly wasn't prepared to look at those yet. In fact, he didn't really look at any of them. He just signed where the nurses told him to sign. They could have handed him anything.

He wore the clothes that Oz had given him, along with the backpack. It turned out Oz had made an extremely fortuitous decision when he purchased the clothes – the nurses had destroyed the clothes Luke was wearing when he was admitted, which had been cut from him in the ambulance on the way to the hospital. The new clothes didn't fit him well, but although he felt a little awkward, he barely gave himself a passing glance in the mirror before he left. It didn't matter.

Prior to leaving, he also discovered that the rest of his possessions had been in a drawer beside his bed the whole time – his wallet and keys (both of which had been handed in by the police after going through his car), his phone, which had also miraculously survived the crash and which he had been using in the hospital room for the last few days, and lastly... Dani's handbag. He put it in the backpack. This was another thing that could wait.

In a haze, he found himself slowly navigating the hospital wards, looking for the exit. He'd also apparently suffered a broken leg in the crash, which had mostly healed by the time he had woken from the coma. He still wore a compression bandage, though, and walked with a limp, but as it was now six weeks since the accident, he was mostly whole.

Mostly.

There was a lot of commotion in the hospital – people scurried about in all directions, as was to be expected. Some were quiet and polite, but most were in a hurry, stress evident in the lines on their faces. Luke fell in neither category – he was certainly in no hurry to get home, but he paid little to no attention to those around him. He simply walked, as if passing through a tornado that paid him little mind, jostling him from time to time when he wasn't quick enough to react.

After an eternity, he reached the hospital foyer. He sighed deeply, looking around. It was busy, but he noticed a row of empty seats, so he sat. He didn't know where his head was at. He didn't know what he wanted to do. All he knew was that he didn't want to go home.

Pulling out his phone, he decided to do something else that needed to be done – he needed to call his boss.

He found the number and pressed the call button.

His boss answered almost immediately. "Luke! How are you, mate? Are you back home already?"

"Gary," Luke responded, somewhat monotone. "Not yet. Just leaving the hospital. I just thought I'd let you know – I'm not coming back to work."

"You quitting? You don't need more time?"

"No." Luke was cold. Emotionless. "I think it's best that I just… finish up here. Thanks for your support to date. Let me know what you need from me, if anything." He hung up, shaking his head and sucking at his bottom lip at the bluntness of his actions.

He sat for a while, watching the rest of the world go about their business. He wasn't angry. He wasn't bitter. He knew it was nobody else's fault that he was in the position he was in… except maybe the truck driver. Even then, he still felt nothing towards that person, whoever it was. He just felt… empty.

He knew he had to leave soon. He couldn't sit in the hospital foyer forever.

Again, he looked at his phone, reluctantly selecting the Uber app. He entered his details, and let the app do the rest. Soon it let him know that his driver, a middle-aged guy named Phil, was a few minutes away in a silver Ford.

Slowly, Luke gathered his things and stood up, once again taking in his surroundings. Nobody paid him much attention, apart from a single elderly man passing by, dragging his IV equipment. He was dressed, if one could use that term, in a loose-fitting hospital gown which barely clung to his skeletal frame. As he ambled past Luke, he looked at him knowingly. Luke saw the years of anguish – the emptiness behind his eyes. When the man had passed, Luke made his way to exit the foyer, towards the drop-off zone outside the hospital.

It was a cool August afternoon, neither hot nor cold, and while there was blue sky and sunlight overhead, it was somewhat cloudy as well. A light breeze blew. Being the main entrance to the hospital, the air was full of the noise of people entering and exiting the hospital, and cars passing by, some honking their horns in frustration, but it may as well have been white noise – Luke paid it no attention. It wasn't long before the silver Ford pulled up in front of him. Luke opened the rear passenger door and climbed in.

His driver was a polite middle-aged man who left Luke to his own devices, allowing Luke to continue staring out the window. He'd seen the view so many times, having lived in the area for most of his life – and Ellen was born in the same hospital – so he wasn't really looking at anything in particular. He just watched the buildings whizz by in a blur.

Twenty or so minutes later, the driver pulled up to the curb in front of Luke's house. It had never appeared so ominous before. The garden was sparse, because neither Luke nor Dani had enjoyed gardening, but today it seemed full of shadows. A kind of panic set in, and Luke felt as if the darkness was creeping in – he saw nothing but the door.

"You all good, buddy?" the driver asked. "This is it, yeah?"

Luke shook his head to dispel the cobwebs and apologised, opening the door to step out. He thanked the driver and closed the door carefully before turning to face the house again. It was now or never.

Pulling his keys from his pocket, he made his way slowly up the path towards the door, dragging his feet. Blood coursed through his veins, pulsating, and his chest tightened. He closed his eyes and inhaled deeply, holding on to the brick wall for support. Exhaling forcefully, he opened his eyes… and then he opened the door.

The silence within the house was violent. Closing the door behind him, he stood looking down the entrance hallway, into the dark. Given his condition, it appeared simply as a black portal. The light around its edges came from the window in the door behind him, but apart from that, the world in front of him was empty. He stood staring at it, wondering if it really was a black hole, a void inside the place he once called home… but he knew this was not the case. He took a few steps into the darkness, and fumbled on the wall for the light switch. His fingers were like sausages. The tension in his chest increased.

As the lights came on, it quickly became apparent that the house had been empty and untouched for almost two months now. Everything was as Luke and his family had left it before they had departed for their fateful trip to the beach. Once again, Luke wept openly, standing alone in the entryway.

It was all too much. He took a deep breath before rushing into the bedroom to grab a suitcase and fill it with clothes. He wasn't picky about the items he chose; he just grabbed the essentials and threw them in the bag. He then went to the bathroom for toiletries. He couldn't stay here by himself. Not yet, at least. He couldn't bear to spend time alone in this house, surrounded by memories, with photos of his loving wife and child staring at him lifelessly from the walls. He couldn't bear to look at them.

Zipping up the bag, he turned and headed to the front door. He made sure the lights were extinguished, and left his home again – this time with no understanding as to when he would be back.

As he passed through his front yard, edging closer to the road, he noticed someone watching him from the house across the street. Old Bill Reilly, the local busybody, was watching through his window, as was his custom. It always struck Luke as odd – did Bill realise that Luke could see him? Bill's silhouette was clear as day. Luke didn't know his story – perhaps he was a widower, and this was the only way he could relate to the world. Still, Luke had always considered it a little creepy.

Defiantly, Luke gave him a wave, and the shadow moved out of sight. Now Bill knew. Perhaps now he wouldn't stick his nose in other people's business... at least, not so obviously.

Bringing up the Uber app again, Luke began to request another ride... but where to? He hadn't thought this far ahead. Wherever he stayed, it needed to be complete with kitchen and laundry facilities, and it needed to be close to a shopping centre – if he had to go out to get groceries, he didn't want to stray far, and he didn't want it to take long. Preferably, he would stay locked up in his own little cocoon until he was ready to brave the world.

He soon found an Adventure Apartment at the outskirts of the city – fully-serviced apartments with in-room laundry and kitchen, but paid by the day like a hotel. A small shopping mall was within walking distance – the kind you would find in a small suburb, mostly intended to serve the immediate needs of locals. This would be perfect. Luke put the details into the app, and less than thirty minutes later, he was standing in front of the Adventure Apartment building.

Making his way to the front desk, he was greeted by a young south-east Asian woman, dressed in a white blouse and a black vest emblazoned with the Adventure logo, a stylised dragon.

"How can I help you today, sir?"

"I... don't have a reservation," Luke mumbled. "I was hoping you might have a room I could book for... maybe two weeks?"

The woman looked puzzled. "Two weeks? And you haven't placed a booking?"

"No. This was… unexpected."

The woman smiled and looked down at her computer. "Well, let's see."

Luke looked at her name badge: Angelina. She didn't look like an Angelina, but then again, he hadn't met an Angelina before, so perhaps this was somewhat judgemental on his part. He wondered where she came from – Malaysia, perhaps, or the Philippines? Not that it mattered.

"We can certainly help you, Mr…" she trailed off, waiting for Luke to fill in the details.

"Nixon," he said. "Luke Nixon."

He went through the motions of checking in, filling out forms, handing over his credit card, smiling and making small talk. Behind it all, though, his mind was inert. Dark. After performing the necessary actions, he made his way to his room on the fifth floor, and inserted his door card to unlock the door.

The room was extremely spacious – more than enough for him, with a separate bedroom and an integrated laundry/bathroom. He unpacked his things and put them away. If he was going to live here for a while, he would at least make it feel a little lived in.

Yet he needed a few necessities – the fridge was empty and his belly was rumbling – so he gathered his wallet and phone, and made his way to the shopping centre.

An hour later, he re-entered the apartment with an armful of shopping bags. Most of the contents were the daily necessities – toothbrush, toothpaste, coffee, milk, eggs, bread, laundry detergent and the like – but he had also tried to select some longer-lasting food. He didn't know how long he could live happily on tuna cans and instant noodles, but at least he could lock himself away for a few days and not have to re-enter the world of the living.

He put away the groceries and looked at the remaining two bags on the counter. Alcohol. Lots of alcohol. It had been some time since he last drank, but it had also been all he could think about since he got out of the hospital. He needed escape. He needed to forget about his troubles and… just be drunk for a while. He was looking forward to it.

He put on some music and drank. A lot.

THE FOLLOWING DAYS were a blur – he rarely noticed when one began and another ended. He was simply at the mercy of the alcohol. He wasn't a nuisance to other guests – he didn't play his music loud, he didn't bang the walls or scream and cry; he simply drank himself into silent oblivion, day after day. He'd pass out, wake up, and have another drink.

But it didn't help. In fact, it seemed to make things

worse. His thoughts were a mix of what-ifs and could-have-beens – he continued to live in the past, and continued to reject the present. This left him with powerfully conflicting emotions, and he often cried himself to sleep on the sofa, which couldn't have been a pretty sight for the cleaners when they came by in the morning. He eventually learned to put the *Do Not Disturb* hanger on the door, where it remained almost permanently.

From time to time, he would spend half a day out in the sun, eating slowly at a local restaurant to allow the cleaners to do their job – clean sheets and towels were a necessity, after all. However, most of his time was spent in his room, mindlessly watching TV or listening to music, drinking all the while.

It was towards the end of the initial two weeks that he had the first of the dreams.

They weren't necessarily pleasant dreams, but they weren't unpleasant, either. However, he would often find himself experiencing the same dream over and over – sometimes even multiple times in the one night. What made them disturbing was their lucidity, and the fact that they all took place in the Adventure Apartment.

Of course, the most disturbing aspect was the content. In every case, Luke found himself walking into the living/dining area from the bedroom, bottle in hand, to find Dani sitting on the couch, crying. Luke would drop the bottle and rush to her, and Dani would look up at him, tears streaming from her eyes, screaming "Wake up!" And he *would* wake up, usually to discover that he had passed out on the couch.

Sometimes the dream played out slightly differently. Dani would scream "Stop!" or "Can't you see?", but the emotion always felt the same. Desperate. The dreams haunted him, and soon they became the focus of Luke's attention, albeit drunken attention.

Why were they recurring? Was his subconscious trying to tell him something? What did Dani mean by the things she said?

When he was a child, Luke would often have strange dreams, but it was so long ago that he had virtually forgotten. In these dreams, he would occasionally see the events of the future, and be able to describe them with a certain amount of detail. He could even make simple predictions based upon them. His family marvelled at his predictions initially, but they eventually began to dismiss them as trivial whenever he brought them up, waiving them off as a child's annoying fantasy as parents often do.

The occasion Luke remembered most clearly was the disappearance of the family dog. He told his father to make sure he locked the gate because one day the dog would run away and never come back. His father laughed it off, but after neglecting to lock up after taking out the trash the very next week, the dog had escaped, never to be seen again. His father had downplayed it at the time – of course the dog would escape if the gate was left open –

but Luke was adamant; he had known it would be his father that would leave the gate open, as he had seen it in a dream. Still – it *was* to be expected. An open gate is an open invitation to a caged animal.

His mother, however, didn't brush these predictions off so simply. She had always told Luke that he was special. In fact, she had told him that they were *all* special – Luke's father, his mother, and himself, but she had never elaborated. Luke regretted not talking more with his mother about this. Eventually he stopped having the dreams.

His older self was sceptical of his childhood experience, and this new recurring dream wasn't a premonition, anyway. Now he was dreaming about his dead wife. There was no future in which she could come back... was there? Even so... why would he still be in this room?

No... it wasn't a premonition. This was something else – most likely his own conscience manifesting as his wife, nagging him from beyond the grave. Maybe he needed to ease up on the alcohol.

As he pondered this, there was a knock at his door. It wasn't room service, who would have left the building by this time, so he wasn't sure who it could be. He hadn't told anyone where he was. He approached the door quietly and looked through the peephole.

It was Oz.

Sighing deeply, he opened the door.

"Heyyyy," he croaked, his throat raw. "How did you find me?"

"Fucking hell, Luke," Oz said in a disappointed tone. "You look like shit."

He pushed past Luke to enter the apartment. "Good to see you cleaned up for me – and the smell in the apartment matches how you look, so I guess you've got some sort of a thing going on here." He waved his hands about like a stage magician. "Seriously, it smells like shit in here."

"Funny." Luke walked to the couch and sat down, frowning. He was glad he had put on some clothes this morning. The last couple of days, he had been wearing an old worn-out T-shirt and underwear. Today he was at least sporting dirty tracksuit pants and… that same T-shirt. No wonder it smelled in here.

Oz, on the other hand, was wearing his work clothes. Navy cargo pants, a white T-shirt, and a black faux-wool jumper, all of which was dirty in the traditional tradesman style. It was probably the only job where it was acceptable – even normal – to be covered in grime, paint, and grease.

"What are you doing, man?" Oz said in concern. "Why are you hiding from me? Have you even been checking your phone?"

Luke gave a long, exasperated sigh. "To be honest, I don't know. I couldn't stay home, so I came here. I… guess I wanted to be left alone."

"And do you still want to be left alone?"

"Not really." This response surprised even Luke. "I mean – I'm not over it. I don't think I'll *ever* be over it. But I think I've gotten whatever I needed to get out of my system." He gestured around the room. "And, uh... this isn't exactly a great way to live, I must admit."

"So what's next – and how can I help?" Oz seemed a little more chipper now, pleased that his friend had come to some realisation, and it was clear that he actually wanted to help. Perhaps he was the only person left that actually cared about Luke... himself included.

"First things first, I've gotta cut down on the drinking, and clean myself up again. I'm not going home – not yet – but I need to return to some semblance of normal living. I need to figure out how to be myself again. Maybe I need to figure out who I am now." He paused before continuing. "I quit my job – not sure if you were aware."

Oz nodded.

"I'm done with sales. That was part of the old me. And now that I'm alone again, I—"

Oz interjected, "You're *not* alone."

"I know, I know, but you know what I mean. Now that I'm... well, *alone* again... I think it's time for a change. I've got plenty of cash. I accepted the truck company's offer, so I'm good for a while at least. I don't need to work just yet. I'm thinking I might study... or travel... I don't know. I really don't. But I need to start by cleaning myself up."

"Well, whatever you choose to do," Oz replied, "I'd like to be part of it. Even if you do travel, let me come with you. At least on one trip – I'm not sure how much time I can take off work, but I want to be with you. You helped me through my shit, now I wanna help you through yours."

The "shit" Oz was referring to was an almost fatal suicide attempt when Oz was in his twenties. Alcoholism mixed with substance abuse, anxiety, and depression weren't a great combo. Oz had slashed his right wrist one night, during a period of sustained introspection, but he had instantly regretted it and called Luke to help. Luke took him to the hospital, spent the night by his side, and had never told a soul. Later, Oz covered the scar with a tattoo, and it had always been their secret. Clearly, Oz wanted to return the favour and be there when Luke needed him most, and he wasn't going to back down. Like it or not, Oz was going to be a major part of his life once again. Secretly, Luke was pretty happy about this. He had great memories of his bachelor life prior to starting a family, although he knew that life was behind both of them.

Their conversation continued for a while, but moved onto less serious, more mundane topics. Luke was thankful for this – this mundane activity was, in effect, part of his returning to normal. He was grateful for the company, and after Oz left, Luke even found his phone, which he had basically ignored for two weeks, plugged in the charger, and turned the sound back on. It vibrated as if possessed, notifying him of weeks of missed calls and messages, all of which were from Oz.

Luke went to the bathroom to look at himself in the mirror. Oz was right. He looked like shit.

# CHAPTER FIVE

A FEW NIGHTS later – after days spent showering, eating right, getting out, and generally being "normal" – Luke had another dream. It was similar in some ways to his previous dreams, particularly in that it was set in the Adventure Apartment, but in many ways it was different.

On this occasion, when he walked into the room, he was no longer holding a bottle. Dani still sat on the couch, but she was no longer crying. She sat with her right arm along the long edge of the couch, looking at Luke. As he got closer to her, her chin shot up and she looked him in the eye and said, "Go home."

And he woke up.

*Go home.* Not what he had been expecting. But he wasn't sure what he would be expecting to hear from his dead wife in a dream. Regardless, he knew he still wasn't ready to go home.

Suddenly, his phone rang, startling him. It was his boss, Gary. He contemplated ignoring it, but there was little to be gained from that. Reluctantly, he picked up the phone.

"Gary, how you doing?" He cringed as he spoke,

feeling a little awkward.

"Good, Luke – how are you?" Gary's voice was brighter than it had been during their previous conversation. Clearly, enough time had elapsed since the accident that he felt more comfortable chatting with Luke. Plus, this time the conversation was on his terms. "Just thought I'd check in – it's been a while since we spoke, and I want to make sure you really have made your mind up." He paused briefly. "Your job's still here if you want it."

Luke was genuinely surprised. He liked Gary, both as a boss and as a colleague, but he hadn't realised that his work itself was appreciated. In fact, he had always seen himself as a number, a cog in a machine, someone that could easily be replaced. Perhaps he had been wrong to feel that way. He was humbled by the gesture.

"Wow, thanks Gary – you didn't have to say that!" he replied, laughing, but then quickly realised this could be taken the wrong way. He cleared his throat and continued, "Seriously – thanks. I really do appreciate you keeping the position open for me while I got on top of things, but the truth is, I'm definitely after a change."

Gary sighed. "I was hoping you wouldn't say that. I had a feeling you would, but I still thought it was worth a try. Is there nothing we can do to get you back?"

"Not really, to be honest. No hard feelings – I enjoyed my time, I just need a change. A big change. I think I'll try a whole new career, I'm just… not sure what yet. I'll take a little break first."

Once the call was over, Luke sat for a while, still surprised that the conversation had even happened. He wasn't sad to be leaving the company, but he was reassured that they had actually wanted him back. It was good to feel wanted again, but it was even better to be able to say no. For the first time in a long time, he actually felt free. He smiled. For the foreseeable future, he had no responsibilities to worry about.

Still, it left him with a problem – when he did return to the working world, what could he actually do instead of sales?

Truly, he thought he could probably do just about anything. In fact, if he played it safe, he could probably live out his remaining days on his inheritance and the payout from the accident alone, but he'd rather live a little, spend a little, and then settle into an easy role until he retired.

THAT NIGHT, HE had another dream. It was almost identical to the last, but it ended on a more desperate note. As he approached Dani, she stood up and grabbed him by the shirt. "GO. HOME. There's something you need to see." Again, he woke suddenly.

Luke found this dream more striking than the previous one. The dreams weren't normal, that much was obvious, but something had changed. Dani's urgency was palpable. It was probably time he went home and had a look around, just to satisfy his curiosity. He slept fitfully for the rest of the night, knowing what was ahead of him.

He woke early the next morning, and got himself ready for the day. Still feeling anxious about the trip, he brought out his trusty whisky flask and filled it, and also a glass that he drank straight away. It burned his throat, and the fumes cleared out his sinuses, but the feeling was refreshing. It was the slap in the face he needed to prepare himself for the day ahead.

Now ready, he gathered the necessities – his phone, keys, and wallet – and slung his backpack over his shoulder, popping the flask in the side pocket. He glanced around the apartment, in case there was anything else he might need for the trip, but the simple fact was that he didn't even know why he was going in the first place. Nodding to himself, he headed toward the door.

A short Uber trip later, he stood once again at the foot of the path that led to the front door of his house. Once again, the door itself appeared oppressive – a looming threat bearing down on him. He felt its weight as if it really were exuding force. As much as he wanted to allow it to repel him, he knew he had to face the house once again. It was either that, or face Dani's spectre in his dreams. He chuckled nervously – he was more afraid of his dream wife. She still had a hold of him.

It was a bright and sunny day, but the house appeared dark, bleak, foreboding. It was deathly quiet. The street was mostly empty, birds chirping happily from the trees. He sighed and took a swig from his flask before taking a few tentative steps towards the door. His legs were heavy, resisting his every movement.

Standing in front of the door, he fumbled for his keys. He realised that now – weeks after he had awoken from his coma, weeks after he had last stepped into his house, and only a few short days after he decided to get his life back on track – he still wasn't quite ready to face the truth, but he knew he had to. His time was up. He'd hidden from reality for long enough. He straightened his back, shook his hands and bounced on his feet, like a runner preparing for a race. He needed to get the blood flowing and the oxygen moving.

Feeling slightly more energised, he opened the door to his house and entered the bleak silence within.

As soon as he walked inside, he realised what he was dreading most – the photos. More than anything else, more than the memories and the smells, it was the photos that Dani had hung on all of the walls.

She had loved photos – she loved to capture every moment the family spent together, she loved making photo books to share with friends and family, and she loved framing special photos and spreading them throughout the house. No matter where he looked, he saw Dani and Ellie's sweet faces looking at him.

It hurt, but he was OK. In fact, he welcomed it this time. He hadn't seen them for so long that it was nice to see their faces, smiling in happier times. He found himself smiling, too, while looking at the photos in the hall near the front door.

The rest of the hallway was dark – very dark, in fact. As a young father, suddenly responsible for a small family unit of his own, safety had been his prime concern. This was particularly true because the house they had bought was in a relatively cheap area of town, among neighbours of similar social stature to himself: single-income families and low-income earners. The people themselves were no major concern, but Luke was aware that these areas tended to attract more crime than others, possibly due to the tendencies of some low-income earners, or possibly because more desperate individuals would target areas less likely to employ security.

As a result, he had seen fit to secure his home with roller shutters on the majority of the windows. While this put his mind at ease during the night (a potential burglar would need to make a hell of a racket in order to break into his house), it would also completely block out the light, plunging the house into complete darkness whenever they were closed, night or day. This wasn't ideal, given Luke's condition, but he always argued that "you take the good with the bad" – it was far more important that the house was secure.

Now, though, he cursed himself, as he couldn't see much more than a couple of feet along the hall, and even then what he could see was murky. Reaching over to flick the nearest light switch, he cursed himself again. It had been several months since he last set foot inside the building, and he had forgotten – or rather neglected – to pay the electricity bill. The blackness in the hallway remained, beckoning.

Still, this was his home – he knew where he kept his personal light sources. There was one in the master bedroom, which was immediately beside the entrance. He could see its door from where he was standing, but he didn't want to leave the front door open while he fumbled about – he still didn't trust anyone, even though it was the middle of the day and the sun was high in the sky.

Closing the front door thrust him into almost complete darkness. He put out his left hand and felt for the wall before slowly taking a couple of steps, his hand sliding along the plaster. Soon enough, he found the door jamb, and turned towards the opening.

The master bedroom was somewhat brighter than the entrance. While he had put shutters on the rest of the windows in the house, he had left the ones facing the street uncovered – mainly because he couldn't afford it at the time, but also due to Dani's position that shutters on the front window would be ugly. This meant that there was light seeping in from around the curtains, brightening the room slightly.

It still wasn't quite bright enough to see perfectly, but he could make out most of the larger objects in the room, such as the bed in front of him and the dresser over to the left.

He walked to the dresser near the window, knowing what was there – his and Dani's favourite photos of Ellie. They both used this dresser for their clothes, so Luke had often looked at his daughter in these photos before heading off for a soulless day at the office, while she slept in her own room in the rear of the house.

Today, he looked at the pictures again, and smiled at his daughter. She was such a cutie – a little treasure, with her whole life ahead of her.

He squinted tears from his eyes and put the photo back on the dresser. Best not to think about that. He needed to focus for now. He needed the lantern beside his bed so that he could search the rest of the house for… whatever Dani had sent him here for.

He headed to the left side of the queen-sized bed, which took up most of the room. The left, closer to the window, was his side. Dani had always felt safer on the inside… "you know, in case someone came in through the window". Luke smiled to himself as he checked the bedside table near the head of the bed. He'd put his phone to charge here every night for years as he slept beside his wife, but it was now covered in a layer of fluffy grey dust.

Painful thoughts kept creeping in. He tried to resist them, but they came in waves. Little thoughts triggered little memories. Little memories triggered pain. He sniffled and shook his head. He had work to do.

Still sitting on the bedside table was the little LED lantern he'd purchased a few years prior. It was small but powerful – he had been surprised at the amount of light it could generate. Pressing the button on the top, the bedroom lit up as if a spotlight had been pointed at him. Perfect.

So… why was he here? What exactly was he looking for? He wandered around the bedroom aimlessly. He wasn't searching for anything in particular, so he just… *floated* from one place to another.

The lantern flickered. The battery was dying – just his luck. Still, he was happy to have a new objective – collecting batteries from the kitchen drawer. He always kept a supply of batteries – not only for his light sources, but also for Ellie's toys. In better times, he'd often joked that perhaps he should have become a battery tycoon – now there was a resource that was always in high demand.

Heading along the hallway, he noted that the lantern lit only his immediate surroundings, whereas normally it could illuminate an area of two to three metres radius. Within this small area, he could see perfectly. Outside of that was profound blackness. It was a weird sensation – as if he were in a bubble of light, or as if things only existed when they were in his presence. Outside of the bubble, perhaps everything was in a state of uncertainty. Only as he moved about did things pop into existence.

The thought made him chuckle.

When he reached the kitchen, he noted the smell. Damn. No electricity meant the food in his freezer had thawed and begun to rot. He made a mental note to call the power company later. Luckily, the smell wasn't overpowering, as the freezer door was closed, but he was going to have to do something about it before he left. No point in putting it off further – it would only get worse. He wasn't looking forward to it.

For now, though, he headed to the drawers near the sink. He bent down to the third drawer – the one traditionally reserved for everything he couldn't think of a place for – ripped the Velcro child-safe lock off the side, and rifled through it for batteries.

Success. For some reason, he had thought he wouldn't find any, as if the house might want him to remain in the dark, but the drawer was full of batteries of all sizes. Soon enough, with the lantern batteries replaced, he stood in a new bubble, larger and brighter than before.

He decided not to clean the freezer just yet – he'd leave that until last, otherwise he'd have to wade through the stench while he searched the rest of the house. He headed towards Ellie's room at the rear of the house. His reasoning was twofold: for one, it would likely be the most difficult room for him to enter, so he may as well get it done first; and secondly, he'd made up his mind to start at the back of the house and work his way forward.

As expected, Ellie's room was heartrending. It was

relatively barren – a change station to one side of the room – which Dani had been nagging him to get rid of for many months – a chest of drawers against the wall in the centre, and her little pink bed on the other side. More memories crept in, and Luke felt his chest tighten once again. He turned and left the room – there was nothing to see here. Nothing but pain, and he'd had enough of that for a lifetime. When the time came, he would need help to clear out this room.

The room beside Ellie's was his study. Originally, he had planned to convert it to a playroom, but that plan had never come to fruition, and now it housed his desk, a bookshelf, and a large TV, which was his pride and joy. Luke liked to spend his time playing video games, and when Dani finally relented and allowed him to buy that gorgeous 60-inch 4K TV he'd had his eye on, he was ecstatic. Today, though, it may as well have been a sheet of cardboard. It no longer gave him the enjoyment it once had. He no longer cared.

*Crash. Thud.*

The sounds were sudden and loud – the sound of breaking glass, and of something large hitting the ground. It wasn't close, but it was within the house. There was only one place it could have come from – the master bedroom, the only room in the house without shutters. The only room with exposed windows.

He turned off the lantern and stood completely still, listening. His heart was pounding, and he struggled to control his breathing. All he could hear were his laboured breaths, which sounded like a chainsaw. He slowed his breathing and strained to listen for sounds from the front of the house… There was the sound of muffled movement, but not much else. It sounded as if someone was moving about the master bedroom, going through drawers. They didn't seem to be in any hurry.

He didn't know what to do – this situation was new to him – but he had nothing to lose. He grabbed the flask from his bag and took another swig in an attempt to calm his nerves. He immediately regretted the decision.

Quietly, he put the lantern in his backpack and both arms through the straps – he didn't want anything in his hands as he moved about, but he didn't want to leave his things behind. In complete darkness, he used his knowledge of his house to navigate his way back. He'd done it plenty of times over the years – in fact, he'd run from the master bedroom to Ellie's room on several occasions when he had been woken by her screaming in the night.

He moved quietly, grimacing at every noise he made, every creak of the floorboards, every breath he took.

The noises in the bedroom had stopped – had the intruder heard him as he fumbled his way in the dark? Part of him hoped they'd been spooked, and were already gone, having leapt back out the window through which they had entered.

As he approached the master bedroom, he noted

there was a lot of light streaming into the hall through its open doorway – clearly, whoever had broken in had left the window exposed.

He stopped short of the doorway and took a few deep breaths. Then he stepped inside.

As he entered the room, he saw the intruder's silhouette from the side against the light from the curtains.

The first thing he noticed was that they were tall – perhaps around seven feet, and broad shouldered. They were standing at the dresser, holding one of the photographs, looking down at it. Either they hadn't noticed Luke enter the room, or they weren't impacted by this in any way – they kept looking down at the photograph.

Luke took a step forward, straightened his posture, and tried to look menacing. Regardless, he knew he was no match for this intruder, but it was too late.

As he came closer, the intruder's features began to clarify…

Whoever it was appeared to be wearing a dress. A lavish, detailed dress made from some fabulously expensive-looking material, probably silk, but Luke's knowledge of textiles was poor. It was deep red and high-collared, skin tight from the shoulder to the hips and down the sleeves, which extended to the wrists. It seemed almost regal, and entirely out of place here. Luke made a sharp intake of breath.

The intruder turned to him, their back to the light, features darker than the surrounding light. They seemed to have some kind of armour on their shoulders, and a horned helmet on their head. Maybe it was this that made them appear so tall and so broad.

They tilted their head to the left as they appraised him.

*{Are you afraid to die, little lamb?}* the voice boomed. It was deeper than any voice Luke had heard before, ringing out as if in chorus with itself, and yet at the same time it sounded like a growl. He felt he could hear two distinct voices within it – one deep and rough, the other light and ethereal. Whoever this was, they didn't think Luke was in any way their equal, and they spat the words as if they hated him…

In addition, he knew this was a language he had not heard before, yet somehow he understood what had been said.

He continued to stand rigidly still, mouth agape. "Wh-what?" he stammered in reply.

The intruder repeated itself: *{Are you afraid to die, little lamb?}*

"What?" Luke said again, incredulous. He was in shock – the voice itself was disturbing enough, and there were too many questions in his head. He couldn't make sense of any of his thoughts. He felt as if he was back in the hospital bed, at risk of passing out.

The intruder shifted its weight, then slowly moved towards him, into the light.

Luke felt his heart wrench. As he had suspected,

whatever stood before him was not human. It did not have armour on its shoulders, and it certainly was not wearing a helmet.

Its head was large and bulbous, the skin as white and shiny as porcelain, though certainly not as fragile. From the front of its forehead rose two bronze-coloured horns, curved but symmetrical. They appeared polished to perfection.

Its eyes were large saucers, almost entirely black, as if the sockets were merely portals into a void within its skull. There were large vertical slits where one would expect a nose, below which was the most complex mouth that Luke had ever set eyes on.

He could only describe the mouth as crab-like. Most of the moving components were hidden behind flattened, hardened components where a person's chin might be. The mandibles (for want of a better word) above them had fangs of their own, which chittered as the creature moved its mouthparts.

Seemingly sensing his discomfort, the creature fluttered the various components of its mouth, and sent a lush, deeply red and moist proboscis searching about its edges, as if licking its lips.

As the creature approached him, raising an arm threateningly, thick and heavy as a log, the voice came again.

*{Answer me!}*

"No!" Luke screamed, covering his face in fear while

pulling back to avoid a blow.

But no blow came. At his scream, the creature recoiled as if it had been struck. It took a step back, its mouthparts chittering.

*{You are Nephilim? He did not tell me. This changes things.}*

It turned and moved faster than Luke would have expected from such a large creature – faster than his eyes could track. It looked like a crimson blur, leaving a trail behind it like smoke that was pulled after it as it went. It was almost as if it were covered in thousands of tiny ribbons, but Luke knew this was not the case. Within the blink of an eye, it had exited through the broken window and was gone.

Shocked, Luke ran to the window, hoping to see where the creature had gone, or to determine whether any of his neighbours had seen it. In short, he wanted to make sure he wasn't going crazy.

It was still bright outside – it was still mid-afternoon, after all. Luke didn't see any of his neighbours, but he wanted a better look at the front of his house as he couldn't see the creature either. Not wanting to cut himself on the glass, he rushed to the front door and along the path that led to the road.

As he did, a large black van came screaming down the road. Stopping at the foot of the path, the side door slid open. Out leapt a single person dressed head-to-toe in black military fatigues, a helmet and goggles obscuring their face. They were holding something in their hands – something long, black, and tubular.

Although Luke had never actually seen one in real life, he knew what a rocket launcher looked like. He had thought this day couldn't get any worse, but it just had. After surviving an encounter with… whatever that thing was, he was now looking down the barrel of a rocket launcher, pointed in his direction by someone that looked very much like they knew how to use it.

From his right, Luke heard someone scream his name, and was tackled roughly to the ground by the waist. Soon after, he watched a rocket pass directly over him as he lay on the ground, a thin trail of black smoke streaming in its wake as it flew. It seemed to travel in slow motion, and he kept watching as it passed straight through the open doorway to his home. After a few seconds of stunned silence, the air shook, and his chest compressed as the rocket hit something deep within. The explosion blew out the roof and the remaining windows in the front room. The front door was blown off its hinge. The very bricks of the house seemed to expand with the force of the explosion, then settle back upon themselves, dust in the air. At least he didn't have to worry about the freezer anymore.

Immediately after firing the rocket, the black-clad individual jumped back into the van, which promptly sped off, leaving Luke and his saviour lying in the dirt.

Only now did Luke feel the pain of being tackled into

a pile of rocks. He groaned as he tried to sit up. Still, he was grateful. It was better than being blown up. His saviour stood above him, offering him a hand to help him up. Luke looked up to say thanks.

"Oh, it's you!" he said, shocked.

"That's an interesting way to thank me for saving your life, but yes, it is me," replied the African nurse from the hospital, dusting herself off.

What a day, Luke thought. After all that happened, he had finally been rescued from certain death by one of the nurses from the hospital.

"I can't hang around," the nurse said. "The police will be here soon, and I don't want to get involved in all of that. I'll find you soon – we really need to talk."

She turned and walked away.

"What's your name?" Luke asked.

She turned and looked over her shoulder without stopping. "Asha."

# CHAPTER SIX

BILL REILLY SAT in an old leather armchair, inhaling deeply on the thick cigar held between his fingers. He'd hoped this day would never come. At his age, he was just waiting for the day he could hang up his kit and retire, spending the rest of his days lounging beside a pool... or something like that. The pool wasn't exactly his style, but he still looked forward to the day he could leave his responsibilities. But... this wasn't that day.

He'd watched over the Nixon family now for some time – ever since they'd set up home in this town six years prior. He knew all about them. In fact, a man in his position knew more about his quarry that anyone would like. More than that, though, he knew that things were stirring among those that were aware of the old ways. He had only hoped it would be someone else's problem.

But now it was very clear that he needed to take action. The accident on the freeway had failed to end the bloodline, which had clearly been the intention, as far as he was concerned. However, it had made his job easier – now he only had to keep watch over the one surviving member of the family. It was a heartless way to look at things, but after everything he'd seen and done in his life, it wasn't worth regretting.

For a while after the accident, everything seemed to have settled. Understandably, Luke hadn't wanted to stay in his home alone, but there were no further attacks on his life during that time. The concerns of Bill's superiors seemed unfounded. In fact, even given the freeway accident, everything had been relatively quiet.

And then there was the explosion. Bill had noticed Luke return home – Bill had done little other than sit in his armchair, which was of course facing the window to allow him to keep his vigil. He had watched as Luke disappeared into the house and closed the door behind him. Not long after, he had seen something that he hadn't expected to see in his lifetime. Something that shouldn't have been there. Something that forced him to pick up the phone and make an immediate report to his superiors.

# CHAPTER SEVEN

THE MOVIES WOULD have you believe that a situation like this blows over pretty quickly. Not so much, in this case. The police kept Luke for as long as they were able to within the law. Having your house destroyed by a rocket launcher was a matter far removed from the average day on the beat, and while Luke had repeatedly insisted that he had no idea who would do this or why, the police didn't seem to believe him. Luke conceded that it was a fair attitude – a rocket launcher was a pretty uncommon weapon in residential areas. Eventually, though, the police had no choice but to release him under observation. He certainly wasn't guilty of the damage himself (there were several witnesses that supported his account of the events, including Bill Reilly), and he definitely didn't need the insurance money.

Sorting out the house itself was another challenge. A few days after the event, Luke returned to sift through the debris for anything he might want to keep. There wasn't much, but not because the house was totally destroyed. The explosion had been fairly central, and the subsequent fire had burned itself out pretty quickly.

The reason there wasn't much left for Luke was because it was a life he wanted to leave behind. He'd lost everything – over the course of just a few short years, he'd lost both parents, his wife, his child, his job (which was his choice after all, but the fact remained), and now… his house. There was virtually nothing left of his old life. So, he grabbed some clothes and some books full of photographs, but he didn't need anything else. In some ways, the rocket launcher attack had simplified his life – not that he was thankful for it, but he wanted to try to put a positive spin on things. Otherwise, he'd end up back at the bottom of a bottle.

Later in the week, he negotiated a payout with his insurance company. This was incredibly difficult, as the circumstances were far from standard. He was able to come to an agreement with them by turning over the title deeds in return for the amount he had advised for cover when he'd first bought the place. His insurance company probably got the better deal, but at least this way required no further action from Luke. It was time to move on.

After all of this, and for the first time since his early twenties – when he'd moved out of his family home to begin life as a bachelor – Luke was completely free and independent. He had no job, no family, no home… he had virtually nothing but the clothes on his back (and, if he was honest, a very respectable bank balance).

Yet even given this newfound independence, he still wasn't quite sure how to feel about it all. Sitting on the couch in the Adventure Apartment he'd been living in for the last however many weeks (and which was now his new home), he felt as empty as he had in the hospital. At least when he was in his twenties he had had goals and desires. Now… he had no direction, and no responsibilities. It was surreal.

He took another sip of whisky and placed the glass back on the coffee table, sighing loudly in defeat. Simultaneously, the doorbell rang. He stood, straightened his clothes in the mirror, and made his way to the door.

He opened the door to Asha, the nurse, who greeted him politely and pushed her way past him into the apartment, seeming in a hurry.

"Uhhh… hi," said Luke incredulously. "Thanks for coming by, I guess? Do I need a check-up or something?" He scratched at the side of his head.

"A check-up?" she replied curtly. "What the fuck are you talking about?" Her tone was intense, which put Luke on edge.

"I… uhhh…" he stammered. "Well, you're a nurse, aren't you?"

She laughed. "Fuck no!" She walked up close, pointing her finger into his chest. "I'm your fucking…" Poke. "Guardian." Poke. "Angel." Poke.

And she plonked herself down on the couch, giggling, obviously pleased with herself. Luke noticed she was sitting in the same place Dani had sat in his dreams. He raised a finger, about to ask her to move, but he pushed the thought away in resignation.

Confused, he approached Asha slowly. Who was this woman? He recalled the first time they had met – when she'd told him that things were not exactly as they seemed. What had she been talking about?

"Well, I'm not sure who was pulling all the strings, but there's a lot you don't know," she said, as if reading his mind.

"Like... what?" Luke inquired.

Asha sighed. "Why don't you pour us a drink?" She gestured to the bottle of Johnny Walker on the table.

Luke obliged, and soon enough they were sipping from their glasses in silence. Asha spoke first.

"So..." she began, "did you talk to him?"

While Luke wasn't certain who she was referring to, he could only assume it was the "thing" in his house.

"Uhh... well, 'he' spoke to me," Luke replied. "I didn't have much chance to respond. Nor could I... think clearly at the time."

"Did he mention why he was trying to kill you?"

"No... but he asked me if I was afraid to die... which was kind of weird."

Looking a little confused herself, Asha took a deep breath before continuing. "Your daughter is alive," she said, sharp and final.

Luke laughed. This was absurd. Over the last few weeks, he had gathered the courage to look up images of the crash online – it had been big news on the day. He was shocked at the pictures. While he could make out his car, it was little more than a pile of twisted metal, torn apart like pastry and spread across the highway. It was horrific. He shuddered at the thought.

In one photo, he'd seen what he thought was probably himself being carried away on a stretcher, and two sheets covering bodies on the ground, one much smaller than the other... The news report had listed a female child among the dead.

He told Asha as much.

"Well, someone was lying." Asha replied sharply. "Your daughter is alive, and he has her. He didn't tell you that?"

Luke took another long sip of whisky, wincing as it hit his throat. He wasn't sure what to say. He wasn't sure what to feel. It just didn't seem right – it didn't seem *real*.

Asha's question lingered, but the pause was long enough for her to decide to move on. "So... you met *the* Dion Wexler, huh?"

Luke glanced at her. Dion Wexler? What was she talking about? Was Dion the guy that destroyed his house?

"Ummm... I doubt it, this was something else," he replied. "At least... I'm not sure he... or it? ...looked like a "Dion", and it never said its name. It only called me..." He fumbled for the word. "Nephilim?"

Asha's eyes widened. She threw back what was left of the whisky and slammed the glass down on the table.

"What... the fuck... are you talking about?"

Slightly taken aback, the pressure began to increase in Luke's skull. He stood and pointed at Asha, clenching his jaw. "Look. I'm confused. *You* come in here asking questions, telling me you're my guardian angel, that my daughter is alive and all sorts of other crap, but the simple fact is – *I don't know why you're here.*"

He noticed he was breathing heavily, and that the muscles in his whole body were tense. He needed answers, but he felt like this was going nowhere. Clearly Asha knew more than she was letting on, but her line of questioning seemed nonsensical.

He took a deep breath and continued, keeping his voice as level as he could manage. "Before I answer any more of your questions, you need to answer some of mine. One: who are you and why are you following me? Two: why did someone blow up my house? And three: what the hell was that demon thing in my bedroom?"

Asha's jaw dropped, and she put a hand to her mouth in disbelief. Regaining composure, she began her response.

"'Demon' is really quite accurate..." She looked off into the distance, lost in thought. "My name is Asha Amani, and I'm a member of the Naacal Collective, an ancient theosophical movement that has been kept well hidden from modern society for several hundred years. Our numbers are small, but our reach and our influence are great.

"Our primary purpose is to monitor the descendants of certain individuals. I was assigned to monitor your family, Luke Nixon, for both yourself and your wife have very special ancestors, whether you are aware of this or not."

Luke laughed. "So… you're going to tell me I'm related to Jesus Christ?"

"Well, yes," she replied. "But so is virtually everyone else on the planet at this point in time. Your ancestors are far more important, and your line of descendancy is very direct – as was your wife's, I should add. This makes your family very rare, and very special indeed."

Luke looked at her blankly. This was stupid, and – if he had anything better to do – a waste of his time. But he *had* nothing better to do. He let Asha continue, resisting the temptation to roll his eyes.

"I'm not going to explain everything to you now – you simply won't believe most of it, and perhaps more importantly… there's too much to explain. But let me say this: the crash on the highway was no accident. I believe it was intended to wipe out your family and end your bloodline. Exactly who perpetrated this – and why – is beyond me, but these facts are pretty clear.

"Now. Dion Wexler. He was once a part of the Naacal Collective as well. In fact, he too was assigned to your family – prior to me. However, he had… disagreements with other members of the Collective, and went rogue. His goals are opposed to ours, but he still would not have tried to kill you – at least, that's what I thought. He needs you. Or perhaps... *needed* you. Regardless, he's not one of the good guys.

"Which leads me to now. I had followed you to your house on the day of the explosion, as I have every time you left this apartment. Distracted, I didn't see who had smashed your front window, but I assumed it was Dion. While I didn't want to get involved too soon, I also needed you alive – but by the time I had decided to help out, you were suddenly standing at the explodey end of a rocket launcher – held by Dion himself, if I'm not mistaken. I couldn't quite make out the face.

"For him to want to kill you, that means he definitely has the child, as I had already suspected."

Luke sighed. None of this sounded like real life. He was just a sales guy who had lost everything in a car accident – there was no great conspiracy, and he was nobody special. But it still didn't answer his final question.

"And the demon thing?" he asked in a flat tone. "How are you going to explain that?"

"Right now? I can't." Asha shook her head at this admission. "I mean – I could, but again, you probably wouldn't believe me. You saw what you saw, so all I can say is that you yourself need to accept that before you can accept anything else I tell you. What I will tell you is that what you saw shouldn't have been there. Or it shouldn't be *here*, is more accurate." She gestured broadly around her, but Luke wasn't quite sure what she meant by it. "I'm guessing Dion has something to do with it, but for now, I'm kind of at a loss."

Luke placed his hands on his knees and stood up.

"Well, this has certainly been illuminating, but I really do have something important to attend to." He gestured to the door. "After you?"

Asha gave an exasperated sigh, but she relented and made her way to the door.

"I know you think this is all bullshit, Luke," she said, turning towards hm as she exited. "But can you afford to ignore it? Your daughter is alive – I'm not joking. Whenever you feel the need to move on from this charade—" she gestured to the room again "—or whatever it is that you need to attend to, just remember, I'll be watching, and I'll be ready."

Luke closed the door inches from her face, and walked back into the living area.

"Good riddance," he said to nobody in particular, pouring himself another drink.

LATER IN THE day, there was another knock at the door. Frustrated, and expecting it to be Asha once again, Luke stormed over to look through the keyhole. It was Oz.

Relieved, he let him in.

They sat and talked for a while, mostly about inane

topics, but soon enough, Oz seemed to note that Luke wasn't his usual self – or at least, the new self he had become since the accident.

"Mate, is everything OK?" he asked. "Maybe it's just the drink, but you seem distracted... and... kind of on edge. You good?"

Luke put his drink down and looked him in the eyes. "Honestly? I don't know if I'm OK, Oz. After everything I've been through, life just doesn't seem to want to leave me alone. But the worst thing? None of it makes any damn sense anymore."

He spent the next twenty minutes or so telling Oz everything that had happened at his house, and the discussion he'd had with Asha that morning. He didn't leave anything out, because he had nothing to hide from Oz, and besides – Luke himself didn't believe it anyway, did he? He wasn't so sure how he felt... And then Oz voiced his greatest concern.

"But... what if she's right?" Oz asked. "Ellie may still be alive – can you afford to ignore that? Regardless of how crazy this Asha lady's story is, it might not be a good idea to ignore that one piece of info."

"I know – that's the hardest part. As much as it all seems bat-shit insane... what if my little girl is out there somewhere, and if she *is*... who the hell is this Dion guy that has her? I just don't know how to feel. It took me so long to come to terms with her loss, and now... I'd be absolutely furious if it turns out that Asha is lying."

"Then let's tackle this together. Whatever you need to do, I'll join you. You don't need to be alone – this way, it'll be two against one if it turns out she's leading you down the wrong path. I'm all you got, bro." He cringed as he said it, but continued, "I won't let you handle this on your own. I'm your family now."

Luke nodded. This idea made perfect sense to him – alone, it would be too much of a weight to bear, but together? It just might work. If Asha was right, he needed to get his daughter back.

As if on cue, Asha entered the room. Did he leave the door unlocked? He hadn't even heard her enter.

"So," she said with a smile. "Where do we start?"

# CHAPTER EIGHT

SADLY, AND PROBABLY as was to be expected, there was no easy place to start. Although Asha assumed that Dion had Ellen, they really didn't know this for certain, nor did they know where to find Dion. So, they decided to use the only resources they had to hand – the Naacal Collective and the local police force.

While Asha disappeared for a few days to check her sources, Luke headed back to the police station to see if they had any clues. At the end of a long day of bureaucracy and sitting in waiting rooms, he returned to the apartment with nothing new to share, and he didn't harbour any expectations of that changing any time soon. He had a feeling that the police had exhausted all leads and did not plan to pursue them any further.

Oz, on the other hand, had gone about his part of the bargain, quitting his job to put all of his efforts into helping Luke find Ellie. Luke had tried to convince him just to take some time off, but Oz had replied with that classic old line, *in for a penny, in for a pound.* As a tradesperson, his skills would always be in high demand. He didn't expect it would be too much trouble to find something when he needed to. It was ballsy, but Luke was appreciative. It meant he really didn't have to do all of this alone, and the weight of responsibility was already getting heavy.

Now, once again sitting alone in his apartment, cradling a glass of whisky in his hands, Luke fought back tears. He felt dizzy, as if he was being slowly sucked down into a whirlpool. After everything he'd gone through during the last few months, he was now putting his trust in a complete stranger. And on top of that, the tale that Asha had told him didn't reflect his reality – or at least reality as he had come to know it. It wasn't so easy to change his understanding of the world – especially when it seemed so *unreal*.

He decided to head off to bed – he could continue banging his head against theoretical brick walls tomorrow.

That night, he had a dream. Yet again, it was lucid, but this dream was different to those he'd had previously. He stood in a long hallway lined with doors, not unlike a cheap hotel. And like a cheap hotel, it was very poorly lit, and Luke struggled to see as he walked along it. Testing a few doors, he found them all to be locked, but something told him that what he was looking for wasn't in any of the rooms anyway. He continued walking down the long, dark hall.

It was quiet, but not silent. Strangely, all he could hear was the whistling of the wind, somewhere between a strong breeze and a light gale, but he felt nothing upon his face. If he was inside this hallway, where was the wind coming from?

Almost imperceptibly, he thought he heard other noises within the wind – a rhythmic drum beat, and a rasping chant. They were quiet enough that he wasn't sure whether he was actually hearing them or whether his brain was misinterpreting the sounds of the wind. He continued down the hall.

Suddenly, the ceiling peeled away, as if being gently removed by a giant, and Luke looked up into space – the night sky was as clear as he had ever seen it, stars spotting the deep black blanket of space, the dense Milky Way forming a clear line across it. Luke felt lost in its infinity, himself a lone consciousness in the wild expanse of space. He closed his eyes for a moment and took a deep breath, trying to centre himself.

Upon opening his eyes, he was shocked to find himself standing at the edge of a cliff; the sounds of wind rushing through a forest behind him, the ocean crashing violently onto rocks below him. It was still night time, and he could hear the wind continue to blow about him, but still he felt nothing on his skin.

The drums were beating louder now, as was the rhythmic chanting within, both now clearly more than a figment of an overactive imagination. He didn't understand the chanting – he wasn't even sure there were words, but the voice itself was somehow both menacing and comforting, sounding not unlike a chant one might hear in a Buddhist temple, rasping and throaty. The sound built, both the drumming and chanting becoming louder until they filled his skull, forcing Luke to put his hands to his ears in a futile attempt to drown it out.

And then it stopped.

Everything. Even the wind. All was silent and still.

To his left, Luke noticed movement and turned to face it, only to find Dani standing there smiling. She wore a thin silken dress that blew in the wind – wind he couldn't feel and could no longer hear.

"Seek the Pyramidion," she said, the vibration of her voice surrounding him.

And Luke woke up, sweating.

His blanket was on the floor, and the sheets were twisted. His damp t-shirt clung to his skin. His heart was beating like a drum, thumping in his chest, and his breathing was irregular. Swinging his legs out of the bed and onto the floor, he took a deep breath and looked around the room.

Empty.

Dark.

Silent.

It was dawn – orange sunlight crept in through the cracks in the curtains, gently lighting the room. He wasn't about to fall asleep again anytime soon, so he had a shower and began his morning ritual, all the while pondering the latest dream.

What the fuck was a Pyramidion anyway? And what was the significance of the cliff? And the spooky hotel hallway?

He wasn't sure anything that had happened in the dream had any real meaning. It may have just been the result of everything happening in his life right now, his brain trying to make sense of a nonsensical series of events. Maybe that was what the doors symbolised: pathways open to him, potential futures. But they were all locked... Still, he couldn't shake the fact that every time his wife had appeared to him to date, she seemed to be doing it for a reason, as if directing him somewhere.

He had to admit that life was interesting right now. He'd lost everything that he had once been, and had somehow became someone else, though not through any choice of his own. But regardless of what he'd been through, he *was* still the same person – just... altered by circumstance. He didn't know what to think anymore.

The doorbell rang.

He looked at his watch – 7:15am. Still early, but not so early that he was the only person awake.

It was Asha. In her usual way, she bustled into the room as if she owned the place, throwing herself onto the couch like a ragdoll.

"Get anything out of the police?" she asked.

"Just a sense that they have no idea what they're doing. No leads on the black van, no ongoing investigation, nothing. At least... nothing they were willing to share.

They didn't seem to care that somebody blew up my house with a rocket launcher."

"Or," replied Asha, dramatically waving her hand in the air, a gesture that Luke was starting to find a little annoying. "Those that *do* care don't want *you* to be involved. They probably sent you from office to office, person to person, until you decided they had no leads and left on your own. I wouldn't be surprised if the Feds had taken over by now – in which case, you're shit outta luck, my boy."

She was probably right. A fully-armoured individual jumping out of a black van and blowing up a house with a rocket launcher – in clear daylight, mind you – was likely something within the jurisdiction of the Federal Police. It was probably something they were *very* interested in. Not to mention the fact that this happened in a suburban street, to a virtual nobody. Luke also didn't tell her that she had effectively summed up his day precisely.

"Hmmm…" Luke frowned, deep in thought. "Do you think I'm a suspect?"

"To the Feds? Of course you are! There are those within certain departments of the Federal Police that we probably don't want chasing you, but we don't really have control over that right now. I'm starting to think you aren't safe here – I think we need to move, and soon."

"Move where exactly?" Luke said with a scowl. "We have no idea where to go – and if they already know I'm here, they're just gonna follow."

He paused to gather his thoughts. "How did it go with your people?"

Asha looked up, a little desperately, Luke concluded. "My people? Nada. Dion Wexler is a ghost. They didn't even know he was in town. He was last seen in Egypt, six months ago."

*Seek the Pyramidion.*

Luke froze. Egypt. That *had* to be it. There was something in Egypt – a Pyramidion, whatever that was – and he had to find it. Dani was giving him another clue, showing him where to go.

He told Asha about the dream, in as much detail as he could manage, ending with the quote from Dani: *Seek the Pyramidion.*

"Well…" she answered slowly. "I guess it's a place to start. But there are many pyramids, and many pyramidion – not just the famous ones in Egypt. But given Dion was just there recently…" She trailed off. Then, suddenly, she stood up. "I know someone in Egypt. We can start there. He's a member of the Collective, but a renowned historian in his own right. He might have some ideas."

She approached Luke and put her hands on his shoulders. "Buckle up, sunshine," she said, smiling. "Things about to get weird. Pack your bags. We're off in thirty minutes."

"We're leaving now?" Luke asked, incredulous. "What about Oz!? We haven't even booked any flights! What about accommodation… I know nothing about

Egypt – I've never even been to Europe before! And I still don't know what a pyramidion is!"

"Remember when you asked me to explain who I was, Luke, and I told you that you wouldn't believe me if I told you everything? Well, here goes… the Naacal Collective has been around for thousands of years. We have power and influence." She smiled again, pausing for effect. "I have my own plane."

"And you, my friend—" she poked him in the chest "—you have the time! Together, we've got everything we need."

It was all a bit too much, and if Luke was honest, he'd had enough of her poking him in the chest. But still… she had a plane? One that could fly them to Egypt? He really hoped she wasn't leading him down the garden path – if she was, he had no idea what she was trying to achieve. Maybe she was just trying to get to his money?

Still, Dani appearing in his dreams was something he now realised he couldn't ignore – and if she was telling him to go to Egypt, then he was going to Egypt. He was going to save Ellie.

He grabbed a large gym bag and threw in some clothes, along with all of the necessities he could think of, which wasn't much. He didn't know what else he would need. He didn't really have anything anymore.

"Don't take everything," Asha chided. "Leave some stuff you might not care to lose, and pay for the next few weeks of accommodation. Perhaps that will throw the

Feds off your trail for a little while. You never know – we may even be back sometime."

Luke looked around the room. He couldn't believe it. Yesterday he had been lost and confused, and today? He was still confused, but it seemed like he was about to head off on his very own adventure. He picked up a photograph of himself, Dani, and Ellie, folded it up, and slipped it into his back pocket. He might need to remind himself that this was all for Ellie.

He also grabbed a torch and his LED lamp – he certainly wasn't going to be in a familiar place, so he might need them in the dark.

Finally, he slung the bag over his shoulder and walked back into the living room.

"I'm ready," he told Asha. "I, uh… guess we can go now. Do we need to swing by your place?"

"Of course. My "place" is in a secret location. With an airstrip. And my gear. You better be ready, though. We won't be coming back. Not for a while."

Opening the door, Luke was shocked to find Oz standing there, a backpack of his own slung over his shoulder, his hand raised as if he was about to rap on the door.

"Don't tell me you were leaving without me?" he asked.

"Well, that was the plan," replied Asha, "but you're here now, so come along. I hope you aren't expected home tonight, because you won't be."

"Nope – I'm done with work, and Tammy is on board about me helping you. I didn't tell her everything, of course – well… I didn't tell her anything, really. I told her we were going on a holiday because you needed to get away. She knows you need some support."

Soon enough, the three of them stood outside the Adventure Apartment building. It was a fine afternoon – as fine as one would want for the start of a new journey. The sky was blue, the sun warmed their faces, and there was a light breeze in the air. People continued about their business, oblivious to the group.

"So…" Luke began. "Should I call an Uber?"

Asha pointed along the road. A wine-red minibus with dark-tinted windows made its way towards them, the driver smiling in a grey suit with gold lining. When it stopped before them, Asha slid the door open. Luke expected a black-clad individual to leap out and drag him inside, but the minibus was empty but for a few rows of black leather seats.

Asha gestured inside. "Your carriage, sir." She smiled again, bowing slightly. When she looked at Oz, the smile faded slightly. "You too. We haven't got all day."

And soon they were all in a minibus – next stop… A secret location, apparently.

# CHAPTER NINE

The trip to Asha's secret lair (which was the only way Luke could think about it, given the circumstances) was fairly uneventful. Asha sat silently for most of the trip, staring at her phone and tapping feverishly on its screen with her thumbs, brow furrowed. Oz, on the other hand, was like an excitable child, chattering endlessly. His conversation was nominally directed at Luke, but in reality he was mostly talking to himself. Luke gave the occasional non-committal response, but paid little attention to Oz and his ramblings. He was simply lost, completely numb.

For the duration of the journey, Luke stared out the window, watching the world pass by. None of it meant anything anymore. Life had revealed some if its great truths. If you could suddenly stop everything one day, move somewhere else, quit your job, and yet the rest of the world continued without you... Then what was the meaning of any of it? All those hours he had spent worrying about customer orders, stressing that his job was at risk, pressing his shirts so that nobody judged him poorly – none of it mattered. The world really didn't care what anyone did – people were merely specks of space-dust that flittered about its surface. Here one day, gone the next.

And the world kept spinning.

He felt small and insignificant, as if he were simply waiting to be expunged. And when that time finally came, still the world would keep spinning.

Soon enough, they pulled up before a small, nondescript building within a forest outside of town. Although Luke had been looking out the window for the whole trip, he had no idea where they were, and to be honest, he didn't feel it mattered. They were here now, and it was time to get out of the minibus.

He got out slowly, then stretched in the sun, which made him feel slightly better. The building in front of him was square and grey, but he couldn't quite work out what it was made from – metal? Wood? Plasterboard? He couldn't tell. But it didn't look like anything special – in fact, if it were made from corrugated iron it wouldn't have looked unlike a large backyard shed, filled with boxes, old tools and spiderwebs. Surrounded as it was by trees and weathered by who knew how many years of wind and rain, it resembled a bunker on the forest moon of Endor, from *Star Wars*. Now it felt like he was on an adventure. However, this glimpse of positivity soon moved on, replaced once again by melancholy.

Behind him, the minibus took off towards its next destination.

"Welcome," said Asha dramatically, "to Outpost Six! One of fifteen similar outposts across the country. Here, we can prepare for our trip while we wait on my pilot. He won't be long."

She walked to the door, beside which was a keypad, which seemed out of place. More than that, though, and most striking of all, the door was clearly made of steel. It looked heavy, with a push bar at waist height, obviously to help opening the thing much easier. Asha tapped in a code, and the door beeped happily. Pushing at the bar, she was able move the door smoothly – perhaps it wasn't as heavy as it looked.

"Gentlemen, a new world awaits inside. You might be surprised by what you find here, but frankly, I expect that much of what you hear and see on this trip will eclipse what's behind these doors. Your world will never be the same."

It seemed to Luke an overly dramatic speech, but he somehow found comfort in her words. *Ridiculous times call for equally ridiculous speeches*, he thought.

He nodded, and stepped inside the grey building. *For Ellie*, he thought.

At first glance, the building didn't seem to contain anything particularly impressive; however, the interior was a stark contrast to the outside – the walls, floor, and ceiling were black and glossy, impeccably clean and reflective, with bright inset downlights illuminating the space. It was strangely bright and clear for an interior so profoundly black.

As he moved inside, though, he noticed there was more to this outpost.

The next room was a large open space, which was missing a wall opposite the entrance. This led into a large hangar, within which sat a small silver jet – at least, it was small by comparison to most passenger aircraft. Lining the walls of the main room were smaller rooms walled off by glass that stretched from floor to ceiling. Some of these rooms contained computers, but it was clear that they were storerooms of some kind, as they were filled with shelves and boxes and other knick-knacks.

One of the rooms on the right contained rows of lockers, and it was here that Asha headed first, disappearing between the rows. Not long after, she returned with a large duffel bag over her shoulder.

"Look around, but don't touch," she said, walking into the hangar. "I'll be back in a moment to answer any questions you may have." She looked at Oz. "Don't. Touch. Anything."

With that, she disappeared around a corner. Luke heard a door hinge squeal.

One of the rooms on the left caught Luke's attention. It didn't seem like the others – there were display cabinets inside, along with a bookshelf. The room seemed to have more colour than the majority of the others, as there were fewer cardboard boxes, so he and Oz set off to investigate while they waited.

Upon entering the room, he noticed a couple of

things. Firstly, everything here was old. Not just antique, but *ancient*. There were rusted pieces of armour, swords and scabbards, as well as bowls and cups made from various materials. Much of the metal was rusted and aged so much that parts had returned to dust, but the original form was still apparent. In some ways it was like a small museum. The display was impeccable, each item carefully placed and positioned for optimal viewing, and yet there were no placards describing what they were.

"Feels like we're back on a school excursion," mused Oz from outside the room, looking through the window. He smiled broadly when he noticed his comment had elicited a grin from Luke.

The books on the shelves were frayed and fragile-looking – some appeared as if they would fall apart if Luke as much as touched them – and there were hundreds of them.

Oz waltzed into the room, whistling in awe. "Well, would you look at this," he said incredulously. "This stuff is amazing!"

He reached out and took a book from the shelf before Luke could warn him against it. It didn't disintegrate. In fact, it was quite hardy, and as Oz turned its yellowed pages, Luke could see that the ink inside had been painstakingly handwritten in a language unknown to him. Calligraphy like this was surely a lost art. Given the flourishes that accompanied the text, Luke envisioned it must have taken a great deal of time to scribe each copy.

He'd never thought about it before, but for the very first time he appreciated the printing press.

In the centre of the room were two dark plinths; large, rectangular prisms of equal height. They appeared to be carved from dark marble, and they were gorgeous in their perfection. Sitting atop them was a glass case, the glass at least an inch thick, slightly distorting the item inside when viewed from an angle. They were affixed to their respective plinths via a metal frame, which glistened with green laser-like lights. Luke assumed this was some sort of sensor. The items inside each case must have been priceless given the security. And yet here they sat, locked away in some little grey outpost in the middle of nowhere.

In stark contrast to the security measure taken to protect them, the items within were simple in design. Beautiful, definitely, but simple nonetheless. One case held a small wooden box, slightly larger than a jewellery box. The wood was dark and still intact; Luke thought it was possibly mahogany. There was a hinge on one side, and a latch on the other, much like any wooden box that you might see anywhere.

The other case contained a small stringed instrument, not much larger than a tabloid newspaper. It was glittering and golden, but Luke wasn't certain if it was plated or made entirely from gold. Even the strings themselves glittered, as if they too were spun from some priceless metal. Strangely, this glass case didn't seem to have the same security device built in.

"It's beautiful," Luke exclaimed without thinking. "A harp. I've never seen one before."

"That's not a harp," replied Oz, this being one of those rare occasions when he knew something Luke didn't. "It's a lyre. But yes… it's exquisite."

Luke turned and looked at Oz, wondering who this was. Who the hell even knew the difference between a lyre and a harp, let alone *Oz*?

They both stood staring at the lyre for a short while, before Luke moved back to the wooden box.

A voice came from the doorway. "Pretty, isn't it?"

Asha walked into the room, surprising both Luke and Oz. She was dressed head to toe in black fatigues, with straps and pockets covering her thighs and torso. Dressed to kill, and looking like she could meet the task with next to no trouble. A short metal baton was strapped to the small of her back, and an empty black scabbard flapped above it. Luke wondered what sword someone like her may need to carry, and what other weaponry she had access to. He had known she was a badass – she carried herself like someone that could handle anything – but now she looked the part. She had also taken the time to tie back her amazing hair; she now had a kind of ponytail, tightly bound in leather, which was wound about its length almost like a tight rod that hung from the back of her head, the rest of her hair tight against her skull. She was an imposing sight.

"But you don't want to open this one," she said. "Hence the extra security." She waved her hand about the glass.

"Why?" asked Oz.

"The last time this box was opened, a lot of people died. It belonged to many individuals over the years, but most famously, it belonged to a woman named Pandora, among other things. The story surrounding the box itself has changed over the years, but the point remains the same – this box is bad news."

Luke laughed incredulously. "*That's* Pandora's Box?" He giggled. "That must make it thousands of years old!"

"Correct." Asha shut him down with a glance. "It is thousands of years old. But it didn't contain any magical mumbo jumbo… just thousands of diseased insects. When it was opened, it released a swarm upon the land, spreading a plague that destroyed entire cities. I'm sure the years have cleansed the box of any traces of the disease, but I don't want to be the one to find out."

"And the lyre…" She gestured to the other glass case. "Much less dangerous, but equally old." She paused in thought, tilting her head in thought. "Perhaps older."

Luke looked at Asha sheepishly. He didn't really believe this was Pandora's Box, but *she* certainly did. He felt bad that he had ridiculed her.

The entrance door opened and a man walked in. He moved quickly through the main area and out the back without so much as glancing at the group.

Asha gestured to the others that it was time to move on. They followed the man into the hangar area.

"That was Raven, my pilot," Asha told them. "He's… not really the talkative type, but he'll warm up to you. Eventually." She smiled. "Maybe."

"What kind of a name is Raven?" asked Oz. Luke was thinking the same thing, though he didn't think this was the right time to ask. He cast a quick glance at Oz, who shrugged and smiled.

"Clearly, it's not his name," said Asha. "It's his call sign. He has a name, just like you do – but he's more than that now. In certain company, if you tell people you know the Raven, they'll know *exactly* who you are talking about."

"Raven is a damned cool nickname," Oz said, and sighed. "I'd be pretty happy with that."

"It's *not* a nickname." Asha shot him a deadly look. "He earned that name. And while you may think it's cool, the story behind it isn't, really…" She laughed and her eyes drifted, recalling some old memory. "Perhaps he'll tell you someday."

At that moment, Raven himself entered the room. He'd obviously done what Asha had done when she first arrived, and headed into a changing room to get ready, but he wasn't wearing the same black fatigues as her. Instead, he wore blue jeans and heavy boots, complemented by a dark polo shirt that was open at the neck and tucked into his jeans. What made him imposing, though, was his sheer size. He looked like a powerlifter – the kind of guy that liked to pick up heavy things in his spare time. His upper torso was immense. His long hair and bearded face completed the tough-guy look, but nobody was going to vocalise this thought.

He looked at Asha, his expression stern. "Let's go."

Asha nodded, and the group headed toward the plane in silence.

While Raven set about doing preliminary check-ups on the outside of the plane, Asha opened the door and set up the stairs before heading in. The men climbed the staircase into the carriage afterwards.

The inside of the cabin was plain, yet still seemed somewhat extravagant, given the quality of the interior. In some ways, Luke thought it resembled some of the long-distance bullet trains he had ridden in Japan, with comfortable chairs that could be rotated to face each other, and small side tables that could be raised between. The main difference, though, was that these chairs were white leather, and looked more comfortable than even the most excessive chairs Luke had seen.

He selected a chair, and Oz sat across from him, peering out the porthole-like window. Things were starting to get real. Luke's mind went to Ellie, and he closed his eyes. He hoped he was on the right path. He felt good about it. He had to – Egypt was the only clue they had.

Soon after, Raven climbed the stairs, closing and

locking the door behind him by pushing down a large metal lever. He turned and faced the group.

"This ain't Emirates," he said gruffly. "Restroom is down the back, and there's drinks in the refrigerator and snacks in… well, somewhere. Help yourself."

With that, he turned and entered the cockpit, again closing the door behind him.

"I guess there's no passport check," mused Oz.

Before long, they were in the air. There was a very short runway behind of the outpost, the whole location clearly designed for a single plane.

Luke had never flown in a small airplane like this before. He shifted in his seat. Everything felt a bit rougher – the take off was bumpier, the turbulence felt stronger.

Asha noticed his discomfort. "There's nothing to worry about," she said, smiling warmly. "Smaller planes are lighter, so they feel the bumps more. But because we're smaller, so we can go much faster. Raven is probably one of the most experienced pilots in the world, so… you're in pretty good hands."

Luke smiled in return, but it didn't help. He'd never liked flying, since he was young. His imagination would run wild, envisioning the worst possible outcomes. He hadn't really grown out of that. To this day, he would experience stomach aches and pains every time he flew, so he often avoided eating, as it never really agreed with him. Most airline preprepared foods smelled terrible as well, which didn't help.

Perhaps a conversation would take his mind off things. He asked Asha who they'd meet in Egypt.

"He's known internally as the Historian. For as long as I've been around – and as far as I know, for as long as the Collective has been in existence – we've all kept our personal identities hidden. For some of us, it's been so long since we last used them, it's almost a memory…" She trailed off, lost in thought. "Anyway… we all play a part. But I know the Historian better than most."

Luke saw an opportunity. "What's yours?" he asked. "Your call sign?"

"I'm one of many trained for combat," she replied, entirely neglecting to answer the question. "I've spoken with the Historian on many occasions. Mostly to learn the history of the Collective, to learn where I fit in… and where *you* fit in. He's one of our lore-keepers. He has perhaps the greatest knowledge of ancient history out of the entire human race, which is why he's the best place to start."

Luke nodded. All of this only raised more questions, but he had no desire to ask anything further. His stomach was doing backflips.

It was getting dark outside. Luke settled in for the long trip, reclining his chair in an attempt to catch some sleep.

# CHAPTER TEN

For likely the last time, Bill locked the door to what had been his home for the last five years. It didn't really mean that much to him – he'd moved so many times throughout his long life that it no longer mattered where he hung his hat. This was just another in a long list of places he had called home.

Still, it was different this time. For most of his life he'd been a Watcher, never interacting, never making his presence known beyond a shadow in the window. It was a quiet existence. For him and countless individuals before him, life had been simple. But now, an ancient evil had shown its face, and the heretics had made their moves. Now was a time for action. He hadn't anticipated this would happen in his lifetime. No, scratch that – he had *hoped* this wouldn't happen in his lifetime.

His initial tutelage had been performed long ago – years of discipline and military training, and he'd been the best of an elite few. But since becoming a Watcher, Bill hadn't spent the subsequent time lazing about, wasting the efforts of his youth. He had studied as he watched. He had trained. He had practiced his fighting arts. And he prayed – all while in front of the window. Much of his life had been spent in a single room of wherever he happened to be living at the time. With regards to his most recent subject, though, he hadn't needed to be so vigilant. He'd known Luke wasn't going far with the few items he'd taken – he'd have to come back sometime. For this reason, Bill had stayed put while Luke lived at the hotel. He was one of very few individuals that knew where Luke was staying, so if anything was going to happen, it would most likely be here, at his house.

And he had been right.

Strangely, when Luke left the hotel in the minivan, Bill hadn't been ordered to give chase directly. His superiors were happy to leave his target in the hands of the woman from the Naacal Collective – better the devil you know. Instead, he and the rest of the Order of Metatron were to travel to the Holy See to regroup before coming to a decision on a course of action. Of course, the fact that Bill had been able to plant a tracking device meant the Order could track them down anyway. There was no immediate hurry. He was good at his job.

The timeline, at least from the Order's perspective, was clear. Dion Wexler's ambition was to reopen a portal to the underworld, and it was expected that he would attempt to do so at the vernal equinox, only two short months away. The where and how were less clear, but given that they had the ability to track Luke easily enough, and that *his* goal would clearly be to track down Dion and his supporters, they had time to regroup.

Bill stood at the roadside and pulled a silver flask from the inside pocket of his jacket. It was a cliché, but he felt he was getting old enough to let someone else take the lead, although he also knew the Patriarchs wouldn't see things his way. *Age is wisdom*, they would say. *The soldiers need a leader.*

He sighed and scratched at his beard, taking a deep swig from the flask and cringing as the fluid bit at his throat. There had been a time, long ago now, when the fire in his belly – the fire of God – seemed eternally stoked within him. He was the soldier destined to end heresy and destroy the demons waiting to break open the door between worlds.

But now? The fire had long since burned itself out. Being a Watcher wasn't exactly an exciting job. Important, sure, but definitely not exciting. And the fire had burned for so long, unfed... so now he was forced to feed it himself. With strong spirits.

He saw his ride approaching and felt his shoulders tense. This was it – the beginning of the end. In two short months, he'd have saved the day and would finally be ready to retire... or else he'd be dead somewhere. He placed his sleek black quiver in the large black duffel bag resting at his feet, but he held on to his bow – it was old, after all. The quiver was designed to be strapped to his thigh, but there was no need for that now.

A small black SUV pulled up in front of him, and a man jumped out of the front passenger seat to collect Bill's bags, offering him a seat in the front. Bill declined, preferring to sit in the back, where he could stretch out and hopefully keep to himself. He placed the bow gently on the seat beside him.

The driver was staring at him in the rear-view mirror. He averted his eyes when he noticed Bill was looking back.

"Good day, Inquisitor Reilly. Please make yourself comfortable."

"Thank you," Bill replied. He pulled his hat down over his eyes and leaned back. He was in no mood for small talk.

# CHAPTER ELEVEN

MUCH TO LUKE'S surprise, he did manage to sleep on the flight, but it was fitful. Nevertheless, it made a long trip a hell of a lot shorter, for which he was grateful. He welcomed not being present for any part of a flight, and he was glad it was over. There was no feeling like the sense of relief when the wheels hit the tarmac. The instant release of tension in his shoulders, neck, and jaw was always a strong reminder that he was not in control when he was in the air.

The plane taxied for what seemed forever after it landed, much longer than on any other flights Luke had taken, although he'd never flown to Egypt before. Looking out the windows, he saw that his surroundings were much as he had expected – deep yellow sand and stone, peppered with small, somewhat decrepit buildings. In the distance, he saw what was likely the airport proper, but the plane was headed in a different direction. Try as he might, he caught no glimpses of pyramids.

Eventually, the plane pulled into a small bunker – which was either carved into a big rock, or had simply been buried in sand and dirt; Luke couldn't quite tell. A hangar door closed behind them, and everyone on board the little plane suddenly sprung to life, as if they had been in limbo until that point.

The hangar was similar to the one they'd left – large enough to accommodate only a single passenger jet and not much else. There were rooms beyond the hangar, but there was no time for looking about; Asha ushered them towards the exit at the rear.

"It's mid-afternoon already. I don't want to waste any time," she muttered, pushing open the heavy door to the outside world.

Luke chuckled to himself. No passport. No customs. Nothing. He had landed less than twenty minutes ago and he was already free to explore Egypt. He could get used to this kind of travel.

As he stood outside the hangar in the blazing sun, a light breeze picked up the dust around him, and he marvelled at the turn his life had taken. He'd long harboured an interest in the ancient world, but it had always been beyond his grasp. Dani had never wanted to travel to this part of the world, and in recent years, it hadn't really been the safest place to visit. But here he was... a whole life away. His eyes watered, and he remembered his purpose.

The weather wasn't quite what he had been expecting. Perhaps he'd seen too many movies, but he was expecting it to be oppressively hot. Yes, it was warm, perhaps a balmy 25 degrees Celsius, but it was far from oppressive.

He smiled as he looked up at the sky. He hated uncomfortably hot weather.

Asha called him over to a beaten-up four-door hatchback, which was apparently their transportation.

"So... from a state-of-the-art jet plane... to *this*?" Luke mused.

"Well, there's no point in drawing attention to ourselves," said Asha. "When in Rome, do as the Romans do." She turned towards a middle-aged Egyptian man standing to one side. "This is Shehab. He's our driver and local guide. He's a part of the Collective, so we've got nothing to hide."

Shehab beamed through an unkempt beard, and extended his hand in greeting. "Ahlan wa Sahlan!" he said. "Welcome to Egypt!"

Oz and Luke squeezed into the back of the car, and they soon found themselves driving through the city. They'd landed on the runway at the Sphinx International Airport near 6th of October City, where the Naacal Collective had its own hangar and special access. The only thing between the hangar and Egypt at large was a small security gate, through which Shehab passed without much delay. Now, traveling through 6th of October itself, Luke once again marvelled at how far he was from home.

The first thing he noticed was the condition of the roads. They were in terrible shape, potholed and uneven, seemingly unfinished in places. Every few kilometres, Shehab had to slow almost to a standstill to drive over a road-wide gap in the asphalt – if it even was asphalt; Luke wasn't quite certain. There seemed to be a number of unspoken road rules – indicators weren't required, it seemed, and road markings (if they were there at all) were really just a guide. Among all this chaos, though, drivers seemed to keep their calm. There was little use of horns. Back home, most of what Luke was witnessing would have led to violence and abuse.

The sky above was clear, a light shade of blue tainted orange toward the horizon, but Luke couldn't tell whether this was due to pollution or sand whipped up by the wind. Everywhere he looked, he saw yellow sand, spotted with palm trees, and every once in a while, a verdant, well-maintained lawn which stood out like a beauty mark on the landscape.

Strangely, while the buildings each had their own design, they were all the same height, as if there was some law in this region regarding the maximum number of floors to which buildings were restricted. Most of the buildings appeared residential, with clothing hanging on lines on many of the balconies, blowing loosely in the wind.

Soon, however, the surroundings changed dramatically. The roads here were paved and new, and the buildings, while still simple in terms of their architecture, were more modern, utilising different coloured bricks and a lot more polished glass.

"Here we are," said Shehab gleefully. "October 6

University. Pride of the city."

Considering what Luke had seen of the rest of the city, this last comment was not surprising. The university looked like another world by comparison.

Slowly, Shehab took the group into the university complex, along roads surrounded by well-kept gardens and faculty sites.

Soon the group found themselves standing in the entry hall to the university. Here, multiple floors were open to ground level, with balconies looking down on the foyer, and light streaming through the windows at the rear. In places along several of the balconies were large, abstract bas-relief murals. This did not look like a place of historical study, but more like a museum of modern art.

Not long after they had entered the building, they were approached by two well-dressed, bearded men. The taller appeared to be an Egyptian native, while the other had a more Southern Asian appearance, likely hailing from India, Pakistan, or Sri Lanka. The taller man nodded to Shehab before introducing himself as the Historian.

He held out a hand to Luke in greeting. "Welcome, Luke Nixon," he said as they shook hands. Luke was surprised to find he had a British accent. "It is a pleasure to finally meet you. This is my colleague, the Tongue, who is in town to assist with a more complex translation I've come across recently."

The other man bowed slightly, reaching his hand out

in silent greeting, smiling broadly. Both men ignored Oz, and acknowledged Asha and Shehab with little more than a nod in their direction.

"Please," urged the Historian, "come to my office, where we can discuss your needs further—" he paused, looking around at the students making their way through the foyer "—in a little more privacy."

Oz shrugged at Luke, clearly a little hurt at being ignored, but he put his arm around his friend's shoulder, and together they followed the two men as they led them through the university. Asha followed on behind, while Shehab returned to his car – Asha could call on him when they needed him next.

Walking through the campus was much like walking through any other university the world over. Wide, almost silent corridors with doors lining the walls soon opened out onto large shared spaces filled with chattering students.

The Historian's office was one campus building over from where they had started, separated from the rest of the university by a plain wooden door, where other doors in the university were more decorative. On the door was a shiny metal plaque with the words *FACULTY STAFF ONLY* printed in red letters.

Inside was a small sitting room, obviously intended as a waiting room, with old metal office chairs lining the white plaster walls. The door on the other side of the room was metal and painted white, with key card access.

That whole side of the room didn't seem to fit in; the walls beside the door appeared to be constructed from brick or stone, while the rest of the building had been plastered. The Historian swiped his card and the group entered the room beyond.

The next room was much more like what Luke had expected to see at a university in Egypt. Framed pieces of papyrus covered in fading hieroglyphics lined the walls. Several more delicate pieces were laid out on a light board for deeper analysis, handheld magnifying glasses lying beside them. On other desks were carvings, statues, canopic jars, blocks of stone with carvings along their sides. Books filled the shelves against the walls, and more were piled up on the desks, some of them lying open.

And paper. There was paper everywhere. It was a mess, but clearly a mess with purpose.

Luke stood beside one of the tables near the entrance, awkwardly looking at the others. He hoped someone else would get things started – he hardly understood why he was even here, beyond a vision in a dream, and he needed to know that this would lead him back to Ellie.

Thankfully, the Historian began the discussion.

"So, Mr Nixon. I've seen your file; I know why you're here. I'm terribly sorry about your wife and daughter." The look on his face appeared sincere. Luke relaxed slightly. "You've come to me now, seeking a Pyramidion, based on advice provided to you in a vision. Do you... do you know which Pyramidion?"

"I don't even know what a Pyramidion is, to be honest," Luke replied, his face beginning to redden.

Oz replied in agreement, if only to remind everybody he was there. "Me neither."

"A Pyramidion is essentially the top of a pyramid or an obelisk – some refer to them as capstones or Benben stones. Many are made from stone, and they are often coated in precious metals. Most pyramids have one – or at least had one at some point. Some of them have gone missing over the years, often only for the metals encasing them…" He drifted off, looking annoyed at so much history being lost to thievery. "Anyway, I have information on all known capstones. We have several on display in The Museum of Egyptian Antiquities."

Excitedly, Oz interrupted. "So why don't we go see them?"

"Well, primarily because we don't need to. I know what is written on these stones, and none contains the information you seek."

"How do you know that?" Luke challenged him. "I mean… I don't even know what information I seek."

"You look for information on the location of your daughter, likely in the hands of Dion Wexler. You seek to understand the intentions of Mr Wexler. You hunt for the identity of the creature that confronted you in your home. All of this is interrelated, and all of this points to information that has been lost to time – lost even to the Naacal, and to the M'jai.

"Tell me," the Historian continued, "what did you encounter that day in your home?"

Luke hadn't thought of that day in a while. Part of him was still processing the fact that there was some mysterious 'file' on him somewhere, filled with everything that had passed between him and Asha. Every meeting. Every discussion. His favourite brand of whisky. It felt like a kind of betrayal. He cast Asha a glance. He'd deal with that another time.

"Well… it was tall. Maybe seven foot. It, uh, held itself in a very confident manner – almost regal. Its skin was white and as smooth as marble, but there were two discoloured horns rising from the top of its head. Its mouth…" He trailed off, searching for words. "It wasn't a normal mouth. It resembled an insect – or a crab, maybe? It wasn't anything like a human mouth that's for sure. And its voice." He shuddered. "Oh God, that voice."

"Interesting. Not really enough to determine precisely who it was that you encountered, but interesting nonetheless." The Historian turned to Asha. "I think you're right. I didn't want to believe it, but it seems clear to me that the gods indeed walk among us once again."

This elicited a snort from the Tongue. "Surely you must be joking," he said, and laughed. "The ancient tomes are clear on this. These creatures were banished – permanently!"

Finally, Asha joined the conversation. "He has no reason to lie, Tongue." Her tone wasn't polite, and she scowled as she spoke. "Not only that, but all of my studies suggest otherwise. The portals can be reopened. And now it's pretty clear that something has come back through."

"Let's not be hasty, Spear," the Historian replied in an even tone. "There is no evidence that a portal has been opened. We don't know how... it... got here. Keep in mind that the majority of portals are buried deep beneath the pyramids. Preparation and time have made them all but impossible to access."

"Except one." Asha's tone was cold.

"Yes... Except one." The Historian turned to the corner of the room where a doorway led into a dark stairwell. Luke walked over to have a closer look. To his surprise, it was a spiral staircase, and it looked old.

"Many years ago, our predecessors, the M'jai, built a staircase to the portal below, surrounded by a small fortress. Over extended periods of time, as the people forgot what was here, the need for fortifications diminished, and the building was downsized. When the Naacal took over, we built a place of study above the portal, which soon grew to become the university. This room is solely owned and accessible by members of the Naacal Collective. In fact, you two—" he gestured to Luke and Oz "—may well be the first non-members to set foot in here for hundreds of years."

Oz was pretty pleased with this, blurting a boisterous "Hell yeah!" and looking to Luke for support. Luke ignored him.

"Let's go down the stairs," he suggested. "I'd like to see, if I's not too dark down there."

"Sure," replied the Historian. "Go for it. The beast didn't arrive from the temple below, I'm quite certain of that – only myself and the Tongue have access to this room. Take your time, have a look around. We'll be here waiting when you return." He walked to the wall, where some electric lanterns hung. "You'll need one of these, though. There's no power down there."

Taking the lantern, Luke nodded his thanks, and turned towards the door. Oz grabbed a lantern of his own, and they made their way slowly down the rickety staircase. Progress was made slower by Luke's poor vision in low light, but they descended at a steady pace. The air grew musty.

At the bottom of the staircase, the walls were no longer brick, but were cut from stone. Luke hadn't noticed the transition, but it certainly explained the change in temperature. While it wasn't cold, there was far less heat in the air, which had become somewhat stagnant.

There was light in here, provided by torches and braziers that hung on the walls, but it was still fairly dark. Many of the tables along the walls were covered in books, although Luke had to get close to make out details. Many were leatherbound, and they were old – like the books Luke and Oz had seen back in Asha's lair. Unlike the room upstairs, though, there was less order here. Some of these books were covered in what had to be years' worth of dust.

He was glad for the electric lantern – it was high-powered, and lit almost the whole room. They probably didn't need more than one, but he was happy for the extra light that Oz's lantern provided.

In the centre of the room was a round slab of granite, above which the light shimmered, as if there was a thick fog there. It was almost as if Luke was looking through an unbroken sheet of water floating in mid-air.

"Do you see that?" he asked Oz.

"See what?"

"The light… it's shimmering." He waved his arm through the area, and watched as the air swirled around where his arm passed through.

"Does it? I don't see anything." Oz approached the slab, a confused expression on his face. He walked directly through the anomaly, and yet appeared to see nothing.

Luke turned to survey the rest of the room. The dust on the ground around the stone slab was disturbed, as if until recently there had been some kind of fence around it. Apart from that, the room was quite empty. However, ahead, in the darkness at the edges of the room, he could see light streaming in from a small alcove. As Oz whistled in awe as he flicked through books at the other end of the room, seemingly enthralled, Luke approached the alcove to investigate.

As he turned the corner into the alcove, he froze. The Historian had referred to this place as a temple, but until now it hadn't seemed like one. Here, though, he could see why he had used this term. The alcove was much larger than he had expected, and at the other end stood two ancient statues of Egyptian deities, still in excellent condition despite the years. Although it had been a while since he had last read up on Egyptian gods, Luke believed them to be Anubis and Ra – the jackal and the hawk. Between them was a large stone bowl, inside of which a fire was burning, sending light flickering within the alcove and out into the room beyond. Standing behind the bowl, between the statues, was the same entity that Luke had encountered before.

It turned to look at him.

*{Are you lost, little lamb?}*

The voice knocked the breath out of him. He froze, mouth agape, and dropped his lantern.

At that, the creature raised its arms above its head, and a black cloud appeared at its feet. It seemed to stream out from within its robes like a swarm of insects. The cloud grew, and within it Luke could see shapes taking form, accompanied by screams unlike anything he'd heard before. Coarse, like white noise. Luke found this noise even more disturbing than the voice of the creature that had summoned them. As the cloud dissipated, it left behind two new creatures, which stood at the feet of the larger one, beside the fire.

As strange as the original creature was, these new ones made it seem almost pedestrian. They each stood on two hooves – they had the feet of a bull, but the legs of a child – and wings hung from their back: leathery, old, and blackened. One had the face of a snarling lion cub, the other that of a bear cub, equally menacing. At the end of their chubby, child-like arms were clawed hands. But more striking than any of this was their skin, which was a deep and unnatural red, like a ripe tomato. Luke recoiled, fearfully taking a step back.

Footsteps rang out behind him, followed by a gasp.

"What. The. Fuck?" Oz croaked.

"I don't know, but I think we need to get the hell out of here!" Luke turned and ran towards Oz, throwing out an arm to pull him along. However, at the same time he felt something hit him in the middle of his back.

Hard.

Falling to the floor, he looked back to see what had hit him. One of the smaller creatures was hovering not far away, looking down at him threateningly. It must have torpedoed itself into his back, knocking him down, and knocking the wind out of him in the process. It swung its claws at Oz, who had rushed in to help yet found himself frozen in fear as the creature approached, lashing out with its claws. Oz screamed in pain as they tore through his clothing and into the flesh beneath. This was enough to pull him out of his stupor, and he fell backwards, kicking his feet as he scrambled to escape.

Grabbing his shoulder in pain, Oz clambered the remaining few feet to reach Luke, who had managed to stand. Behind them, heavy footsteps came from the staircase while the creatures edged towards them, their hooves clacking on the stone floor. The larger creature was nowhere to be seen.

Suddenly, the Historian burst out of the staircase, followed closely by Asha.

"Spear," he called. "Cherubim!" He pointed towards the alcove.

Asha flew into action, pulling a knife from her waistband and hurling it at the creature nearest to Luke. The blade flew like an arrow and pierced the creature between the eyes, sending it hurtling backwards due to the momentum.

As Asha approached the two men, her free hand pulled a pistol from a holster at her hip, and she fired two shots in quick succession as Luke and Oz watched helplessly. Both bullets appeared to hit the second creature in exactly the same place: its left eye. It, too, fell backward.

Both creatures dissolved to become black cloud, which soon dissipated as if it had never been there in the first place. Asha retrieved her knife from the dust.

"Well, one thing's for certain," she said as she examined the blade. "There's no question about it – for one reason or another, at least one of the ancient gods once again walks the Earth."

# CHAPTER TWELVE

Shortly after the excitement by the portal, the team regrouped upstairs, sitting on chairs retrieved from nearby rooms. Asha tended to Oz's shoulder – thankfully, the claws hadn't damaged too much of the muscle and the majority of the damage was only skin deep, but it still looked painful. The edges of the broken skin were blackened and swollen, and glistened in the light.

Luke sat in mute disbelief, staring at the floor. This wasn't the first time he'd seen the creature, but it didn't make it any easier to accept. And now it was attacking them with demons conjured from the air?

While everything seemed to be going from bad to worse, it was clear they were on the right track. Luke shook his head and looked back up at the group.

"I'm sorry," he began, "but I really need to know what's going on. I know what I saw, but none of it makes any sense – going downstairs somehow raised more questions than it answered."

The Historian nodded. "That's fair. Totally understandable. To be honest, even for those of us in the Collective, this is a lot to take in. We've studied these creatures for centuries, but even given everything we've been told to believe, it's still hard to accept the reality of things like this until you see it with your own eyes…

"However," he continued, "it's not so simple to explain everything in one sitting. Impossible even. Needless to say, things aren't as they seem. The creatures you saw are among many that once inhabited the Earth. But many thousands of years ago, our ancestors were able to banish them back to their own realm, and they haven't been seen since. The Naacal Collective has existed ever since, to retain the knowledge of the past, and to remain vigilant for their return. Although… having seen them now, I'm not sure we are entirely prepared."

Luke stood and began pacing between the tables. "What are they, though? You've called them gods, demons, beasts – surely they can't be all of these things?"

The Tongue, who had been sitting silently in a dark corner until this point, said, "Why not? For the last two thousand years or so, humans have operated in the belief that there were inherently 'good' gods and 'bad' gods, but that doesn't make sense. In the end… there were just *gods*, as far as we know. Why would one god punish those who defy its enemy? These creatures – these gods, these… *demons*, whatever you want to call them – are more or less the same as us, except they possess a kind of magic. They do what benefits them most – sometimes at the benefit of others, sometimes not. The Greco-Roman religions captured their essence best. They are powerful beings... but flawed."

Luke sat down again, exasperated. "Then why did we banish them?"

"Because we were effectively their slaves. We had no autonomy, and so we overthrew the powers that be... and closed the portals behind them. Sadly, the portals can't really be closed per se, so we did the next best thing... We buried the portals, and built massive monuments upon them, designed to exert celestial power over them."

Luke took this in. Nobody spoke. The Historian stared into the distance. Asha finished tending Oz, who winced as he put his ruined T-shirt back on.

"So..." Oz said, gritting his teeth as he pulled his head through the T-shirt hole. "Spear, huh?"

"Well... *the* Spear, if we're being technical," answered Asha in return, smiling at Oz for what Luke thought was possibly the first time. "Since the inception of the Naacal Collective, there have always been twelve in the Prime Council, the keepers of the Truth. You've now met three of us: the Historian, the Tongue, and myself, the Spear. In addition, there are hundreds of apprentices across the globe, including Shehab. If a member of the Prime Council passes away or abdicates their role, their next in line will assume their position, and so on, over and over. It made sense when all we were guarding was information and artifacts. Now, though... we may need more Spears."

Again, the room grew silent. For a while, the group

sat in silence, before Luke asked the question that was on everybody's lips.

"What now?"

It was the Historian who responded. "Now? The trail is cold, but I guess we continue along the path we had started upon – probably starting with the Pyramidion. There are other paths we could follow…" He trailed off, looking over at the Tongue. "What about the Prophet?"

"Heresy!" the Tongue spat in disgust. "The Prophet is lost to this world, and regardless, he never spoke of anything that would help with our current… predicament."

"True." The Historian lapsed into thoughtful silence. "Then I guess we continue with our search for the Pyramidion."

He walked over to one of the tables, upon which was a large piece of stone the size of a bucket. He traced his finger along hieroglyphs carved into the stone before speaking again.

"Many Pyramidion feature hieroglyphs such as these," he said, "but most of them are in worship of the sun god, Ra, or in respect to the Pharaoh housed within the pyramid beneath it. Few, however, have instructions for… various things. One such pyramid did not have a Pyramidion at its summit, but an altar. On this altar was inscribed the location of a hidden pyramid that has never been found. It is believed that this pyramid contains the instructions for opening the portals, hence the reason it was buried, and the altar destroyed – so that man would never again be subject to the gods."

He turned towards the group, a smile forming on his lips. "But I have a copy of the inscription on the altar. It's locked away in my other office in the museum, in a lockbox to which only the Historian has access."

Asha gasped. "That must be what Dion is searching for!"

"But…" Luke said, "wouldn't he have already found it, if one of those things is here?"

"No," replied the Historian. "Those creatures can be summoned, if you have their seal. This knowledge is known to the Prime Council, but hidden from the rest of the Collective and mankind at large. Dion Wexler was, until recently, the Spear's predecessor. It is likely he had located one such seal."

The group decided to head to the Egyptian Museum in Cairo. It was getting late, but the severity of the day's events suggested that there was no time to waste. Asha, Luke, and Oz squeezed back into Shehab's beaten-up hatchback. The Historian and the Tongue rode together separately.

The drive into Cairo was long and uneventful. The traffic was horrific – Luke didn't think he could have driven here, as people did whatever they wanted, whenever they wanted. He saw a taxi reverse for hundreds of metres on a major thoroughfare, honking its horn to notify oncoming traffic, presumably because the driver had missed a turn. The other cars simply drove around it, as if this were nothing out of the ordinary.

Finally, Shehab pulled up in front of a spiked metal fence surrounding a large pink building of European design, which had an arched entryway and a dome at the top of the main structure. It was striking in its garishness. Beside the large entry gates were two guardhouses, which perhaps acted as ticket booths during the day. They waited a minute or two in silence, then a black sedan pulled up behind them. The Historian and the Tongue jumped out, and headed towards the gate.

As the museum was closed, the guards were being difficult, despite the fact they clearly knew the Historian. However, the Historian had his ways, and a quick call to the museum director led to profuse apologies, and the gates soon opened to reveal a gorgeous garden area leading to the arched entryway.

The Historian led the way, leading the six silently through the immense structure.

Luke was in awe. From the moment he entered the building, he was greeted by thousands of objects of antiquity. The walls in the first hall were lined with statues and sarcophagi, while others had rows of wooden display cases filled with thousands upon thousands of priceless artifacts. To someone with an interest in the region and its history, it was mind-blowing.

However, the Historian scolded Luke whenever he stopped to inspect an item. While Oz and Luke stared around them, mouths agape, the rest of the group pressed on silently, with barely a glance at the wonders they passed. Luke made a note to return here when he had more time – with Ellie by his side.

Eventually, they made their way into a private section of the museum. They passed dark offices filled with books, and soon found themselves in a massive storeroom. Floor-to-ceiling shelves surrounded them, holding rows of wooden containers. Luke wondered what was inside – how many thousands of precious items there were here, hidden away, considered of less interest to potential visitors than the items currently on display.

The group approached a black door at the rear of the storeroom. It was out of the way, to the side of the main walkway, and boxes were piled up to the left and right of it. A sign on the door read STRICTLY NO ADMITTANCE.

The Historian looked up at a camera on the wall, nodded, then pulled out a key card and held it to a small box below the door handle. It beeped in acceptance, and a small green light lit up. He opened the door and entered a short corridor with doors on the left and right.

"The secret storage area of the Historian," he said in a reverent tone. "Not many in the Prime Council are aware of its existence. Don't touch *anything*."

He watched the rest of the group file into the corridor before opening the door on the left. The main entry door closed behind them, and locked with a loud click.

"Everything is extremely well organised, but I don't find myself here very often. Please, make yourself comfortable while I track down the right document. And again – you can look, but don't touch." He sat before an aging computer terminal, and began tapping at the keys.

"So…" Oz began, a grin on his face, clearly about to stir the pot. "Have you got the Holy Grail in here or what? Excalibur?"

This earned a sharp glance from Asha. "Now is not the time," she responded abruptly. "If you want a history lesson based on the lies created to keep mankind in the dark, feel free to head back out into the museum. But don't expect any help from us."

Oz blushed. "Sorry. I was just trying to lighten the mood."

"Why are you even here, Oz?" asked Asha abruptly. She had a dark look in her eyes – she'd likely been harbouring this question for some time.

The question seemed to take Oz by surprise, but he maintained his resolve. "For Luke, Asha. As much as you and your wonderful friends are helping him, he doesn't *know* you. He knows *me*. I'm here for Luke."

Asha nodded in response. The dark look was gone.

The Historian stood up, an expression of elation on his face. "Found it!" he exclaimed. "It's in the other room." He looked over at Oz, pointing towards a dark corner of the room. "One of the grails is over there." He disappeared across the hall, followed by the Tongue.

Oz shot a questioning look at Luke and mouthed, "*One* of the grails?" before moving to the corner the Historian had indicated to get a closer look. Sitting the shelf was a polished wooden wine cup. It looked neither old nor new, flashy nor cheap. It was kind of dull. Shrugging his shoulders, Oz made his way into the other room to see what the Historian had hidden away.

Luke saw this as an opportunity to talk to Asha. Taking a deep breath, he said, "What exactly does the Spear do, anyway?"

"The Spear wields the sword for the Prime Council. We undergo heavy combat and weapons training, and are tasked with monitoring the bloodline. No harm may fall upon my charges."

"And that includes noting down every little aspect of my life, personal or not, for the rest of the Collective to read?" He looked at Asha firmly, hoping his eyes said what remained unspoken.

"Luke," Asha replied carefully, "it is important that we know as much about you as possible. I understand this is, to some degree, a violation of your privacy, but—"

"To some degree!" Luke raged. "To *some* degree?! Everyone in your little group knows my pain. Perhaps they all know how I dealt with it, do they? Perhaps you took photos of me passed out on my couch and shared them for a laugh – locked doors never seemed to stop you!"

Asha put her hands out, palms up, trying to placate

him. "Of course not, Luke. Look – I can understand why you'd be disappointed, but I only shared what I felt was relevant. The details are less important."

Luke sighed and leaned against the desk behind him.

"If something were to happen to me, Luke… If I were to die, then someone else would be assigned as the Spear. They would need to know everything important right from the get-go so that they could hit the ground running. So that they could *protect* you and continue searching for your daughter."

Luke sighed and nodded. He wasn't happy with the situation, but he had to admit it made sense.

"Before," he said, "you said the Spear wields the sword. Where's your sword? All I see is an empty scabbard on your back."

Asha gritted her teeth. "Dion took the sword when he left us. I keep the scabbard as a reminder that I need to get it back. It's just another of my responsibilities."

Luke nodded once again.

Oz re-entered the room. "They kicked me out," he said, shrugging his shoulders. "I don't think the Tongue likes me…"

*Bang.*

A gunshot rang out from the other room, followed quickly by the sounds of scuffling and footsteps running down the corridor. Luke and Asha sprung up and out the door, Asha holding her sidearm. At the end of the corridor stood the Tongue, pointing a pistol in their direction as he heaved open the heavy entry door.

"You're too late," he shouted, wild-eyed. "The Collective is old and scared, and far too weak to do anything with the knowledge they have. With this, Dion will finally be able open the portal!" He fired off a shot before turning to run through the doorway. The heavy door slammed closed behind him.

Luke stood in shock. He looked at the door frame beside him, where a bullet hole smoked only inches from his right eye, and sawdust floated down from where the bullet had buried itself. Close call. There was a lump in his throat; he felt as if his heart had lodged itself there.

The group hurried into the other room to find the Historian lying on his side, a small pool of blood spreading beneath him. Asha threw herself on the floor, carefully turning him onto his back and lifting his head.

"I'm sorry," he said through gritted teeth stained with blood. "I didn't know we had a traitor amongst us..." He coughed. "He took the instructions." Another cough. "I'm sorry." Each cough shook his entire body, and he winced in pain.

He turned his head to look at Luke. "Nephilim. Go see the Prophet." He coughed again. Now he didn't seem to respond to the pain, and he wheezed as he spoke.

Asha said, "But *where*, Salim? Where should we find the Prophet?"

The answer came slowly and quietly as the life seeped from the Historian's body. "Find... a... bokor."

# CHAPTER THIRTEEN

SHEHAB DROPPED THE remaining members of the group off at a nearby hotel before returning to deal with the fallout. As it turns out, he was the Historian's apprentice, and it was quite likely that the duties of the Historian would be transferred to him, so it was only fitting that he spent time with police and museum authorities. The extended powers of the Collective saw to it that the rest of the group appeared not to have been there at all; any records that suggested otherwise were amended.

Asha, Luke, and Oz sat in their shared hotel room, attempting to process recent events. While Asha was very strong-willed, she was clearly distraught at the loss of the Historian.

"Salim was my friend," she said wistfully. "In many ways, he raised me – he taught me the Truth and kept me under his wing. He was a father figure to me… or an older brother. I can't believe he's gone. And the Tongue! How could I be so stupid – why didn't I see this coming? Another person abdicating their role in pursuit of their own interests. This isn't going to be pretty…" She jumped from her chair and began pacing around the room.

Luke made an attempt to change the subject. "What can we do now?" he asked. "The Historian wouldn't want the Tongue to get away with this, but we lost the transcript... What's our plan B? Do we even have one?"

Asha sat down on the edge of the bed. "Well, first... we wait," she said. "I can't leave until I've spoken with the Prime Council – and given the circumstances, they'll probably send the Executioner."

At the mention of this new name, Luke and Oz glanced at each other with raised eyebrows.

"Then..." she continued, "I guess we look for the Prophet. That's what Salim told us to do."

"What's a bokor?" Oz asked solemnly. "I heard the Historian say we need to look for a Bokor or something."

"A bokor..." Asha repeated, "is a spooky witch doctor, my friend. A voodoo priest, if you will. A sorcerer. A summoner. Someone with the ability to commune with the spirit world. Salim wants us to find him there, I think, in the spirit world." She glanced at Luke. "As you are keenly aware, death is not necessarily the end – particularly for the Nephilim. Hence all the dreams you've had since your wife passed. And Salim's bloodline was also strong – not quite as strong as yours, but strong nonetheless. You must meet him in the spirit realm, and he will tell you how to find the Prophet."

"Why can't he just... haunt my dreams, or whatever?" Luke asked.

"I'm... not really certain, to be honest. You probably

need a strong connection with someone to be able to do that. I expect he just doesn't know you well enough… so you're gonna need some help."

Luke was overwhelmed. Looking at the clock, he saw it was well past midnight. After all of the day's excitement, he needed to rest. The three each picked a bed, and Luke fell swiftly into a deep sleep.

IN THE MORNING there was an unexpectedly early knock at the door. It was Shehab, looking tired and unkempt. He was accompanied by someone new: a tall, muscular, and strikingly handsome Asian man, dressed in black fatigues, like Asha. He was bald, and while he looked stoic, there was a kindness in his eyes. Luke liked him immediately.

"Spear," said the newcomer, nodding at Asha.

"Axe," she replied. Looking towards Luke and Oz and gesturing to the newcomer, she said, "Gentlemen, this is the Executioner. We usually call him Axe. He'll be joining us for a little while, although his primary focus is on locating the Tongue and bringing him to justice. At present, our target leads us down the same path. You should be glad to have him on your side – make sure you don't end up in his sights." She clearly held him in high regard.

Shehab went over the details of the previous night,

and what he'd gone through after the others had left. He had already been unofficially promoted to the role of Historian, but his official inauguration would be decided at a later date – when the dust had settled. He had collected Axe from the airport first thing this morning, and briefed him on the way. It was expected that the Tongue had already left the country.

"Worse still," he continued, "is that the Historian was keeping something from us. Nothing as serious as the Tongue's defection, let me be clear, but I discovered that he already had his suspicions and did not share them with us. The Prime Council was aware of his concerns, of course, so I expect he just didn't have the right opportunity to share his concerns with the rest of us, as the Tongue didn't leave his side yesterday. I think his plan was for you to discover this on your own when you went down to the portal – it had clearly been disturbed. I guess he hadn't expected the demon to be there…" He trailed off.

The Executioner picked up the explanation. "The Tongue disappeared almost immediately upon leaving the museum. Having such a long history within the Collective, he knew our ways all too well, and effectively disappeared without a trace. Whether or not he is still in the country is unknown, but it is expected that he will next meet with the traitor, Dion Wexler. Sadly, we are now several steps behind Dion, and without a hell of a lot of luck, we aren't likely to catch up any time soon."

He let out a long sigh. "However… I hear the Tongue was strongly opposed to us meeting with the Prophet. There *must* be a reason for this."

The group fell silent, until Shehab spoke up. "Does anybody actually know a bokor?"

"Well," Asha began uncertainly, "I guess I know *of* one. But does it need to be a bokor? What about a different kind of medium – perhaps something a little more… local?"

"Salim knew his business, Spear. If he says we need to seek a bokor, then we need to seek a bokor."

"Let me make a few calls."

With that, Asha left the room. Luke and Oz looked at Axe awkwardly, not knowing what to say. What had started out as an adventure was becoming more serious by the minute, and Luke was still trying to decide how he felt about it all. What made this even more difficult was what he had seen below the university – had he hallucinated those tiny monsters?

He decided to ask Shehab, if only to pass the time. "So… when we were down by the portal, something attacked me. What were those little things?"

Shehab took a deep breath. "The Cherubim. Within the hierarchy of the gods, there are several levels – history has referred to some as angels and others as demons, but in the end, they all serve the same purpose: to aid or support their master.

"Each of these demon-gods has their own regimen of

lower-tier creatures. The Seraphim are their direct guards, the highest of the order. Should their master fall, a new leader will generally rise from their ranks. Below them lie the Cherubim – the expendable army. These spiteful creatures have no will of their own, and exist at the whim of their master. They are imbued with hatred and aggression, and are rarely conjured into existence, to the best of our knowledge.

"All of that said, none of these creatures have been seen in over… a thousand years, perhaps? Possibly more."

"Why are they here now, then?"

"It has something to do with Dion Wexler, but this seems extreme even for him. During his time in the Council, I hear he was difficult… but given I was merely an apprentice at the time, I wasn't privy to the details, sadly. I'm afraid I'm not quite sure why he elected to summon this creature."

A voice came from the doorway.

"Power."

It was Asha. She had returned partway through the discussion and stood leaning against the door frame. "He wants power. Part of the reason we withhold the Truth from the rest of the population is that this was bound to happen at some time or another. Effectively, he wants to become a god, or at the very least, control the gods. If he can seize their power, he can take over our world. Or better yet, if he can become as powerful as they are, he can confront them on their own turf. They have even more power in their world.

She walked into the room and stood beside Luke.

"Anyway, I've got the information I needed. We need to head to Haiti next. There's a bokor there who is known to have a relationship with the Loa Baron Samedi, and he has agreed to help us contact Salim. But we've got to get moving – with every passing day, the connection gets weaker."

She already carried her bag on her shoulder. Oz noticed this and looked at his wristwatch. "What – now?" he asked incredulously. It was still only 9am and they were yet to even have breakfast.

"Now. Raven is waiting for us at the airport."

# CHAPTER FOURTEEN

THE TRIP TO the airport was a little more comfortable – rather than squeezing into Shehab's tiny car once again, the group had called a local limousine service, who returned them to their hangar in some semblance of style. Shehab had said his goodbyes at the hotel to return to the university to manage his affairs – he had a lot to learn and a dizzying array of new responsibilities.

The rest of the group, now including Axe, passed through the facility and were soon seated comfortably aboard Raven's jet. Arriving here had taken a little longer than expected, mostly because Oz had complained enough to force a detour along the way, for breakfast. To be fair, the food had made everyone feel a little better and afterwards they all agreed it was the right decision. However, this meant Raven had missed his initial schedule and was now awaiting approval for the next available window for departure. The atmosphere in the cockpit was tense – nobody dared go near him to ask any questions.

In contrast, the cabin was abuzz with conversation. Asha was informing Axe about events of the last few weeks, and Oz was opening up to Luke about what had happened before he had left home.

"Well, I kind of lied," he began, squirming a little. "Not about everything. Just… about Tammy." He paused. "We kind of… broke up."

"Not over me, I hope?" Luke asked. "I mean, I'm glad you came, but not if it was at the expense of your relationship."

"No, no, it wasn't that. We actually broke up a few weeks earlier – I just didn't want to lay it on you straight away. You had enough to worry about. I spent the last couple of weeks in a hotel, too. But it's all good! It was a long time coming, if I'm honest… And, well, it means I can be here, now – fully. If we were still together, part of me would be back home with her. This way, it's you and me against the world. Well, against this Dion guy, anyway."

Luke stared at his friend, unsure what to say. Oz hadn't been with Tammy for long, really – maybe only a year or two – and Luke hadn't really gotten to know her well. Still, he had liked her. She had seemed good for Oz.

"I'm… sorry, man. I liked Tammy."

Oz looked a little sad. "Yeah, I did too… but I guess I can't change the past. But what I *can* do is help you get Ellie back. You know me – I'm an only child. You're like… my brother."

Raven burst out of the cockpit. "Seatbelts, princesses. We're off." He turned around quickly and closed the door behind him. Oz shrugged his shoulders and put on his seatbelt.

Within minutes, the plane moved towards the runway, and the group was on their way to Haiti.

A FEW HOURS into the flight, Luke turned to Asha and Axe, both of whom were now stirring after taking a short nap. *I guess when you're used to a life like this, you take your sleep when you can get it*, Luke mused.

"So… help me understand," he began. "Why, exactly, are we going to Haiti?"

Asha sighed. "Well… as I mentioned earlier, death is not necessarily the end. Not for anybody, but especially not for the Nephilim. Salim had a strong bloodline, so he knows he can reach you in the spirit realm, even though that's not necessarily a place he wants to hang around in. And while there are many that claim to contact the spirit realm, only bokor can merge the two realities, so to speak.

"Given we need to speak with the dead, we need to enlist the help of Baron Samedi, the gatekeeper to the spirit realm, and there is one such bokor in Haiti that can help us. It's unlikely to be an enjoyable experience—" her lips curled in a sly grin "—depending on what you enjoy."

Luke let this information sink in before asking the real question that was on his lips. "What's a Nephilim, anyway? You all keep calling me that, but I've got no idea what it is."

"Ah. I've been waiting for you to ask." She shifted in her seat to face him front on, and took a deep breath.

"Well. I don't even know where to start with this one…" She sighed. "OK. According to early versions of the Hebrew Bible, the Nephilim were the result of the coupling between the sons of God and the daughters of men. Others have called the Nephilim giants, fallen warriors, or the children of angels and demons. As with everything passed down across the religions, there's some truth in this, but it was tainted by dogma over time.

"The truth is, the Nephilim are human descendants of an ancient bloodline, from a time when the gods shared the Earth with humanity. Given the amount of time that has elapsed since those days, everyone alive today has some relation to that bloodline, but some – direct descendants of the original Nephilim – are special. Some are true Nephilim." She paused, looking at Luke intently.

Luke ignored the pregnant pause. "Why does it matter?"

"It matters because…." She drifted off, deep in thought. "It matters because of the relationship between the gods and the Nephilim."

Abruptly, Luke heard a ping, followed by Raven's gruff voice over the intercom. "Buckle up – there's a storm ahead. It's a big one, so we'll be knocked about a bit."

As the plane began to shake, Luke tightened his seatbelt and gripped the armrests. Turbulence made him uncomfortable, to say the least. Outside it was light enough that Luke could see the rain streaking across the windows. Flashes lit up the sky from time to time, but the plane flew on unhindered. Luke closed his eyes and took a deep breath, reminding himself that there were more than 100,000 flights around the world every day, and that he was safer in the sky than on the ground… but every bump made his chest tighten.

He sat this way for a while, paying attention to each breath in and out, trying not to think about the fact he was hurtling through the sky at a phenomenal speed in what was effectively just a metal tube. He began to count backwards from 100, breathing slowly all the while.

Once he'd reached zero, he opened his eyes and looked around him. Oz had his eyes closed and his headphones on, possibly asleep, seemingly oblivious to the world. Axe and Asha had begun playing cards. Nobody else seemed at all phased by the turbulence, even as the lighting in the cabin flickered and the modular components rattled.

The turbulence continued for another thirty minutes, and Luke fell asleep for the remainder of the trip, jolting awake as the wheels hit the tarmac. He scowled and squinted at the sunlight that streamed through the window.

The plane soon pulled into a small hangar and came to a stop.

"Seriously?" asked Oz incredulously. "You guys have your own hangar in *Haiti*?"

Asha laughed. "Not quite. We just called in a favour."

Luke soon found himself descending the stairs onto a dusty concrete area within the hangar. A loud engine whirred as the hangar doors closed. Behind him was a doorway leading into the main building, and standing at each side of the door were two very large men in army fatigues and khaki berets, holding equally large automatic rifles. The men looked straight ahead and paid the group no attention, yet Luke felt very insecure.

Asha passed between them briskly, gesturing at Luke and Oz. The two men jogged to catch up to her and soon found themselves in a room that Axe referred to as the "mess hall", which was effectively a small kitchen.

Asha gestured to a door on the right. "There are toilets and a shower in there, if you want to freshen up. We've got about forty-five minutes before our guide arrives – you're going to want to be as alert as possible. There's food and drink in here as well."

It wasn't exactly the most well-equipped of facilities, but Luke was especially happy to feel hot water on his back. It had been a few days since he had been able to have a shower, and he was a bit ripe. For the first time in a long while, he was alone with his thoughts, and he wept quietly in the shower.

✕

AFTER THE GUIDE arrived, the four soon found themselves in an old black jeep, open to the elements. Thankfully, it was a gorgeous day, clear and calm – sunny, but far from hot. The jeep was rather cosy. Oz was seated between Asha and Axe, the two soldiers of the Collective facing to either side, scanning the streets. Somehow, Luke had scored himself the front seat.

The driver introduced himself as Junior, their guide for the day. As they drove from the airport towards Port-au-Prince, Luke marvelled at how much their surroundings differed from Egypt. Only yesterday he had been in a sandy, windswept concrete jungle, and now he was driving through a lush, green and colourful – yet equally unkempt – landscape. He felt he ought to pinch himself to make sure it was real.

Of course, Haiti wasn't in great repair. The region had struggled to recover after the massive earthquake that had hit the region in 2010, followed by hurricanes and other disasters in subsequent years. The people had rebuilt where they could, and carried on with their days with a quiet pride, but the struggle was evident, not only in the rubble strewn about the city, but on the faces of the people. Life was hard for these people who had fought for their identity, only to find their struggles were far from over.

Junior talked of the origins of Haiti as he drove – how

the local African population in the region, who were mostly slaves at the time, had begun the Haitian Revolution at the turn of the 19th century. He talked about how they were able to fight off the French forces – led by Napoleon Bonaparte himself! – to take the country for themselves. This had then resulted in the formation of government, but unfortunately one that had seen its own fair share of trouble over the years. As a result, the Haitian people were poor, but proud. And they continued their traditions that had been passed down over hundreds of years – including the practice of vodou.

Luke could see this pride everywhere he looked. While Haiti was poor, it had its own identity, full of colour and craft. In the distance loomed a mountain range, and crawling up its side was a series of houses with tiled roofs of varying colour, making the mountainside look like a pageant. This defined Luke's experience of Haiti: from a distance majestic and beautiful, whereas up close, the cracks were clear.

All the stories Luke had heard in regards to Haiti, and to the rest of the Caribbean, was that it was a hotbed of "voodoo" and other such practices. However, driving through Port-au-Prince, all he saw were Christian churches, with large crosses upon their steeples, looking down upon the city in all directions. References to Jesus himself were evident on virtually every street.

Noticing his confusion, Junior said, in his Cajun-like drawl. "My friend, vodou is not practiced as openly as it once was. But it is here – in every street, on every corner. Many of the people you see here will have attended some form of vodou celebration… but they might not admit it." He laughed.

"I will take you to meet a very famous bokor. One you wouldn't find without a guide." His smile faded. "Someone you wouldn't find a way back from without a guide, either."

The jeep pulled up in front of a large white wall. Painted in black was a sign that read *Cimetiere de Port-au-Prince*.

Oz snorted. "A cemetery?"

Junior smiled as he exited the jeep. "Yes, the Grand Cemetery of Port-au-Prince. You want to meet le Baron, you come to his home. But you knock first. And you always bring respect."

As the group stood outside the cemetery, a group of locals rushed towards them, showing off jewellery, watches, and other adornments, and calling out phrases such as "My friend!" and "Finest goods!" in their hope of offloading their cheap wares upon unsuspecting tourists. Junior scowled and addressed them in Haitian Creole, and the group scattered.

"Sorry about that," he said, laughing and shrugging his shoulders. "People need to live."

Luke looked again at the wall that surrounded the cemetery. Graffiti covered some sections, depicting crosses, skeletons, and snakes. He couldn't tell if these were invocations of the Loa, or protection spells, or simply a celebration of death. Regardless, the images didn't unsettle him. The fact he was about to walk into the cemetery to meet a man that would help him enter the spirit world... *that* was what was unsettling him.

Junior gestured towards a black metal gate not far from where they stood, and they all lumbered up the incline to enter the cemetery.

# CHAPTER FIFTEEN

BILL REILLY WALKED briskly through the Leonardo da Vinci International Airport in Rome, winding through corridors not open to the general public. On the roof of the building was a helipad, from which he would catch his ride to the Holy See. There were many ways to get there, of course, but the matter was urgent and he was already late. The Patriarchs were waiting, and the other soldiers had already arrived.

He hated helicopters. They were loud, bumpy, and more than a little uncomfortable, but sometimes they were a necessity. And the view was always magnificent. Even so, he hated them.

Thankfully, it was an extremely short trip from the airport to the Holy See, so Bill had little to complain about. He soon found himself standing in the exceedingly well-kept gardens of Vatican City, waving at the pilot in thanks as she took the helicopter on its next journey. Behind him stood the walls of the city, which partitioned the area off from Rome, and in front of him lay the seat of the Catholic Church, to which the Order of Metatron paid fealty.

He was far from the throngs of tourists; St Peter's Basilica was on the opposite side of the city, and with it, the crowds of the faithful wielding cameras, drinking in religious experience under the watchful eye of the obelisk, a relic from another time, and curiously, another set of gods.

Before Bill stood a large tower, itself a structure of grandeur, originally built in the Middle Ages, but reconstructed much more recently, hence its perfect condition. It was known as St John's Tower, a building most publicly used to house the Pope and other such heads of the Church when other living quarters were under repair. However, as with all ancient structures, there was more to the tower than met the eye; its underground chamber had been gifted to the Order of Metatron several hundred years prior, for its exceptional service to the Church. It remained the Order's central headquarters.

Although the Order was an institute linked to the Holy See, it was not controlled, nor publicly acknowledged, by the Church at large. Like the Naacal Collective and its Prime Council, much of the world was blissfully unaware of its existence.

Nodding at the Swiss Guard holding vigil at the entrance to the tower, Bill made his way beyond a solid wooden door that would likely have been overlooked by many that entered the foyer, their gazes overwhelmed by other wonders. Behind this door was a spiral staircase, leading below ground, electric torches lighting the way, their design mimicking wooden torches of old, even down to their minor flicker which added to the ambiance.

Some way down, the air musty but cold, Bill stood in front of another door, knowing that on the other side was the Assembly of Metatron, a kind of war room designed for just such an occasion. He pulled out his flask and took a swig. The time was now. Sighing, he pushed the door open and entered.

"Our Assembly is complete," said a deep voice from the other side of the room. It was a presentable man in a black cassock with crimson piping. His grey hair was neatly brushed to one side, and he offered a broad, toothy grin, revealing impeccable teeth. "Inquisitor, take your seat. There is little time for formality – the others have been briefed on events up to the time you left your post."

Bill took an empty seat at the table, which was massive and intricate, with thick wooden edging featuring a marble inlay. Exquisite etchings covered the table, each richly coated in gold leaf. A single, inch-thick layer of glass lay over the top as protection, as well as to provide a flat surface.

Around the table sat a total of twenty men, ten to each side, plus the man that had admitted Bill, who was seated at the head of the table. Attached to the wall behind him, in strikingly contrast to the antiquity on show in the rest of the room, was a large flatscreen display, upon which glared a photograph of Luke Nixon.

"This photograph was taken this morning just outside the Ritz-Carlton in Cairo. Last night, Salim Elrashidy, also known as the Historian of the Naacal Prime Council, was shot and killed inside the Museum of Egyptian Antiquities. It is understood he was shot by another member of the Naacal Collective – someone aligned with Dion Wexler and his group of radicals. We do not yet know who.

"Elrashidy had met with Nixon prior to his death, and provided him with some direction, although again, it is unclear at this stage what this involved."

He paused, cleared his throat, and pointed a small handheld device at the display. The image switched to a photograph of Luke Nixon flanked by two individuals in black fatigues.

"As you can see, Nixon and the Spear have now been joined by the Executioner, all of whom we now expect to be in pursuit of the killer."

He turned and faced the group once again.

"What we don't know is whether or not this group knows where to go next, or what their plans are. We are aware that Wexler has summoned a demon, but we also know that he has not yet learned how to open a portal to the underworld. It is understood that the Naacal Prime Council believes Ellen Nixon to be alive and in the hands of Wexler, which is a grave concern.

"With the vernal equinox less than two months away, we don't have much time to find out what Wexler knows, where he is, and how to stop him. I feel that Luke Nixon is our best bet for now, as he likely has more information than the rest of us."

He stood and walked slowly around the table. On reaching Bill's chair, he stopped, and placed his hands upon Bill's shoulders.

"Inquisitor. You have done a fine job to date."

Bill squirmed slightly at the compliment.

"Your watch may be finished; however, your job is far from over. Follow Luke Nixon. Stay with him, but don't let him know of your presence. You will need to place a listening device somewhere that won't be discovered. We need to understand their plans."

Bill coughed quietly to clear his throat. "Father. Surely you don't mean I am to go alone? Can't I take one or two men for added protection?"

"No, Inquisitor, you cannot. One man is risky enough. Two or three will not go undetected, not when you're following them so closely. However, your brothers will also be working – they will be sent in pairs to the locations of the remaining known portals. I expect Wexler will need to show up at one of these eventually. Hopefully you will all converge on the same place at the same time, at which point you won't be wanting for 'protection'."

The manner in which he spat the last word made Bill squirm. The Patriarch was clearly calling him a coward.

"Yes, Father. I understand." Bill tried to add steel to

his tone, but his voice wavered. Perhaps he *was* a coward.

The rest of the meeting passed without much fanfare. Bill greeted a few old friends, many of whom he hadn't seen in more than twenty years. Some of the younger soldiers revered him, much as they might a celebrity – after all, he was the man in possession of Apollo's bow. The bow itself, though, was the real target of their reverence. Now likely thousands of years old, it was still as gorgeous as the day it was made. It wasn't gold, as many had once believed, but merely coated in gold. The material beneath was unknown. Many thought it was wood, but Bill didn't believe so, although it was definitely organic. Bill had always thought it was some kind of tusk – not quite as thick and hard as an elephant's, but a tusk nonetheless. And the string itself? Rumour said that it was made of fine strands of demon hair, twisted and taut. Regardless of the truth, it was strong. Bill had had the bow for more than twenty-five years – the string had always been taut and had never frayed or snapped. To the best of his knowledge, it was still the original string from whenever the weapon was originally made.

As the room slowly emptied, Bill was eventually ushered out of the Holy See altogether, and sent off to a local hotel to prepare for the next day of travel.

After a fine meal at the hotel restaurant, followed by a relaxing shower, Bill sat before the large wooden desk in his hotel room, a bottle of red wine in front of him, and his small notebook computer open.

On loading into his tracking software, Bill stopped and held his breath. Luke Nixon was now in Haiti, and there was only one reason the Prime Council would send him there. Clearly, the Historian had not managed to impart his advice before he departed.

This made his job even more difficult. While Haiti was a religious place, it was also a hotbed for… alternative spirituality. One man's demon was another man's god. Cursing, he grabbed the wine bottle with his left hand and brought it to his lips, taking a deep draught.

# CHAPTER SIXTEEN

THE GRAND CEMETERY was both confronting and surprising. At first glance, it was a cemetery much like any other – gravestones and mausoleums were in abundance. However, when Luke looked beyond the external facade and moved deeper within the cemetery, he discovered much more than that. For one, most cemeteries in which he had spent any amount of time (including the time he spent standing in front of his wife's grave in the weeks that followed his release from hospital) were drab, depressing places; concrete gravestones arranged in an orderly fashion, interspersed with the odd marble chest or vault signifying the more financially sound of the deceased and their families. Here and there, graves would be adorned with flowers, some fresh, some wilting, many as dead and decayed as those they were placed to remember.

This cemetery was different. Sure, there were plenty of gravestones, but they were far from well organised – centuries of death and poor planning meant that it resembled more of a labyrinth of grave sites and passageways between tombs. However, it was also quite colourful; many of the tombs and mausoleums were tiled with varying patterns, from simple checkerboard patterns to others as spectacular as rainbows. Luke smiled at seeing them. He recalled the housing that spread up the mountainside, adding a smattering of colour to the greenery. Here, the colours brightened up the otherwise dreary and serious graveyard.

Of course, this wasn't the only thing of note. Decades of poverty, internal struggles, and natural disasters meant that many of the graves, tombs, and mausoleums were in disrepair, some heavily fire damaged, others deteriorating in ways he couldn't determine – perhaps simply by time.

Then there was the smell. At first it was only mildly disagreeable, but in places it was acrid; damaged mausoleums and flooding did not make a good mix. Luke noticed several tombs and vaults that remained flooded, the water likely having been there for some time. Occasionally, the air became putrid, and seemed to get stuck in his sinuses; he kept getting a whiff of the stench even when he'd moved well away from these areas. He did his best not to retch.

More than all of this, the enduring poverty meant that many of those within the cemetery were not there to visit relatives. They had put up tarpaulins, and cardboard and metal sheeting, and set up their own home. Luke did his best not to stare.

Junior noted Luke's concern and fell back to walk beside him as they made their way through the rabbit warren.

"It's a humble life… and, in many ways, dangerous. But these people mean no harm." He looked about at the faces that peered at them from around corners of the labyrinth of tombs. "Well… most of them, anyway." He smiled and gave Luke a pat on the back before returning to the lead.

Luke shrugged. It didn't make him feel any more comfortable. Every person they passed would stop what they were doing and watch them silently. It didn't sit well with him – he shouldn't have been here, but for whatever reason, here he was.

Occasionally, he would turn and see someone looking back at him – the same man each time: a tall, thin man in denim jeans and an open denim vest, his teeth crooked and yellow, and his eyes dark and sunken. He didn't seem to be following the group, yet he was always within sight… watching. Luke kept an eye on him and moved closer to Asha and the Axe.

After a few twists and turns, Junior led the group down a short flight of stairs to an open area. In the centre of the space was a small concrete altar. This was a place of offering, and much like Haiti as a whole – or, at least, what Luke had experienced of it – it represented a mixture of religions. A large wooden crucifix dominated the altar, but in front of it lay a large, flat, bronze plate, blackened from years of offerings. Small bones lay strewn about the altar, which itself was stained with a black substance. Luke could only imagine it was old blood.

Junior stood in front of the altar. He placed something small in the plate and said a silent prayer before turning to face the group.

"Like I said. First you must knock. Pay your respects to the dead – this is their home, after all, and you are trespassing. You do not need to make an offering, but you all need to state your intentions. The Loa are always listening."

He turned and ascended a nearby set of steps, then stopped leaning against a tomb that effectively formed a wall beside them. Asha made her way to the altar, clasped her hands in front of her, and bowed her head. Her lips moved as she communed silently with the gods.

Oz made to go next, but hesitated. He turned to Junior. "Who exactly do we pray to? I'm, uh, not religious."

Junior smiled at him. "Religion has nothing to do with it, my friend. We talk to the spirit world. We ask their permission to be here – as I said before, this is their home."

While this discussion took place, Axe had briefly said his piece, and stepped back to stand beside Asha. Oz now stood in front of the altar. He made the sign of the cross with his left hand, which Luke thought was strange. He'd known Oz for most of his life, and he'd never been religious. Still, it was a common gesture, so perhaps it was something Oz had seen in a movie. Even more unexpectedly, though, Oz spoke aloud.

"Spirits. Until today, I didn't really believe you even

existed. But here we are!" He chuckled lightly. "I've seen some shit recently that has made me rethink my position on a lot of things. And more than anything, my friend needs to find his daughter, who was lost to him. I think we need to pass through here in order to find her – at least, I hope so. So... please. Let us do what we need to do, and soon we'll be gone. We mean no disrespect."

Once again, he made the sign of the cross awkwardly, then stepped towards Junior, who nodded and smiled gently in approval. Junior made a gesture to continue, and the group started to move on as Luke stepped in front of the altar.

He wasn't sure what to say. His mother had raised him as a Christian. They'd attended church every Sunday for most of his life, and his mother had prayed the rosary every night. She did it privately, but as a child, Luke had heard her repetitive whispering through the walls as he lay in bed, trying to sleep. As he got older, though, Luke had questioned his faith, eventually settling on *confused*. He'd never really abandoned his religion, but he didn't quite subscribe to the newsletter either. He hadn't prayed in at least fifteen years. In fact, he hadn't even said any kind of prayer after he lost Dani and Ellie...

He closed his eyes and swallowed. "Uh... I don't know why I'm here and I don't even understand what I'm here to do. But I hope you're OK with it. I lost my whole family recently, so... Any help you can provide – even if only to let us through – is greatly appreciated."

Opening his eyes, he noticed the rest of the group had gone, but he was not alone. The man in the denim vest was standing beside the altar, leering at him expectantly. How he'd sidled up here so silently was beyond Luke. Beside the stranger were two other men, hunger in their yellowed eyes.

Luke surveyed his surroundings, evaluating his options. There weren't many – the three men had blocked off all of the exits, and behind Luke was the wall of a mausoleum.

The man in the denim vest spoke, his accent drawling.

"Mah friend… there's no need to be afraid. We not gunna hurt you. Juss give us some cassssh—" he paused, tilting his head to the right "—and we leave you alone." He smiled with his mouth, but his eyes betrayed him. His friends took a few tentative steps towards Luke. One of them pulled a large, serrated hunting knife from a sheath attached to the back of his pants.

Luke's heart skipped a beat. He wasn't sure what to do – he certainly wasn't going to give them anything, and he could tell that he wouldn't be able to reason with them. But he also wasn't sure if his friends were still within shouting distance, or if they could get here before these guys attacked. If he was stabbed by that knife even once, it was going to do a lot of damage. He'd never been in a situation like this before. He didn't want to die, after all he'd been through – he couldn't leave Ellie to whatever fate Dion had in store for her.

One of the two accomplices – the one without the knife – moved in quickly, pinning Luke up against the wall of the mausoleum, his forearm pressed up against his throat. Luke could feel the heat of the man's breath on his face, and could smell the rum within it. The other man edged closer, showing off the blade, which glinted in the sun, though it was far from clean. Luke didn't want to get stabbed by a rusty blade – nor *any* blade, come to think of it.

Abruptly, he heard a scream of "Get back, you scum!" and saw Junior jump out from behind a vault near the man in the denim jacket, swinging a large piece of old wood. It connected with the back of the man's head with a mighty clunk, and the man fell forward against the altar. Blood spilled down his neck. The attack had split the skin at the base of his skull. The man gestured for his friends to come to his aid. Junior yelled at them in his native tongue, and the men ran away, carrying their injured leader, likely off to find some medical assistance… or at least some dirty bandages.

"You could have killed him!" Luke said, exasperated. He wasn't sure if he was thankful or frightened.

"Could have done, yes," replied Junior wistfully. "Should have done, maybe. Not like he didn't deserve it – I see bad things in that man's eyes." He looked down at the drops of blood on the altar. "Looks like we gave le Baron a real offering. It's good!"

He smiled and clapped his hand on Luke's back, pushing him towards the rest of the group, who were gathered at the top of the steps. Luke stumbled along, his hands trembling.

THE REMAINDER OF the trip through the labyrinthine graveyard was uneventful; nobody followed them after the encounter at the altar, and it wasn't long before they found themselves somewhere near the middle of the cemetery – or so Junior told them. Luke felt as if they'd walked for an eternity. As far as he was concerned, they might as well have entered another dimension altogether – no cemetery could be this big, could it? He felt as if he was at the centre of the universe, and the universe consisted only of graves.

They approached a small, white stucco building. There were plants around the entrance, and Luke could see an open area out the back. At the rear of this area was a large tree, covered in what must have been hundreds of offerings. It was hard to tell exactly what they were from this distance. Regardless, it was clear that they'd reached their destination.

Junior opened the door and the group entered a small room, well-lit due to the lack of a wall on one side of the building, the warm light of the day streaming in. On the opposite side of the room, against a wall with a window looking out upon the cemetery, was a dark-stained pine chaise lounge. Lounging upon it was an old balding man in a very loud Hawaiian-style shirt. He held a thick cigar in one hand and a glass of some kind of brown liquor in the other. He smiled broadly as Junior entered the room, although his eyes were hidden behind wide black sunglasses.

Junior smiled in return, turning towards the group as they entered, and gesturing towards the man on the chair. "Everyone, this is Emmanuel Narcisse! He is the bokor you seek. He is well-loved by the Loa. If anyone can get you access to Guinee, the spirit world, he can."

Asha stepped forward. "Bonjour, Monsieur Narcisse. We hope you can help us. Our friend here—" she gestured to Luke "—needs to reach the spirit world to speak with a friend of ours. We hope the Baron will grant him leave." She proffered a bottle of rum and a box of cigars, which she seemed to have produced from nowhere. Luke hadn't noticed her carrying these items before now.

The old man started laughing – it was boisterous and hearty laughter, with a depth that only a man with the broadest of chests could produce. "My dear – I would do anything for *you*!" His smile became even broader, and he moved his sunglasses down his nose so that he could look her directly in the eyes, repeating, "Anything." He sat back and laughed again, salaciously. "But why do you ask for him? Is he mute? Let the man speak for himself!"

Asha stiffened, clearly unimpressed at his candour. She turned towards the door and stuttered. "L... Luke?"

Luke stepped forward, pulling his shoulders back and lifting his chin in an attempt to appear confident, but it only made him feel more self-conscious.

"Sir. I don't know what else to say. A friend of ours recently died, and he asked me to look for him in the spirit world. I'm hoping he will help me find my daughter, who was taken from me."

The old man wasn't even looking at him. He was puffing on his cigar, blowing smoke rings and watching them as they rose in the stillness of the summer's day. He waved the glass of liquor at Luke. "Yes, yes, but *why*? Why the fuck should I annoy Baron Samedi for you? He is not a spirit to be trifled with." Luke felt his eyes burrowing into him, even through the glasses. Emmanuel Narcisse was an intimidating man.

Luke opened his mouth to respond, but stopped himself before any sound came out. Why *was* he here? Why did he need to talk to a bokor? Wasn't his missing daughter enough?

He decided on the truth. "I'm here... because that's what everyone else is telling me to do." He felt sheepish saying it, weak willed.

The bokor put the cigar between his teeth and placed the glass on the table beside him. Standing up, he clapped loudly as he approached Luke, pointing his finger and smiling broadly. "Ha!" he said, somehow managing clarity despite the inch-thick cigar between his teeth. "Now there's the truth!"

He took the cigar from his mouth, walked up close to Luke and put his hand on his shoulder, bringing him in closer.

"So…" he whispered softly, so that only Luke could hear, "why are you really here?"

"I want to see my wife. She died earlier this year, and she's been haunting my dreams."

"And you want to bring her back?"

"N-no…" Luke stammered, confused. "Can I?"

"No, my friend, you cannot. But if she wants to speak with you, and if the Baron lets you, you can talk with her one last time. Of course… this does mean she will no longer 'haunt' your dreams, as you have put it. Is this what you truly want?"

Luke hesitated. "Yes."

"Then it shall be done. And what about your other dead… 'friend'?"

Luke blinked. He felt as if time had paused. Everything apart from himself and the bokor was a blur. "I… uh… Can I see both? Like I said, he's helping me find my daughter… and there's this demon that's chasing me…" He felt foolish even saying the word 'demon'.

Suddenly, the world around him snapped back into clarity. The bokor took his hand from Luke's shoulder and walked towards Asha.

"What's this about a demon?"

Asha stood her ground. "This is what I was trying to tell you. Someone is trying to reopen to gates to the underworld. One of the elder gods already walks the Earth. We need to find out how to stop it, and only our friend had the answers we were seeking… but he died."

"Then…" the bokor began, turning back to Luke again, pointing with his thick thumb. "Why him?"

"He is of the old blood."

The bokor's eyes widened as the pieces fell into place. "The Loa speak of the old gods, and of the old blood. These are dark times. And dark times call for dark ceremonies. I will do what you ask."

He turned and began to walk towards the door. "Make yourselves at home while I prepare."

# CHAPTER SEVENTEEN

Emmanuel returned later in the afternoon, this time with an entourage of young Haitian men and women carrying various items required for the ceremony. They carried boxes of varying sizes, more than a few bottles of rum, and a live chicken, which one of the men was holding by its legs as it flapped its wings in protest. Upon entering the open area, the man let the chicken loose. It ran for a few metres before shaking its feathers and regaining its composure. It soon began pecking at the dusty ground.

Emmanuel himself had changed. He was no longer wearing the flamboyant Hawaiian shirt; now he wore a plain white shirt, open at the collar, and a black suit jacket – with tails, but this was paired, somewhat oddly, with black shorts. It was hot, after all. On his head he wore a top hat, and his face was painted with the familiar black-and-white skull that evoked the image of Baron Samedi. He still hid behind dark glasses, but he also wore a pair of clean white gloves. He now looked like what Luke had expected from a "voodoo priest", and although the top hat and gloves did seem a little ridiculous to Luke,

Emmanuel now had a far more intimidating aura.

In fact, he'd changed more than just his clothes. He now also wore a different countenance. Where previously he had been relaxed and welcoming, he now held himself with a more tense and erect posture, and his movements were slower and more calculated.

Then there was his voice. It was still cheerful, but his drawl was more pronounced, slower, more nasal. He seemed like a different person, and it was evident to Luke that he had taken on the persona of Baron Samedi. The other Haitians in attendance treated him with equal parts reverence and fear.

Yet he still held that thick cigar in one hand and the glass of brown liquor in the other. He took a sip from the glass and placed the cigar between his teeth, gesturing for the group to follow him outside as he puffed on it.

The sun was a little lower in the sky now. It wasn't quite dark, but the few trees surrounding the clearing cast long, grey shadows across the dusty ground. Old wooden chairs had been brought into the area and were strewn about the place with no apparent regard to any kind of organisation. Towards the back of the space, near the large tree that had first captured Luke's attention, there was now a small altar covered in a purple silk cloth. The edges of the cloth were frayed, perhaps having been scraping across the ground for years, but it was otherwise well kept.

On top of the altar were a few items that appeared

strange to Luke. There was a blackened human skull, and although it could arguably have been painted, Luke was certain it had been blackened by fire, and that it was a real skull. Beside it stood a bronze crucifix. Despite knowing that voodoo and Christianity were often found hand in hand in Haiti, it was still strange to see. Beside this was a bowl of peanuts, and a bowl of what looked like M&Ms. This arrangement of objects was surrounded by candles – black, purple, white, and red – in various states of use.

Junior approached Luke from behind and placed several bottles of white rum on the altar. "Gifts," he said, "for the Baron, and the ceremony, from me. You're welcome." He smiled a toothy yellow smile and took some bottles of red wine from a bag he had slung over his shoulder, placing them on the table as well.

A solid hand clapped Luke on the shoulder. He winced.

"These offerings are good, my friend," came a nasal voice over his shoulder. "But can a broken little man like you keep up with me?" It was Emmanuel. He laughed; a deep and boisterous booming sound. "We shall find out!"

He offered Luke a glass, seemingly from out of nowhere. "Now… drink."

Luke hesitated. "Uh… no thanks," he replied, taking a step back. "I'm trying to cut down."

"*Bullshit*," came the curt reply. "I can see it in your eyes, my friend. Besides, this is not a request." He pushed the glass into Luke's chest forcibly. "*Drink*."

Junior, who had sidled up beside Luke, whispered in his ear, "This is all part of the ceremony. You need to drink with the Baron. And you need to do what he says. *Everything*. When the time is right, he will let you – and only you – pass the gates of Guinee."

Reluctantly, Luke reached over and grabbed a bottle of rum. He sighed as he unscrewed the cap and poured himself a small glass. Emmanuel laughed and grabbed the bottle as Luke slowed the pour, forcing him to fill the glass to the brim. He raised his own glass and waited for Luke to join him in a toast.

"To fun," he said, a broad smile spreading across his face.

Luke brought his glass to the bokor's, who clinked them together, spilling a great deal of rum in the process. They both took a sip, and the bokor put his finger under Luke's glass, forcing him to take a longer draught. He didn't force too much on him, and then he laughed as he walked off towards the rest of the group.

"Now… everyone," he began, "it's time to drink and celebrate. Drink, and dance, and be merry!" He turned to Asha. "*All* at my ceremony must drink – especially you, my pretty. Yours is an important role." He winked.

Asha looked confused. Luke could see that she, too, was reluctant to join the festivities. She hesitantly approached the altar. There was no choice – this needed to succeed.

Soon enough, the group was talking and laughing; all the while, the Haitian natives continued about their business, setting up a bunch of traditional tanbou drums and then lighting a fire in the middle of the space. Before Luke had even finished his first glass of rum, the room was filled with women in plain white dresses and men dressed entirely in black, some with faces painted white, all of whom were drinking and talking loudly, broad smiles upon their faces.

Then the drumming started.

At first it seemed celebratory, and people sang and danced to the beat, drinking and laughing, and generally having a good time. Over time, though, the beat took on a life of its own, and the rhythm – along with the encroaching darkness – changed the atmosphere of the ceremony significantly.

The alcohol didn't help, either. As Luke drained each glass, the bokor would always appear, as if shadowing his every move. His glass would be refilled, and the celebration would continue. Conversations and people and activities began to blur. The fire was burning brightly now, and the shadows it cast made it unclear whether more people had arrived to join the festivities. The darkness pressed around the edges of the clearing, blotting out the rest of the cemetery. The celebration existed within a bubble in the infinite darkness, a sense to which Luke was well accustomed.

Luke soon found himself standing near the tree that

had caught his eye earlier in the day. It was covered in red ribbons and other pieces of material but, alarmingly, it was also covered in dolls. It was an old tree, perhaps two metres wide at its base, and it was tall. All the way up its trunk were dolls that appeared to have been crucified upon it. Some were tied with the red ribbons, others with wire. Some were old, and dirty, and in disrepair, while others appeared new. Higher in the tree, the bodies of the dolls reduced in number, but were replaced by bones. Human bones. Skulls, mainly, but Luke could make out some larger bones as well: limbs and spinal columns. He shuddered.

When he registered the complete lack of light beyond the tree, his fear of the darkness returned, and he turned back towards the fire, stumbling slightly as he made his way toward the safe and welcoming light.

Emmanuel laughed deeply from somewhere beside the fire. He watched as Luke made his way over to Asha and the Axe.

But Luke was stopped by a young Haitian man who had picked up the chicken and was waving it around the congregation, shaking it in the faces of the people dancing around the fire. Luke's vision was faltering – scenes were playing out like a slideshow, but this may have been an effect of the flickering light of the fire… or perhaps there was something in his drink? He looked down at the glass in his hand and threw it into the fire. Again, the bokor's laughter echoed in his ears.

The chicken was thrust in his face, squawking and flapping its wings in desperation. The man holding it reached behind his back with his free hand, and pulled a knife from his pants. A quick flick of his wrist saw him open a deep vertical gash down the length of the chicken's neck, and he held the chicken over the flames as it bled out, protesting in agony. A spurt of warm blood from the gash had hit Luke on the left cheek, and he wiped it away in horror as he watched the scene play out before him. He'd been a vegetarian for several years, as a result of Dani's protestations. She was vegan when they met, and although it took many years of pleading for Luke to change his ways, he eventually came to the conclusion he would prefer not to eat dead flesh. Watching now, he shed a quiet tear as he watched the chicken slowly become still. He'd never watched something die before.

The man dropped the carcass in the fire.

Emmanuel, as perfectly timed as ever, slid up behind Luke, and put a new glass of rum in his hand. "Drink," he said with a sly grin, "and talk to your friends. I can take you through the gates soon." He put his hands on Luke's shoulders and led him over to Asha, Axe, and Oz, who were having a surprisingly heated discussion about food.

"I'm sorry, but mustard is the money sauce – ketchup is cheap and boring and I won't hear another word about it." Oz turned as Luke entered the circle. "What do you think, Luke?"

"I... don't care," Luke replied matter-of-factly.

Asha burst into laughter.

Emmanuel remained standing beside Luke. The discussion lapsed into awkward silence.

"Don't mind me," said Emmanuel with a smile. "I'm just a silent..." he paused and looked Asha up and down, smacking his lips "...observer."

Asha squirmed. She clearly wasn't used to this kind of attention – she didn't like it and she didn't want it. She edged away from him.

"Oh, come now, beautiful child," continued Emmanuel. "Don't be like that. I need you to loosen up for the celebration. The door won't open for him—" he gestured to Luke "—without your participation. Le Baron *demands* it." He pulled another glass of rum seemingly from the air, and handed it to her. "Time is of the essence."

Timidly, Asha took the glass and drank deeply. She was somewhat unsteady on her feet.

To the group's surprise – and to Emmanuel's apparent delight – Asha broke off and began dancing around the fire, her body coiling slowly to the beat, not unlike the smoke that rose from the fire in the stillness of the night. Luke felt blood rush to his face and he looked away.

At the same time, Emmanuel put his hand on his shoulder. "No. Don't look away. Drink it in, my friend. The Loa do not let you cross into Guinee without a sacrifice. Every demand requires a sacrifice – you didn't think this service came free, did you?"

Luke looked at him, brow furrowed. He wasn't sure what he had expected. What kind of sacrifice did they want from him?

"Go to her. Dance with her. Feel the music. Let it take you where it will."

Luke gasped as he realised what the Baron was asking. It hadn't even been a year since he'd lost Dani – he was in no mood to flirt with another woman. Not only would it feel like cheating on her memory, he intended to see Dani herself soon, if this was all real. He felt his heart beat wildly in his chest and stammered as he tried to come up with an appropriate response. Junior's words from earlier in the day echoed in his ears: *You need to do what he says. Everything.* He sighed, and knocked back what was left in his glass.

Before he knew it, he was dancing. He *never* danced – he always felt stupid – but tonight, the rhythm took him as if he was caught in the current of a river. His head was spinning. He felt like a marionette, as if someone was controlling his movements. Only the sounds of the drums and the Baron's laughter filled his head. All he saw was fire, and Asha. In his mind the pair of them were serpents, coiling around each other, snapping at each other.

And then they were in each other's arms, and he felt the warmth of her lips pressed against his, and the rush of her breath, and his ears filled with the bokor's laughter, swelling to drown out the drums. A tear slid down his cheek.

Suddenly, everything stopped and fell silent. His sight became disconnected, as if his consciousness had been pulled out of his body. He floated backward, watching the scene before him shrink as he became enveloped in darkness.

Eventually, everything around him was black. There was no light, no stars to suggest he was even outside. He was nowhere. Luke lifted his hands to his face, then was shocked at his own touch. He didn't even feel the resistance of the air against his skin and was unable to determine his own movement or position. In many ways, it was sickening – he experienced no gravity, and was unsure if he was floating, standing, lying down, or anything in between. He merely existed. And yet the touch of his hands on his face suggested that wherever he was, he was there in the flesh, which was even more perplexing. He began to feel dizzy and nauseous. He panicked and released a frustrated whimper. He couldn't even close his eyes to try to orient himself.

A voice rang out, loud and authoritative. It was clearly Baron Samedi, and yet it was no longer Emmanuel. The voice seemed to vibrate through every aspect of his being.

"Relax, fool," the voice began. "This is what you wanted. Perhaps you should be more careful what you wish for, no?" The Baron laughed. In this place, where his voice was everything, his laughter had power. If Luke were standing, it would have brought him to his knees.

"Now, I take you into Guinee. Your sacrifice is accepted."

Suddenly, Luke was deposited unceremoniously back into reality – or some form of it, at least. He found himself on his hands and knees in a dark, barren landscape. It was empty of buildings and other structures, but it didn't lack inhabitants. It was an open plain filled with long grass and pathways, lit by what appeared to be stars. Everywhere he looked he saw the familiar blue tinge that he associated with the dark of night, yet he saw no moon in the sky.

The sky itself, however, was a wondrous sight. He doubted he'd seen that many stars in the course of his lifetime. He was entranced for a moment... until he heard the screaming.

He wondered how he hadn't noticed it before. All of the sounds he could hear were screams. He heard distant sorrowful wails on the wind, punctuated by screams of stark horror from different directions, some near and some far.

Then he noticed the man standing before him. This was Baron Samedi – the same spirit that Emmanuel had channelled, but here, now, in the flesh. Like Emmanuel, he wore a white shirt and tuxedo, yet in this case, the Baron had opted for full-length pants. He also wore a fabulous silken top hat and puffed on a huge cigar. Despite the darkness, he wore sunglasses. His face appeared tattooed with a white skull. Luke shuddered. The Baron was leaning against the long, black walking stick held in his left hand.

"The screams you hear," he said, "are mostly the screams of the... recently departed. Mostly."

He inhaled long and deep from his cigar, the smoke pouring out his mouth as he continued, "Some people don't realise they are dead, you see. It takes some time to... adjust. That is why *we* are here. The Loa. We help the lost souls make the transition to... whatever comes next. But we almost never let a living soul in here. This is not a place for the living. Find your wife, find your friend..." he inhaled from his cigar again "...and then get the fuck out."

The implied threat wasn't lost on Luke. He looked around. He had no idea where to start looking, but he chose a direction and started to walk.

As he moved along his chosen path, shapes began to take form around him. Black, cloudy wisps, but all bipedal. Humanoid. The spirits of the recently departed.

They groped at him, pulling at his clothes. Arms reached from the ground, grasping at his legs. He moved faster to avoid them, pushing into the long grass. Ahead of him, at the end of the path he was mindlessly following, stood a lone figure.

As Luke approached it, the other forms fell away. Eventually, he stood before the apparition, which remained unmoving. The surrounding area was a fifteen-metre radius clearing, the edges of which were a haze of black mist.

The form solidified. It was Dani. She was crying. Luke fell to his knees, tears flowing from his eyes uncontrollably. He couldn't look at her from shame.

"My love," Dani said, "look at me."

He raised his face, and saw that she was smiling.

"Come to me."

Soon, he was once again in her embrace, and the two were both crying again, their sobs shaking their bodies.

Dani pulled away to look into Luke's eyes. "Don't worry about what you did to get here – it was the price you had to pay. And I'm glad you did."

"I'm so sorry… I had no control over myself." He continued to cry with shame and anger.

"Shhh… I know. But forget about it for now. You're here with me, and we don't have much time. I've missed you."

"I need you," Luke replied. "I can't live without you. I didn't deserve to survive."

"Don't be silly. You did survive, and so did our daughter. I love you, and I miss you, but you need to go on without me. Ellie needs you – I need you to find her. And I need to move on… I can't stay here, Luke."

Luke drew a deep breath and looked Dani in the eyes. He could tell that she was truly happy. It wasn't only in her eyes; it emanated from her entire being. Her happiness was infectious, and he smiled back, his own mood lifting.

From behind him, Baron Samedi said, "Time is up,

kids. It's time for your wife to move on. Be glad. She goes to a better place, and very few people get a chance to say goodbye like this."

Luke and Dani kissed once more, for the last time. It wasn't a lustful kiss, breathless and wanting, yet it was more filled with passion than any other kiss they had ever shared. Luke had no real sense of time, and despite their final embrace lasting for what felt like hours, he didn't want it to end. But it did end – suddenly, and without warning, Dani became incorporeal, and Luke stumbled forward at the loss of her weight to counterbalance him. Ghost Dani sighed, took a step back and looked a final time into Luke's eyes, a solitary tear running down her right cheek.

"I love you, Luke. Go find our daughter, and live your life."

"I love you too, Dani." Luke smiled wistfully as he watched her slowly fade away. He knew she was finally gone. Where he had once felt loss and pain, he now felt gladness. The loss still remained, but he had the closure he needed, and his experience here in Guinee had helped him to understand that there truly was more to life – so much he didn't know. He still wasn't happy with Baron Samedi and the sacrifice he had forced upon him, but he let that go in order to focus on the moment.

For the first time since Dani had passed, he smiled with real happiness. He rubbed his eyes. Soon, he heard footsteps in the dirt behind him. Turning, he was greeted by Salim.

"I knew you'd come, Nephilim. And... I'm sorry for the price you had to pay."

"Me too." Luke noted a tinge of anger in his own voice. "But it was worth it, in the end. Not only did I get to say my goodbyes to my wife, but... I get it now. It's all real. And I need to get my daughter back."

"Yes, you do." The ghost of Salim walked closer and put his hand on Luke's shoulder, grasping it with a strength that Luke wasn't expecting. "My knowledge of the Pyramidion and the translation of the instructions on the altar are lost, sadly. I was unable to commit anything to memory before the Tongue betrayed me." He grimaced and raised his fist in anger. "Bastard!" He put this raised hand on Luke's other shoulder and looked him directly in the eyes. "But there is still one that will know what must be done, provided he hasn't been driven mad."

"The Prophet... why would he be mad? Who is he?"

"Who indeed? The Prophet was imprisoned many thousands of years ago by the very beings that once again knock at our door."

Luke gasped. "Thousands of years? How do you know he's even still alive?"

"Because he's one of them. He was imprisoned and forgotten. Much of humanity has forgotten him, but we know the Truth. You will find him at the bottom of the Barhout well in Yemen, a place some regard as myth. Tell Asha she may need to make him an offering – or at least give him something that may spark his memory. I'm sure he is not the same man that he once was. Go now. I have nothing more to share."

"Thank you, Salim," Luke said, "and… I'm sorry."

Salim smiled. "Don't be. I knew the peril of my station. Now go – find your daughter. And don't let Wexler achieve his goal."

With that, he faded away.

And everything went black again.

# CHAPTER EIGHTEEN

LUKE AWOKE WITH a pounding headache, which was no surprise given the amount of alcohol he'd consumed. What was surprising, though, was that he was back on board the jet, laid out on a couch at its rear. How long had he been out for?

Groggily, he tried to sit up, which only served to intensify the pounding in his head. His mouth was dry. He looked around for a glass of water; at home, he always kept a glass of water on his bedside table.

As if on cue, Oz entered the cabin, which was sectioned off from the front area by two partitions with a plain grey curtain hanging between them. Luke hadn't even noticed this on either of his initial trips in the plane. Oz held out a bottle of water. Luke took it gratefully and drank the whole thing in one go.

"Must have been quite the trip," Oz quipped. "You've been out for more than a day."

"What?" replied Luke. "Really?"

"Yeah, we've already made one stop-off. You came out of your funky little trance babbling some kind of nonsense before you passed out, and the next day we were off. That was early yesterday morning. It's now... somewhere around noon the next day?"

"Damn... No wonder my head hurts." Luke stood up and stretched. He stumbled slightly, and realised the plane was in flight. His bones creaked and his muscles ached, but he still felt some relief. He found the toilet at the back of the cabin and freshened up at the small sink. It wasn't much, but again, it helped.

He returned to Oz and gestured towards the curtain. "Everyone else..."

"...is in there, yeah."

Pulling aside the curtain, Luke emerged into the front of the cabin, and took his usual seat. Asha was seated diagonally opposite, but she seemed reluctant to look him in the eyes.

"I'm not upset with you, Asha," Luke began. "I think everything that happened was part of Samedi's plan the whole time. His 'entertainment' was the price I had to pay to get what we wanted. But we got it, and better still – I got to say goodbye to Dani." He smiled at the memory. "Although part of me wants to go back and punch Emmanuel and wipe that smirk off his face."

"Thanks, Luke. I don't think I was in full control of myself, if I'm honest. Something about the music carried me away – and something else took my place. But it doesn't make it OK, so I want you to know I'm sorry. And if you ever get the chance to punch Emmanuel, I'd like to join you... to punch him myself, I mean."

She sighed loudly, then raised her voice as she continued, "Anyway… now we go to see the Prophet. And everything that has happened up until now will soon pale in comparison."

Luke looked out the window and tried not to think of what had happened between himself and Asha. He focused on the view – he had always enjoyed looking at the clouds from above. The fluffy landscape was a seemingly infinite world of white. In the past, he would have taken photos on his smartphone, intending to share them with his wife when he got home. But of course, he'd get home and realise it wasn't really all that interesting, and he'd never look at them again. He laughed to himself at the simplicity of it all. Now, his phone stayed in his pocket and he simply drank in the view, a single tear rolling down his cheek.

THE LIGHT WANED and day gave way to evening, and Luke noticed the plane enter its descent. He took another look out the window, but there wasn't much to see: sandy dunes for miles, with dusty, rocky hills in the distance, and not much else. He didn't think it was possible, but there seemed to be less here than there had been in Egypt.

Raven's voice rang out over the speaker. "Coming in to land, folks. You know what to do."

They all sat back and put their seatbelts on. Luke said

a silent prayer to whatever may be out there (he was starting to believe that there may well be something, given all he'd seen), and held on to the armrests, white knuckled. He closed his eyes and tried to meditate – something else he liked to do on interstate business trips in days gone by. It helped settle his nerves during the long, boring descent.

Soon, the tyres touched the tarmac. Raven had taken the plane down as smooth as silk, for which Luke was thankful. Once again, he felt the tension melt from his chest. He looked over to Asha.

"So…" she began, "you flown in a helicopter before?" She laughed at his look of horror. "Oh, don't worry. Axe and I will protect you. And Raven will be flying, so you know you have nothing to worry about." She laughed again.

Luke frowned. "Why all the laughter, then?"

After a short taxi, the plane came to a halt. Luke was a little shocked to note that they seemed to have stopped out in the open. Raven appeared from the cockpit, stretching his spine. "I hope you're comfy, coz this old bird's your accommodation for the night." He patted the wall lovingly and headed towards the rear of the cabin. "I call the couch." He disappeared through the curtain.

Luke and Oz glanced at each other. At first Luke wondered whether Raven might have been joking, but when Asha began to recline her chair, and Axe gathered his things and followed Raven, it became immediately apparent that he'd been serious.

The two fumbled with their chairs for a while before they figured out the required combination of button presses and levers to put the seats into full recline. It wasn't the most comfortable bed, but it was better than nothing; much better than trying to get some sleep in economy seats on commercial flights. It wasn't long before Oz and Asha drifted off to sleep. It had been a long couple of days for them, although Luke assumed they had slept in real beds last night.

Luke, on the other hand, had spent the better part of the previous thirty-six hours passed out on the couch. He was sore from his experiences of the last few days, but he certainly wasn't tired. He closed his eyes and let his brain take over – he needed to work through some of what had happened. He had to come to terms with the fact that everything he had thought he knew about the world was probably wrong, and that now his life was in danger. What else was out there? Vampires? Zombies? Werewolves? He knew he was being a little ridiculous, but everything he'd experienced within the last forty-eight hours had itself bordered on the ridiculous. But one thing remained clear: he had to save Ellie.

Hours later, Luke himself having managed to fall asleep, the group was awoken by a menacing siren that filled the cabin with violent, ear-splitting sound. Oz fell off his reclined seat, his hands to his ears, grimacing in pain. Asha jumped to her feet, already wide awake and primed for confrontation. Luke simply sat up, concerned, his muscles taut and sore.

Raven and Axe rushed through the curtain, almost tripping over Oz in the process. Raven went to the window beside Asha's chair and pulled up the shade. Bright light filled the cabin. The siren stopped.

Then a voice came over a megaphone. It spoke in Arabic, so Luke wasn't certain of what was being said, but he could tell from the tone the speaker wasn't offering them a morning coffee. Axe and Asha rushed to the door and began the unlocking procedure.

"Stay inside," Asha said firmly to Luke and Oz. "Axe and I will handle this. Raven knows what to do, so listen to what he says."

The door opened and the stairs descended into place. Asha and Axe exited with their hands in the air, Asha yelling a response in Arabic. Shortly afterwards, Luke once again heard the sounds of heavy footsteps on the stairs. Somehow, he could tell that they were not friendly. Three men entered the cabin, dressed in camouflage fatigues, each wearing a green flak helmet and pointing a menacing assault rifle in the direction of the group.

Luke and Oz threw their hands in the air, while Raven took a step in front of them, raising his own hands slowly.

The three men continued yelling at them in Arabic.

"Stay here and don't move," Raven translated for Luke and Oz.

The soldiers stood completely still, each with a rifle trained on one of the three.

After several tense minutes, another man entered the cabin, followed closely by Asha and Axe. While this man was dressed much like his companions, he was not wearing a flak helmet. He had a long, neatly tended beard, and wore reflective aviator glasses. He shouted something at his men in Arabic. They turned and left the cabin, but the newcomer stayed.

"Gentlemen," Asha began, "this is Colonel Saleh Hassan of the UAE Armed Forces. While we did call ahead to announce our intentions, he was not informed. On changing of the guard this morning, the Colonel was alerted that we had stopped here, seemingly without approval. He has apologised for his error, but he asks that we leave as soon as possible."

"Seems to be a common request," quipped Luke quietly.

"I see," said the Colonel, speaking in a perfect British accent. "Then perhaps my concern is not unwarranted. You have twenty-four hours. I want you gone by dawn tomorrow morning."

Just as suddenly as he had appeared, he turned and left the cabin. Seconds later, Luke heard a vehicle speeding away.

"Well... that was quite the welcome," Luke said.

Asha chuckled, the tension leaving her face. "Well. We're up. Time to go."

"Is this Yemen?"

"Yep. Grab your stuff – let's go."

Luke shook his head, eyes wide. He wasn't sure he even knew where Yemen was. He definitely couldn't point it out on a map. And yet... here he was.

Asha, Axe, and Raven got to work readying themselves for the day. Their planned rest before their leisurely trip to the well had been cut short, replaced by a strong desire to get the job done. They each carried large rucksacks slung across their shoulders.

Raven approached Oz and Luke, a black rucksack in each hand, and thrust them towards the bewildered men. Luke took one bag awkwardly, misjudging the weight, wondering what he was getting himself into. He threw the bag over his shoulder, hefted it to adjust its weight, and followed the rest of the crew onto the dusty tarmac.

Not far from the plane was a series of helipads, several of which were empty, but upon each of the others was a large, black helicopter. Luke didn't have a great deal of knowledge about helicopters, but these clearly weren't your run-of-the-mill vehicles that you'd book for a leisure flight over a city on a bright sunny morning. These were military transport helicopters – the type that could be fitted with mounted machine guns, should the mission require it.

They approached the nearest helipad. Another man in camo fatigues and a flak helmet stood to one side, leaning against a dusty jeep, smoking a cigarette. Raven walked over to him, and the two chatted.

It wasn't long before Raven returned to the group. "We're taking this one," he said, motioning to the nearest vehicle. "Let's go."

It was the first time Luke had ridden in a helicopter, and he already hoped it would be his last. The inside was cramped and loud, despite the headsets they each wore in order to communicate with each other and to partially block out the deafening sound of the blades as they cut through the air.

It was also quite bumpy. For someone that didn't like flying, this was less than ideal. Each shift in direction impacted the momentum of the passengers, and Luke felt the metal bars beneath the seat cushion digging into his thighs.

"So how long is this going to take, roughly?" Luke asked Asha.

"Two, maybe three hours, tops. One way, of course."

"And where are we going exactly? What is this Barhout well?"

Asha shifted in her seat, leaning closer as if she were going to whisper a secret, despite the cacophony that meant that all communication needed to be shouted across the headset communication channel. Luke wondered why they didn't shut the doors.

"It's an old shaft. Ancient, even. I'm not gonna guess how it was created, but the locals think it's a kind of portal to Hell. Some think it's a portal for the Djinn to enter our world from the underworld. It's hundreds of feet wide, with sheer rock walls. And the smell that comes out of it turns people away. It's deep, and nobody can really see the bottom, but when the sun is high in the sky you can see plants lining the walls, and water forming black puddles in some ledges along the way.

"Some have tried to descend into the well, but blacked out before they could get even halfway – mostly due to the gases. Smarter attempts were made more recently with gas masks, but some of these men never returned, and those that did were unable to speak of what they'd seen – they'd gone mad." She leaned back into her seat. "Or, at least... that's what the locals say."

"And what's 'the Truth'?" Luke asked, making quotation marks with his fingers.

Asha laughed. "You catch on quick, my friend. The Truth, or so I have been told, is that the Prophet was imprisoned there many thousands of years ago over a quarrel with the gods, immediately prior to their banishment. I don't know the details of what the quarrel was, but I do know what the Prophet was."

"One of the gods, I assume?"

Asha nodded. "But the well itself is situated in the middle of nowhere – hundreds of miles of desert in all directions. People rarely go there. In fact, it's probably lost to time – it doesn't feature on most maps. The Yemeni government denies its existence."

Axe leaned in. "The Arabic desert is so vast and empty… I'd say there are hundreds of ancient sites lost to time, buried by the sands, too small to show up on satellite maps."

Luke sat back, pressing his head against the headrest. It occurred to him that he was running from one demon god straight into the hands of another – but at least this one was in some kind of prison. He shuddered at the idea.

He stared through the open door and watched as the sand dunes passed by, occasionally interrupted by a cactus or twiggy plant.

Time crept on without incident; Oz and Axe discussed their favourite foods, a topic they always seemed to return to. In fact, they appeared quite chummy when it came to food – perhaps they were kindred souls. Asha and Luke looked out at the brightly-lit landscape, avoiding eye contact with one another.

"Here it is – Barhout well," came Raven's voice over the headset. "I'll do a quick fly-by so you can all get a good look down into it, then I'll put us down over to the side, wherever I can find a flat enough surface."

The group edged closer to the open doors, hanging

on to the railings at the side and peering over the edge, each hoping to get a glimpse of the well. They all got their wish soon enough.

It clearly wasn't a well – or rather, it wasn't man-made. Luke estimated it was about a hundred metres wide, and deeper still, simply a hole into blackness, for all he could see. The strangest aspect was the sheerness of the walls. It looked like a borehole – something you might see on a mine site, or as part of initial work for a roadway tunnel. It all looked so… cleanly cut.

Greenery jutted out from the edges of the cliff here and there, spotting the walls like blemishes. Luke noted that this was possibly the greenest plant life he had seen that day. In the very centre of the well was a large rock, pointing upward like a spear. Perhaps it had begun as a stalagmite that grew over the years, but it was more likely that it had actually eroded over time. There were no plants to break up its plain yellow surface. At the very least, this rock proved there was a ground down there, somewhere.

Raven put the chopper down about fifty feet from the opening – the area was mostly flat in every direction, so it didn't appear to matter where he put it. Luke was glad when the sound of the blades gradually lessened in volume as they spun down.

The group exited the helicopter and stood near the opening – all except Raven, who had pulled out a book and sat reading in the back of the chopper. Axe was hammering some very large metal spikes – which to Luke appeared capable of inducing tetanus – into the rocky soil, likely to act as an anchor for their ropes.

Rock-climbing. Another first for Luke.

Asha pulled a harness from her pack, and gestured to Luke to look in his own rucksack. He pulled out a harness of his own and examined it. It was a messy jumble of thick rope, padding, metal hooks, and carabiners. He had no idea which end was which. He tried his best to untangle it, feeling stupid all the while, but holding on to his desire to pretend he knew what he was doing.

Asha walked over to him after she had fitted her own harness, and showed him which part needed to go where. It was actually very simple, and more surprisingly, extremely lightweight. Luke almost didn't even notice it was on. Asha moved over to help Oz.

By this time, Axe had hammered the four tethers into the ground and tested them for stability. He called Raven over and got him to double-check his work while he fitted his own harness.

Satisfied, Raven returned to his book while Axe connected lengths of cable to the anchors, and threw them over the edge. He put on a gas mask and urged the others to do the same. Thankfully, the top-of-the-line equipment was fitted with communication devices.

"OK, who goes first?" Axe asked Asha.

"I'll go – with Luke. I'll teach him as we go," Asha replied. "Then you follow with Oz. We'll take these two on the left."

Axe agreed, and soon the four of them were standing at the top of a deep, dark hole into the Earth, with nothing but a cable connecting them to the world above.

"Uh… how do we get back up?" Oz asked. Rappelling was one thing, but climbing back up would be another thing entirely.

"Don't worry," replied Asha. "Raven will sort that out while we're doing our thing. Let's just get down there."

Luke didn't like the sound of that, and he grunted his disagreement as Asha fitted the rappelling device to his harness. It was all a bit too much. He didn't think he could climb a hundred feet, let alone a hundred metres – or two hundred, or whatever the case may be. In fact, he didn't think he could even drop into the well in the first place.

His resolve was about to be tested, though. He found himself kneeling at the edge of the cliff, rappelling device in hand, helmet on his head, rucksack on his back, feeling more than a little out of his depth. He could hear Asha's voice in his headset, gently coaxing him down, having already descended slightly into the well herself.

He thought of Dani; her final words to him, which felt like a lifetime ago: "Go find our daughter…"

He thought of Ellie, and wondered if she was being looked after. She was still young, after all. She needed to be fed. But she needed more than that, and he wasn't sure she was getting it. She needed people to give her care and attention. People to wash her and her clothes.

People to love her.

He thought of the Tongue and the monster, and the fact that they likely had his little girl. He gritted his teeth.

Shedding a silent tear, he got to his feet and backed slowly towards the edge of the cliff. He held his breath and gripped his rappelling device tightly, ensuring the lock was in place… and then he stepped over the edge.

Ever so slowly, he let rope through the device, and took a slow step downwards. Step by step, he gained confidence. He wasn't able to leap away from the wall to let himself fall like Asha did, but as he learned, he began to move faster.

He was relying too much on his muscles. He tensed as he descended, assuming that by holding the rope tighter he was preventing himself from falling. About halfway down, he grew tired, and found it hard to breathe through the mask. Asha coached him, telling him to take a rest, and finally convinced him to relax and let the rope take his weight. He felt a little foolish noting that he could have spared so much energy.

After what seemed like hours, Luke's feet touched the bottom of the well. He'd descended more than two hundred meters by his estimation, and the opening above them looked so far away, like the disc of the moon at night. At the bottom it was dark, with very little light able to reach the ground. Luke felt his fears creeping in when he realised he couldn't see a thing, and his hands shook as he reached up to his helmet. He flicked the switch at the side to turn on the lamp on at the front of his helmet, once again feeling foolish that he hadn't done this sooner as it would have brightened the lower sections of his descent.

"Alright," he heard Asha say over the headset. "Luke and I are on the floor of the well. How far off are you?"

"About halfway, I guess," Axe replied. "Oz is starting to get the hang of things. We won't be too long."

"Sure thing, we'll set up the flood lights."

Asha and Luke rummaged in their rucksacks and each pulled out the portable floodlights they were carrying. Asha pointed out where each should be placed. They met near where they had reached the bottom of the well, and Asha flicked the switch, illuminating half of the well with bright white light – light it likely hadn't seen in centuries, if at all.

Luke froze.

On the other side of the circular space, nestled within a darkened alcove and chained to the wall by all four of its limbs, was a giant of a man, easily eight or nine feet tall, but in perfect proportion. It hung there, held up by its restraints, head drooping towards the ground, its long, filthy, dreadlocked hair reaching to the ground. Even completely limp, it was held aloft, unable to rest even on its knees. Waking in such a position could only result in agony. On its back were the stumps of what could only have once been the wings of an angel. Now they were simply sharp, broken appendages, blackened at the edges.

Luke's couldn't tell if it was alive or dead. The grey pallor of its skin made it look like a statue, a creature carved from stone long ago.

Asha, too, appeared awestruck. She took a tentative step towards the creature, her mouth agape, her eyes shining. *Are they tears of happiness?* Luke wondered. She noticed him staring, and composed herself.

"This is a god once revered by many. A god still looked upon favourably by history and legend." Her voice held a tinge of sadness. "And here he is. Here he has always been, forgotten by humanity, but not by us. It is an honour to be standing here… but it's also a sign that times are changing. After three thousand years of status quo, the future is uncertain." She paused, as if taking stock of what she'd just said.

"Who is he?' Luke asked.

Before she could answer, Asha was interrupted by the appearance of Oz and Axe.

"What in the holy fuck is that?" said Oz, his usual playfulness absent. He sounded utterly fearful.

"Let's find out, shall we?" Asha took several steps towards the creature before calling to it in a language that was foreign to Luke – yet at the same time it was one that he could understand. It was the language that the demon had spoken.

*{Awake, Prophet. Awake, O god of light, o oracle, wonder of music and artifice. Awake, o healer, for we have use of you once again.}*

The creature stirred, which came as something of a shock to Luke. Although he had been aware that this was the Prophet they were seeking, it had been so still. Inanimate. Lifeless.

The creature raised its head wearily, and looked slowly around. Every movement it made seemed to cause it pain.

*{Go away.}*

Its sonorous voice filled the room and pounded in Luke's chest, yet the creature's sense of defeat was clear. It groaned again as it moved its right foot across the cavern floor, repositioning itself to get a look at those that had interrupted its rest. There was a rumbling as it moved. The sound was like rocks grating in the depths of the Earth. Luke felt fear creeping up as his throat tightened.

*{Your kind let them chain me here. You left me to eternity. I hate you almost as much as I hate my brothers and sisters for their betrayal.}*

He spat a huge gob of slime that hit the floor in front of them and exploded like a water balloon.

Asha knelt to rummage through her rucksack. *{I have a gift, beautiful one.}*

The creature laughed. *{Beautiful? Perhaps once. But that was beaten out of me. You have nothing that I would want. Go away.}*

Now that its face was in the light, Luke could see that it *was* beautiful; the perfect example of an ancient Greek or Roman god. Every line of its face was perfectly symmetrical, and remained unblemished, even after all these years. The matted hair notwithstanding, Luke could believe that this was a god – at the very least an angel, hence the wings.

Asha had found what she was looking for, and held it up to the light. It was the lyre that Luke and Oz had been admiring before they took off on this adventure, a lifetime ago.

*{Is that… my lyre?}* The creature seemed almost reverent. It reached out with its arms, which were held back by the chains only metres from where they were standing. *{Give it to me. It's mine.}*

*{Only if you promise to help. I'll leave this with you. But you must help us.}* Asha was very firm.

A thought struck Luke suddenly. *{Apollo.}* He spoke the language without even meaning to, without even trying. The group looked at him incredulously, as did the creature.

*{Oh… I haven't been called that in a long time…}* He stood on both feet now, and it became apparent that he could only bring his hands together while standing upright.

"Alright, I'm fucking confused," Oz blurted. "What the hell is all this gibberish – and why the hell does it seem like I'm the only person that can't understand it?"

"It is the language of the gods, Oz," replied Asha. "It is native only to the gods and to Nephilim of pure blood. The rest of us had to study it for years." She and Axe both laughed.

*{Nephilim?}* The creature that was once Apollo seemed intrigued. It continued to stare at Luke. *{So... the bloodline remains. How quaint. Now I'm interested. Give me my lyre, and ask what you will.}*

Asha took a step closer, and handed it the lyre. Luke noticed that some colour returned to its face as it took it in its hands.

And then it began to play.

It was music unlike anything Luke had heard before, and it was magical. From what Luke could remember of Greek myth, Apollo was known for his love of music, and his skill with the lyre... and it showed. Even after thousands of years of solitude, the music he played was pure beauty, pure genius.

Asha gestured with open hands as she pleaded with Apollo. *{The elder gods threaten to re-enter our world. One of them walks the Earth as we speak. One of the lapsed faithful plans to enact the instructions on the ancient hidden Pyramidion, and we plan to stop him. But we need to know its location.}*

*{Ahhh... I see now. And you think – because I laid the Pyramidion after we buried the portals – that I will tell you its location? And what if* you *are actually the ones who plan to open the portals? You seem to have your very own Nephilim right here.}* He gestured to Luke. *{No. It will take more than that. I made a pact to keep these locations secret.}*

*{YES!}* Asha was elated, and called Axe over to her

side. *{You did! You made a pact with* us.*}*

Both Asha and Axe ripped open their jackets, pulling their shirts to one side, exposing the top of their left breast. Upon both was a large tattoo, about the size of a large apple, entirely in black. The Eye of Ra.

*{Followers of Ra. Hmmm… Are you the M'Jai, the Naacal?}*

*{What's left of it, yes. Ra didn't survive your uprising.}*

*{I know…}* He seemed genuinely sad. *{I hope it was worth it.}*

*{It was. All of that happened three thousand years ago, and our world has prospered ever since, mostly without any interference from the elder gods.}*

*{Three thousand years…}* Apollo stopped playing, and slipped the lyre into what was left of the material about his waist. *{I will help you.}*

He gestured for Asha to come forward, and put his giant hands to her temples. She whimpered slightly as he mumbled something quietly. Axe stepped forward to help her, but Asha put out her arm to stop him. Soon, Apollo removed his hands and dropped them by his side, chains clanking.

There was a sudden whooshing sound behind them, followed by a thunk, and then Luke saw an arrow protruding from the right side of Apollo's chest. The rage of betrayal filled its eyes.

*{No, this isn't us!}* shouted Asha, but it was too late. She was still close to the god.

Apollo swung his mighty arm and knocked her across the cavern. She collided with the rock wall and crumpled to the ground. Axe received the same treatment with the creature's other arm, and Apollo stood and screamed its defiance.

Gunshots rang out. Some kind of grenade bounced towards Apollo, and Luke and Oz dove to either side in fear. The floodlights, along with the lights on their helmets, exploded, and the area was thrust into almost total darkness, the feeble light from the opening too weak to illuminate the space at the bottom. As for Luke, he may as well have been blind.

# CHAPTER NINETEEN

LUKE FELT HE was living a nightmare. He was two hundred meters below the surface of Yemen, deep in the middle of the unmapped desert. His two protectors were out cold – if they were still alive at all. At least one person nearby was in possession of a variety of weaponry (not to forget the very angry god screaming in its chains), and he couldn't even see his own hand when he held it in front of his face. His heart beat against the walls of his chest as if it were trying to escape.

"Luke?" came a whisper off to his right. "Is that you?"

It was Oz. He was close. Luke reached out a hand and felt a shoulder, and Oz grabbed him in an embrace. They both fell to the ground.

"Crawl over here with me," Oz said. "I can see the wall. I've got you."

At least there was enough light for one of the two to see. Luke put all of his trust into his friend.

"What else can you see?" Luke asked, panic creeping into his voice.

"There's someone climbing down the big rock in the centre. I can see their silhouette, but not much else. Asha and Axe... they aren't moving."

Luke could hear someone moving about the cavern, along with Apollo, who was grunting and stamping his feet in the dust.

*{As if eternal solitude wasn't enough – now you torture me with arrows?}*

*{Silence, demon!}* came another voice, a man's voice – the person making their way down the rockface. Luke heard him leap the final few feet, landing in the dust with a thud.

*{False prophet. False god. I'm not here to torture you – I bring with me the wrath of the one true God.}*

Apollo laughed derisively. He spat once again. *{Ah, you're one of them. Don't you feel like a fool, seeing me here in the flesh? Where is your god now? The creators, if they ever existed, left long before the age of memory. There is only my kind... and your kind. Nothing more. For eternity.}*

*{Silence! No more of your lies, demon. I only came to show you this... before I kill you with it.}* Luke heard the man's footsteps as he approached Apollo.

*{How dare you call me demon? I was a god! One of few that fought to defend the Nephilim and their kind! Your kind!}* Apollo stomped and the cavern walls shook.

Suddenly, the area was flooded with light, which soon faded to an extremely bright shade of amber. The man had lit a handheld flare and dropped it at Apollo's feet.

Luke could make out the man now – he was standing

about fifteen feet away. Like Axe and Asha, he was dressed from head to toe in black, including a black combat helmet. On each of his shoulders was a large red cross, which extended down the length of his arms and wrapped around his biceps. A sleek automatic weapon hung across his chest, very close to the body but within easy reach. Slung over his shoulder was a very impressive-looking bow, and strapped to his right leg was a quiver with four black arrows poking out of the top. Somehow, the man looked familiar, but the flickering light of the flare made it difficult for Luke to figure out.

The man removed the bow from his shoulder, and held it up. It glittered in the flickering light. *{Do you recognise this?}*

*{That... is mine. It is not fit for the hands of mortals!}* Apollo raged once more, swinging his arms and wrestling with his chains. Rocks fell about the cavern and cracking sounds came from deep within the walls of the cave.

*{Now, now – we can't have any of that,}* the man said, taking a few cautious steps back. *{Clearly your bow is fit for the hands of mere mortals. Those that walk in the light.}* He reached down to his right leg and pulled an arrow from the quiver. This one wasn't like the others. This one was gold. *{And as an added bonus, I also have the only ancient golden arrow ever found.}*

Apollo's rage was superhuman. It was chaos – the pent-up rage of a god long forgotten. The rage was the result of eternal punishment, unleashed in an instant. In the waning light of the flickering flare, now more red than amber, light seemed to skip a beat like a strobe. His movements were unnatural, and as the light of the flare began to fade entirely, Luke saw what he had been dreading all along – one of the ancient chains had pulled loose from the wall in a shower of dirt and stones, flying loose in an arc before Apollo like a weapon.

Sensing the danger, the man ducked under the chain as it swung in his direction. He soon regained his composure and loosed the arrow he had notched. It found its target, lodging deep into Apollo's heart.

His hand now free, Apollo reached up and felt the arrow protruding from his chest. *{How ironic. Punished by the gods and killed by those I sought to protect – and by my own weapons, no less! Let this be a lesson to you, Nephilim.}* He cast a look in Luke's direction. *{Don't trust anyone. Not even yourself.}*

At that, it reached to the cloth around its waist, pulled out the lyre, and began to play a melody. It was the last song that Apollo would ever play. It was melancholy, and brief.

The stranger approached Luke and Oz. "I didn't come for you – continue on your hunt. I'll see you again, but next time I may not be so friendly." He turned and began to climb back up the rocky mound in the centre of the cavern.

Startled, Luke and Oz got back on their feet. Oz found their rucksacks and rummaged for a torch. Luke was surprised to find that they each had another head-mounted lamp in their bag – he supposed there was no such thing as being *too* prepared. Who could have predicted that some ninja armed to the teeth would come after them and kill the Prophet?

They fitted the new headlamps to their helmets and switched them on. It was a little awkward for Luke, given his eyesight, but as he got used to the light of the lamp he decided he would keep one on him at all times – minus the helmet, of course. It was like his own personal set of headlights. He could only see what was right in front of him, but that was a damn sight better than nothing.

Satisfied, they looked for Axe and Asha.

Axe wasn't far from where they were standing. He was already starting to rouse when Luke reached him. He waved them away and told them to look after Asha.

She was slightly worse for wear, as some of the rubble had landed on top of her. Regardless, Asha was beginning to push herself to her knees, shaking the dust that had settled on her hair, as the two men approached. She sat up and brushed off her clothes, testing her back and legs and wincing at the pain she encountered.

"What the hell happened?" she asked, looking more than a little confused. "Did… did you two fight off the attackers?"

Luke snorted. "No. Some guy appeared and talked to Apollo… before killing him with an arrow."

"Some guy killed him with an arrow… What was he

wearing? What kind of bow did he have?"

Luke described the man's clothes and the glittering bow. Oz chimed in from time to time, perhaps a little too excited about some of the more impressive aspects of the man's appearance, but Asha shushed him.

"A red cross on the arm and a golden bow. Interesting – they didn't just send any Inquisitor, they sent *him*. That's gonna be a problem."

"He and I have unfinished business," Axe said. "I might be able to close out three contracts in one mission. Nice."

Asha stood up and stretched her legs. She approached Apollo, and groaned as she picked up the chains that he'd pulled from the wall. She prodded him in the chest with one of her feet to roll him over. He still looked perfect, unblemished. The wound had healed around the area where the arrow had struck, but he was clearly dead.

"And here he'll lie forever, untouched by time." She looked over at Luke and Oz. "The flesh of the gods does not rot. Over time his skin may harden and may even turn to stone, but here he'll lie…"

They collected their gear while Axe made a call to Raven on some kind of handheld radio transmitter. Raven had been caught off guard himself, but nothing had been damaged or taken, so he lowered cables to pull the group back up to ground level.

The group was all business for a while as the motorised cables pulled each of them up to the lip of the hole, and before Luke knew it, they were on the trip back to the airport.

Oz was the first to speak, after thirty minutes of painful silence, as if each person had been occupied licking their wounds.

"We didn't just go there for nothing, did we? I mean… did that thing even tell us where to go?"

Asha smiled. It was the kind of smile that someone gives when they have a very cool secret to share. "Nope – we got more than enough information. I think at our next stop, Axe is gonna finish his business. And Luke?" She looked over at Luke, who raised his head when he heard his name over the headset. "You should find your daughter. We're back on track."

# CHAPTER TWENTY

Bill sat on the tiny balcony of a dilapidated old hotel on Yonaguni Island, Japan, shivering slightly due to the evening ocean breeze. While it wasn't much to look at now, the hotel had likely been a lavish mansion in the 1960s. The current owners had had the building renovated to provide bed and board to a couple of paying tenants – whoever saw fit to visit such a place, so far from the beaten path. It was a small island, hard to get to, and with little to do or see unless you knew what you were looking for. It was, however, the westernmost part of Japan, if that was enough to entice a visit, but for most, it was a backwater island that saw few visitors.

This was also an apt description for the hotel itself. It had seen better days, with tiles missing from its red roof, and cracks in the white stucco paint on the exterior walls. Even the plants in the garden had seen better days.

Still, for Bill's requirements – it was fine. There was a bed, and a window with a balcony from which he could look out upon the ocean, sipping whisky and smoking a cigar. And better yet, the owners left him well and truly alone.

Having successfully planted a listening bug during his previous incursion, not only did he know the location of his quarry, but he knew exactly what their plans were. He'd followed them, of course, after they left Yemen, making sure to stay far enough behind so as not to be noticed. Given the tiny town in which he was staying, he found it amusing that he was currently sitting less than a hundred metres from their hotel. Those premises were slightly better than his, from a certain point of view, but it didn't matter to him. All he needed was a desk and a bed, and he was happy.

His job was simple, really: to follow the group until they found Dion Wexler and put an end to his plans. From there, he had free reign over whatever he wanted to do to the Council members, but preferably Nixon was to be presented to the Order.

He knew that the group had planned to head out early the following morning, and he knew where they would be headed, but even then, he didn't really have to follow them. After all, it was very likely that Wexler had already passed through here. But there was something strange about this location that caught his interest. Not far from where he sat watching the ocean was a virtually unknown pyramid, forgotten by mankind – and perhaps more surprisingly, forgotten by the Order of Metatron and the Naacal Council – mainly because it was almost entirely submerged in the Philippine Sea.

It was not the only pyramid in Asia, of course, but

what made it notable was that it had been forgotten. It seemed to Bill that this was a deliberate act on somebody's part. Someone or something had buried this pyramid many years ago, and worked hard to purge its existence from collective memory.

And yet, here they were. The Prophet had not forgotten, and some obscure Mayan altar had references to it inscribed on its surface, for those that could read the tongue of the gods. History was finding ways to unearth itself.

Bill had taken pride in killing Apollo. It was his duty as Inquisitor of the Order, for one thing, but he also felt sorry for the damned thing. He laughed to himself at that thought – he had indeed felt pity for a demon. Apollo had been imprisoned in the well, alive, for thousands of years, punished for betraying his own kind. Punished for eternity. Bill felt a twinge of guilt at the knowledge that he had been imprisoned for helping humanity, but the fact remained – he was a false prophet, a false god.

Bill scoffed at the thought as he put out his cigar. Evil. Pure evil.

Yawning, he looked out once more upon the beach before returning to his room and closing the sliding door behind him. He noticed a flashing alert on his phone – he'd received a communication from his superiors as a result of his most recent report.

He settled down at the desk and opened his laptop, pouring himself a glass of red wine as the machine whirred to life. He'd finished the glass and poured another before checking his emails.

The message was simple.

*Follow the Nixon group into the monument. Find details of temple worship. Secrecy is of utmost importance.*

He laughed, a boisterous, loud bellow that irritated his throat, and then he coughed deeply several times. One of these days he'd quit smoking. Or perhaps he wouldn't – in his line of work, he encountered more immediate threats to his life on a daily basis. Still, how was he expected to sneak his way into an underwater temple without being seen? What if there was only a single room in there? The fact that no entry point had been found to date made the idea even more preposterous.

He sighed, sat back in his chair and took a sip of wine. Despite his concerns, the fact that he was going to be one of the first people to enter this place in thousands of years excited him. Perhaps there was treasure to be found. But more importantly, there absolutely had to be something there that needed to be buried and hidden from the world. What was it?

He drained his glass and slammed it down on the desk. He was ready for bed. Tomorrow was going to be a busy day – a strenuous day – and he needed to check his equipment before he even thought of lying down. After all, it had been a few years since he last used any diving equipment, and dammit, he was getting too old for this shit.

# CHAPTER TWENTY-ONE

LUKE WOKE IN yet another hotel, sore and feeling sorry for himself. He'd spent the previous day with Asha performing a crash course in scuba-diving. He was the only one in the group with no experience – knowledge of scuba-diving was an aspect of Oz that even he hadn't been aware of, although it had been some time since Oz had last gone diving, apparently.

It had taken a while for the group to arrive here. On leaving Yemen, they'd flown straight to Osaka, where they'd gathered equipment from a local Council outpost. The organisation was truly rich beyond Luke's comprehension, and beyond secretive. It had roots that spread everywhere, or so it seemed, and yet in every surreptitious Google search that Luke had attempted, he had been unable to find a single mention of them. And yet here they were; the influence of the Prime Council and the Naacal Collective was evidence in itself.

After a night's rest at a hotel in Osaka, the group flew down to Yonaguni island, fresh and well fed.

At first, Luke had had no idea why there were here, in such a backwater place. It was quiet and peaceful, but there was nothing to see beside the locals. These were mainly elderly Japanese men and women who had likely lived on the island for most of their lives, only for their children to abandon them for the bright lights of the big cities. They were simple people, but they seemed happy, from what Luke could tell. But, boy, did they welcome foreigners.

Luke had learned that the very thing they were here to see – the Yonaguni Monument – was a relatively famous attraction. It didn't attract many tourists, as reflected in the town's dowdiness and lack of hotels, but it certainly attracted the more hardcore divers looking for something new. And, of course, scientists and historians.

The hullabaloo had died down in the years since its discovery; many geologists had argued that the monument was simply a natural formation of layered sandstone, a result of earthquakes in the region over the years, and investigations had subsequently quietened down. However, there was some consensus among scientists and historians that the features appeared to be man-made, though modern history had relegated this theory to pseudoscience. Officially, it was natural.

Fewer and fewer people came to see the monument besides the occasional thrill-seeker, but the people of the island welcomed visitors nonetheless, knowing that foreigners tended to spend while out and about – and this town certainly needed financial stimulus.

Not long after they'd arrived, though, Luke had found

himself in another helicopter – far sooner than he had hoped. This time, Raven flew them only a short distance and set them down near the edge of a cliff overlooking the ocean. As he approached the edge and looked out at the craggy rocks jutting out of the sea, and the waves crashing upon them, Luke froze. This was where Dani had taken him in that dream, so long ago.

*Seek the Pyramidion.*

It hit him again. He was on the right track. Dani had shown him where to go, and he was still on the path to save Ellie.

He'd spent the rest of the day learning about diving equipment, followed by that arduous crash course. He wasn't sure how capable he would prove to be; he'd practiced to around 20 metres, which was as far as he would like to go, but the top of the pyramid structure started at a depth of 26 metres, and they had no idea how much further they would need to travel to find an entrance… if there even was an entrance to find.

The rest of the group assured him he would be fine; Axe would lead the party, followed by Asha. She would hold one end of a tether and Luke would hold the other, enabling her to pull him along if he began to slow the group – and it was generally assumed that he *was* likely to slow the group. Oz would follow behind, in case Luke lost the tether. Simple! Or at least that's what Luke had been told.

And, of course, Raven would once again hold the fort back at the chopper.

A few hours of training, a couple of hours of eating and drinking with the locals – not because any of them wanted to, but because they were expected to – and they were off to bed.

When he headed into the kitchen area of the hotel room, it was clear to Luke that he wasn't the only member of the group feeling sorry for himself. Oz was rubbing his legs and cursing his lack of practice, and both Axe and Asha looked like they needed more sleep. It was the first time these two superheroes had looked less than super.

They quickly loaded up their gear and headed to the rooftop – this was the only hotel in town with a helipad. Luke was certain they were pretty lucky to find *any* place in town that had a helipad, but he kept his thoughts to himself. On the short trip over to the site, they loaded up on energy bars and electrolyte drinks. It would likely be a few hours before they would be able to eat again.

They landed in the same rocky clearing as the day before, but now there was a small dinghy tied to one of the rocks. It wasn't your run-of-the-mill dinghy; it was jet black, with a shiny outboard engine. While he had no idea how the boat had suddenly appeared overnight, Luke had experienced enough Council dealings now that it didn't come as a surprise. He shrugged it off and carried his gear over.

Thankfully, it was a calm morning. Given their early arrival, it was cold, but by the time the group was fully decked out in their scuba gear, Luke could barely feel it. The tide came in slowly and waves gently lapped the rocks. The sea air was invigorating.

It took a while to get into the boat – Luke had practiced diving the day before by walking directly into the sea, so he had no idea how to get into or out of the boat with all of his equipment – but without too much trouble, they were soon on their way, each testing their headsets with Raven as they went. As it turned out, they didn't have to travel far, as the diving location was only around 200 metres from where they had set down, although it was behind a large rock jutting out of the ocean, putting Raven out of sight.

"Alright," came Raven's gruff voice over Luke's headset, "you're on your own now. Good luck."

Axe dropped a heavy-looking anchor over the side of the boat while Asha ensured that Oz and Luke were ready to go.

With a nod to Asha, Axe dropped backwards from the boat, barely causing a splash and sinking into the depths. Asha grabbed her end of the lengthy tether, putting her hand through a loop and tightening it around her wrist. A heartbeat later, she too had disappeared beneath the surface. Oz clapped Luke on the shoulder and smiled – though Luke couldn't see his mouth given their facial apparatus, he saw the edges of his friend's eyes soften. He smiled back, glad that Oz was here with him. Then he took his end of the tether, strapped it to his wrist, and followed Asha into the water.

It wasn't long before the group had reached and broken Luke's previous dive record of 20 metres. Though they had woken early, the sun had now risen fully, so there was enough light in the water to guide their dive, and for Luke to see around him, for which he was grateful. It was one thing to be blind above ground, but underwater?

Luke heard Axe over his headset. "Doesn't look like much of a pyramid."

Looking down, Luke understood the sentiment immediately. In many ways, the monument resembled a massive staircase with giant steps. It certainly didn't look like a pyramid, unless it had toppled at some point… but that would have required the pyramid to be solid internally. Still, Luke was no historian, nor a geologist, so he didn't really know what he was looking at. Either way, though, he could tell it was old.

The large grey stones looked too cleanly cut to be natural, and were stacked in such a way that they seemed to be aligned with purpose. More than this, though, the light that streamed in from above traced ethereal designs that appeared to move across the surface.

As a group, they made their way over to one side of the monument, where the ground dropped away. Here, Luke could see what looked like steep ramps and steps that led further down, while a little further off in the distance, he saw a star-shaped formation jutting out of the rocks, larger than two people lying head-to-toe.

As they dove deeper, though, he was surprised to reach the seafloor. While the monument was far from small, it was a pebble by comparison to the Great Pyramid of Giza. Still, given they had no idea where to look, this was an advantage – they could split up and cover the whole area fairly quickly.

Axe and Oz had the harder course, as their search would require some deeper diving on the side they had chosen. Oz admitted that he wasn't confident in himself, given he may need to go deeper than his accredited 50-metre limit, but it was generally accepted that Luke would be best paired with Asha, so the groups went their separate ways.

As he swam along, it became clearer to Luke that there was no way the monument was a natural formation. There were clear passageways, about the width of two people walking side-by-side, each of which led to a set of stone steps. There was too much design here to be natural, strange though the design may have been.

More than that, though, elements of the stones seemed to be carved into other kinds of natural formations. At one location, Luke saw what looked like a stone turtle, and many stones appeared to have carvings in them that defied explanation, to his untrained eye. He wondered how this site had come to be ignored by science. Was this once again the influence of the Prime Council – had they led others to agree that this was a natural formation in order to keep prying eyes away? It was the only thing that made sense. It seemed quite evident that what he was looking at, while simplistic in design, had been created by the hands of an ancient culture.

He continued on, marvelling at the sights, once again confused by what his life had become in only a few short months, when he suddenly came into contact with Asha. Surprisingly, given her stature, she was like an immovable object herself. She nodded for Luke to look in the direction she was facing.

In front of them was a wall that at first glance appeared to have fallen apart, revealing a passageway within the pyramid. At the end of this passageway was yet another stone stairway – but this one led downwards. On closer inspection, the opening in the wall appeared to have been created by some kind of underwater explosion. Someone had beaten them to it, which was to be expected. Perhaps the details on the altar inscription contained more than just the location of the site; it may have also identified an entry point. Dion was once again two steps ahead, but they couldn't be certain how recently he'd been here.

Concerned, Asha placed a beacon on the wall, let Axe know that they were investigating a potential entrance, and made her way into the murky darkness. She cursed as she went, complaining that it was hard enough to see already.

Luke found her remarks almost amusing. Although there was plenty of light under the surface, the masks that the group wore limited their field of vision severely – but all this felt somewhat normal to Luke. The peripheral vision that the mask blocked were the very areas that Luke struggled to see in normal circumstances, so he felt quite at home. Even now, heading into the dark, following the light of his head-mounted torch, he still felt comfortable. His disability seemed to have prepared him for something, at last.

But the further they went, the darker it got, and they seemed to be descending for a hell of a long time, exceeding 50 metres depth, which Luke found somewhat alarming. Then the ground below them levelled out, and they came to the end of the passageway, which continued to the left – a portal into darkness where no light could penetrate. It appeared an abyss, a penetrating blackness. Fearless, Asha continued inside.

After a short distance, they found the base of a new stairway leading upwards. At first, Luke thought they had simply found the way back out, but he noticed there was no sunlight coming from the top. Before he had turned the corner, he'd taken a quick look back at where he had come from, and seen the murky light which struggled to reach the bottom of the stairs. Looking back now, Luke could just make out that light. These new stairs didn't lead out – they led further in. They'd definitely found an entrance.

Luke's eyes were firmly focused on the stairs as he ascended, and when his head suddenly broke through the surface of the water, it took him several moments to adjust to his unexpected change in weight. He floated about for a moment, looking at Asha, who appeared to be deciding what her plans were.

"Axe," she called over the headset. "We're inside. Head to our beacon, and follow the stairs down, then up. I'm going to find somewhere to leave our equipment while we wait for you. But stay sharp – it's pretty clear that Dion got here before us... and he may still be here."

There was a brief response. The stone walls impaired the communications system slightly, but Luke got the gist. Slowly, he and Asha climbed out of the water, the weight of the equipment on their backs setting back in.

Having emerged fully, Asha sat on one of the steps and removed her fins, gesturing to Luke to do the same. Navigating the stairs would be difficult otherwise, he supposed, so he followed her instructions. Remembering that his headlamp had a brighter setting, he looked upward and pressed the button. Thankfully, there were only about another ten steps to the top.

His feet freed, Luke giggled unashamedly and rushed up the remaining steps, dropping his fins at the top and peeling the heavy oxygen tank from his back, unhooking everything in order, as per instructions.

"Leave the headset on," Asha's voice rang out in his ears. She set her gear down beside his and stretched her back.

As Luke turned around, he gasped. Standing on the other side of the room, its back to the wall, arms outstretched, was the creature that had been following him. Somehow, it had arrived here before them to stand in the dark.

"It's just a statue, Luke," Asha said with a laugh. "Anyone would think you'd seen a ghost."

"That's the one," was all Luke could muster in reply. "That's... the one I saw."

"*This* is who Dion summoned?" replied Asha incredulously. "I wonder if that was intentional... or if that was the only sigil he had found."

She approached the statue to inspect it, walking around its base. Luke was horrified – it was so lifelike, from its perfectly symmetrical horns to the smooth, almost skull-like appearance of its face... and the horrible, nightmarish mouth. He felt as if it was taunting him. Judging him.

A noise behind them startled him, and he turned around to find Oz and Axe placing their gear on the stone floor. There was a sense of elation in Oz's eyes, they were wide with wonder, and he was smiling from ear to ear. They were inside an ancient pyramid, surrounded by artifacts that perhaps hadn't been seen in thousands of years. It was very cool. Luke smiled and nodded in acknowledgment.

"OK," Asha said, and grinned, "if you two teenage dirtbags are ready, we can go find what we're here for."

"Teenage dirtbags, eh?" said Oz. "Says a lot about your taste in music there, Asha. Careful."

At the back of the room, on either side of the statue, were two dark pathways that led further into the monument. Luke assumed they would lead to the same room somewhere behind the statue but, in the interests of saving time, they split into the same groups as before, Axe and Oz taking the left-hand path, and Asha and Luke the right.

The path was dark, and there were hieroglyphs along the walls. Luke was enamoured by everything he saw, much like he had been at the museum in Egypt. But again, like then, he didn't exactly have time for tourism.

As they made their way down the hall, he came across a section of the wall that was different from the others. Not only was this text not in hieroglyphs, he could actually read it, although it was in a script he hadn't seen before. The message concerned the old gods.

"Woah, woah – Asha, look at this!"

"Yes, I see it. We can both read it. It's not so important right now."

Luke frowned. He wanted to spend some time reading over the information on this wall, but he knew this was all likely old news to Asha – and of course they were in the middle of a key exploration and there was no time for a history lesson. Still, the few sentences he had time to read were eye opening. Blasphemous to many, he was sure. He wondered if this was part of the Truth.

He turned to follow Asha along the hall. Fifteen or twenty meters further, the passage opened into a small room – but it was a dead end. A large mural on the rear wall was surrounded on both sides by more glyphs. Apart from that, the room was empty, except for iron braziers attached to each of the side walls.

This time, Asha appeared more interested in the mural and the hieroglyphs, as it was clearly related to the entity that was following Luke, and it had something to do with the portals.

"Interesting…" she murmured as she read the information on the left side of the wall. "Moloch, the demon that Dion summoned, was assigned to be the guardian of the portal on their side. He was granted the land on all sides of the portal by Enki, who was crowned king at the time. Clearly there was a reason Wexler chose him."

Their headsets crackled with an incoming transmission.

It was Axe. "We need you guys… uh… *now*. We aren't alone here." He was whispering, but his urgency was clear. Asha looked at Luke, and they both turned and ran back the way they had come. Suddenly, a muffled sound rang out along the hall.

Gunfire.

They found Axe and Oz in a large room a similar distance down the hallway as the mural room. However, this room was a great deal larger, and was dominated by a large pyramid-shaped stone in the centre of the room. It was a Pyramidion, and Luke was absolutely certain this was the one he had been searching for. He took a deep breath, his eyes wide. The Pyramidion was covered in dust, but it was clearly coated in some kind of reflective metal, possibly silver or platinum. It was breathtaking, standing approximately two metres tall, reflecting the headlamps of all who stood in the room. Lining the base, faded with time but still clear to the naked eye, was a row of hieroglyphics, and some text in the script he had encountered earlier.

But this wasn't all that was in the room. On its far side stood Dion Wexler and the Tongue, both smiling at this turn of events, and both holding short semi-automatic weapons. Their weapons were pointed at Axe, who was down on one knee on the left side of the room, clutching at his side. He was bleeding. In one hand, he held his namesake, a nasty-looking axe made entirely of black metal. Every part of it looked sharp, including the handle. He grimaced and held it threateningly, pointing it across the room.

In the darkness, Luke couldn't quite make out Dion's features, but he and the Tongue were dressed much like the rest of them: black scuba gear, gadgets strapped about their torsos, weapons holstered to their thighs. Their diving apparatus was stacked against the wall behind them.

On the right-hand side of the room, beside the great Pyramidion, stood the demon Moloch. It stared at Axe in defiance, unmoving. Its left hand, claws and all, were tightly wrapped around Oz's neck, who knelt motionless at the beast's feet, gasping for breath.

"*Oz!*" Luke couldn't help but scream out for his friend, and suddenly all eyes fell upon him and Asha.

"I'm fine," Oz groaned as the beast tightened its grip on his neck.

Asha reached behind her back and retrieved the short metal baton that Luke had noticed all those weeks ago. When she pressed a button on its handle, the baton underwent a series of changes. It was extendable, but its size belied its true form. After a series of clicks and clacks, it extended silently to around six feet. At a twist of her wrist, it underwent a final transformation, blades spiralling from the tip. The Spear. It was as menacing as it was mesmerising.

From the other side of the room, a voice rang out. It was Dion Wexler.

"Moloch, end this. Kill the Axe." Arrogance dripped from every word. He sighed. "We have places to be."

The beast turned, and in a swift, effortless motion, threw Oz at the Tongue, who placed a knee on his back and immobilised him with a pair of handcuffs. He pulled Oz to his knees and pointed his weapon at the back of his head, the muzzle pressing against his skull.

Moloch strode across the room without a care in the world. His legs were clearly moving beneath the long, shiny robe, but it almost appeared as if he was gliding.

Axe rose to his feet, brandishing his weapon at the beast. As he came closer, he leapt into action with a flurry of kicks and acrobatics that ended with a backhand swing of his axe. It would have thrown most opponents off guard and ended in their bloody demise, but the beast merely took a step back as if it had complete control of the flow of time, and stepped in to grab Axe by the elbow as he swung his arm for a final blow.

A slash with its claws took Axe's head clean off his shoulders.

Luke fell to his knees in disbelief.

"Eric!" shouted Asha. Then she too jumped into action, leaping around her spear like a drill, a horizontal spiral, as she sped towards Moloch. It was a sight to behold, and given she was uninjured, Moloch took her a little more seriously, leaping back to stand beside Dion and the Tongue, knocking Asha to the ground with the back of his hand as he did so.

"We have no time for this, Asha," Dion said. "As always, your efforts have been admirable, but also sloppy and ineffective. And now you'll drown in this temple. I would have preferred it not to end this way, but…" He sighed again. He shrugged his shoulders and walked over to Axe's body, taking the sword from the scabbard on his back. "Finally," he said, "the last piece of the puzzle."

Abruptly, a noise rang out from behind Luke, followed by a rush of wind. He heard a *thunk* as an arrow found its home in the Tongue's left eye socket. It didn't kill him, and he reached up with his left hand, touching the shaft of the arrow in horror before finding the mangled and bloodied flesh at its base where his eye had once been. Shocked noises came from his throat.

The next arrow silenced those sounds, striking him directly in the centre of his throat, just above the collar bone. Absolute precision. The Tongue dropped backwards, dead.

Rushing to grab Oz, Dion yelled, "Now!"

The beast conjured a portal, a bright shimmering light that floated in the air about a foot above the ground. Dion pulled Oz into the portal with Moloch, and the three teleported from the room, leaving Luke, Asha, and the black-clad stranger standing in desperation amongst the slain.

Asha slowly climbed to her feet, staring intently at the stranger. "How do you always seem to know where we are?"

"We have no time for that right now," he replied, tilting his head towards the ceiling.

Luke followed his gaze. Two devices were attached to the ceiling at equal distances across its length, each with a little light that flashed red in the darkness.

Dion had rigged the place to explode.

# CHAPTER TWENTY-TWO

"Fucking *run!*"

Asha was wide-eyed as she ran to the Axe's body. She looked at it for a second, at the pool of blood that had bloomed around his shoulders, before reaching over and grabbing the weapon that was his namesake. Then she too turned and ran from the room.

As she entered the hallway leading to the antechamber, a hideous noise rocked the walls, causing the three to stop in shock, checking the walls around them to ensure they held. Luke looked back to the large room from which they'd come, and laughed when he saw that the ceiling had not collapsed, nor had any water begun to enter the chamber. The explosion seemed to have been ineffective. Asha pushed him further down the hall and urged him to continue running.

As they reached the end of the hall, a deep cracking sound echoed from the walls like the rolling sound of an earthquake. A rush of dusty air billowed into the room, signifying that the ceiling had indeed come down. Water trickled into the antechamber – not in a rush as Luke had feared, but more like a slow stream that picked up some of the flippers that lay near the door. The room at the end of the tunnel had likely been blocked with stone, preventing the hallway from being filled with water instantly.

"Get your gear on – hurry!" urged Asha. Luke realised that it wouldn't be long before the stairway filled, followed not long after by the antechamber itself… which was especially worrying, as the water already seemed to be rushing past their feet faster than it had been.

Luke lifted the oxygen tank onto his back and shouldered the straps, but froze when he realised he didn't know how to reconnect everything. The stranger glanced at him and grabbed one of the two remaining kits, his own smaller unit having washed away with the stream of water. Asha grabbed Luke and, in a controlled panic, began connecting the tubes.

The water was now climbing their legs. The stairway was already full.

Asha looked Luke in the eyes. "Go, now. Don't wait for me, but I won't be far behind. Go straight up to the boat and climb in."

"But…" Luke was wide-eyed, pleading.

"Go!" She pushed Luke and he turned, diving into the stairwell. The stranger followed.

Asha, now alone, looked about for some flippers, which

she hooked to a carabiner on her belt. She put her head underwater to check the tanks, then froze, suddenly realising her fate. Some large stones had been dislodged and had travelled down the hall along with the water, crushing the remaining kit against the walls. They were beyond repair. Her only hope was to swim out using only the air in her lungs.

She knew it was a lost cause, but she had no choice but to try. Struggling to put her flippers on underwater, she rose to fill her lungs and was shocked to find the water was now at shoulder level. She took as deep a breath as her lungs could accommodate, and dove for the stairway.

It wasn't far to the first corner, and she made it there fairly easily, letting out small amounts of air as she went. By the time she reached the stairwell that led out into the open, however, her lungs had just about given up, and her head had begun to pound. Darkness began to creep in at her peripheral vision, and she stopped, unable to progress any further.

Suddenly, something grabbed her left arm, and she felt herself being pulled along underwater. And then everything went black.

LUKE SURFACED AROUND 100 metres from the dinghy. The sun had risen fully and the sky was clear and blue. A light breeze blew, but all Luke could hear was the crashing of the waves against the large black rock to his right, which had initially blocked their view of Raven when they first embarked on this mission. Their little boat floated nearby the rock. Slowly, he made his way over, and struggled to pull himself into it. When he finally got in, he lay in the bottom of the boat and tried to catch his breath, his eyes fixed on the cerulean sky. Overcome with emotion, he sobbed uncontrollably.

Soon after, he heard splashing from not far away, followed by a man's voice calling out for help. Luke sat up to see the stranger swimming towards him, tearing off his mask as he did so.

"Help me get her into the boat!" he yelled. Then Luke saw that he was dragging Asha behind him. She was completely limp, and her skin was pale. Luke's heart skipped a beat. He tore off his own mask and reached out to pull Asha into the boat, struggling with her dead weight. The stranger followed, and immediately began CPR.

For several tense moments, Luke sat and watched, holding his breath. While Oz was his tether to the real world, Asha was his shield. Suddenly he felt very alone, sitting in a boat far away from mainland Japan, with people he neither knew nor trusted. He didn't even know if he could save Ellie now. In a moment, he had once again lost everything. It was all he could do to keep the little crystal of sanity in his mind from cracking.

The stranger sat back and watched as a stream of water came pouring from Asha's mouth, followed by a cough and a deep intake of breath. The stranger started up the motor and they made their way towards Raven, who Luke imagined by this point was probably losing his mind – they had lost contact with him once they entered the pyramid. Asha coughed continually, almost unconsciously.

"The Inquisitor? What the fuck is he doing here?" shouted Raven when they were within earshot, gesturing at the stranger. "And where is everyone else?"

"He saved Asha's life, Raven," replied Luke solemnly. "Help us get her on to the chopper. She needs to rest."

They continued to work silently, but all the while Luke kept looking at the Inquisitor, sure he had seen him somewhere before.

LATER, WHEN LUKE had awoken from a sorely-needed afternoon nap – fitful though it was – he sat down beside Raven at their hotel room table and walked him through everything that had happened. While he had explained some of the details on the short flight back – mainly that that Axe had been killed and that Oz had been taken – he had been in no mood to go into detail then. However, Luke knew Raven deserved more than that.

Upon hearing the whole story, Raven rummaged

through his backpack and pulled out a bottle of whisky. Pouring two glasses, he slid one over to Luke and raised his glass.

"To Eric. A formidable soldier, a hard-as-nails Axe, and…" He sighed, gathering his thoughts. "And a good friend." Luke saw tears in his eyes; he suspected the men had been more than just friends. He'd rarely seen Raven respond to any situation with anything other than stoicism. It was good to know that there was an emotional human being in there.

He felt a shudder in his chest, and tears welled in his own eyes. The two charged their glasses and downed the whisky in a single shot, grimacing as the liquid hit their throats. Thankfully, it was good whisky, so the bite was short-lived.

The door to the bathroom opened, and steam poured out. Luke's eyes brightened and he watched the door expectantly, but it wasn't Asha that stepped out, but the Inquisitor. An old man wearing black cargo pants, a white towel draped over his bare shoulders. But he wasn't just any old man – he was easily as fit and strong-looking as Axe had been, and Luke blushed a little as he realised how poorly he compared.

And then realisation struck him.

"Bill?" he asked. "Bill fucking Reilly? What the…"

Bill sighed.

"Yeah. That's me." He grabbed both ends of the towel and sat down at the table. "You got one of those for me, Raven?"

"Who the hell are you?" asked Luke, his mind still boggling at the realisation that his nosy old neighbour was some kind of badass warrior.

Raven growled, but he acquiesced, pouring three more glasses. "He's an Inquisitor of the Sacred Order of Metatron, a secret sect of Christian warriors. They don't believe in the Truth, only the parts that came after."

"And…" Luke took a sip from his glass, "you two know each other?"

"We've all been around. I didn't always work for the Prime Council." Raven emptied his glass and slammed it back down on the table. "After what you did to me in Yemen, old man, I shouldn't be so friendly."

"Well," Bill replied thoughtfully, "I don't think you would have let me down into the well if I asked, would you?" He let the question go unanswered for a second before continuing, "Desperate times call for desperate measures. I made sure not to hurt you, but I had to…" He paused. "…incapacitate you." He drained his glass, wincing briefly.

Raven only grunted in reply.

The old man continued, "Luke, I am indeed an Inquisitor of the Sacred Order of Metatron, and wielder of Apollo's bow. The Order is the sword that sits at the right hand of God. We are the safekeepers of His kingdom." He gestured at Raven, who filled the glasses once again. "For many years, I was assigned as a Watcher. I had proven myself in battle as a young man, and was given free rein to monitor yourself and your wife in my twilight years, or so I was told. I don't think fifty-eight is so old these days – and of course I was younger than that when I was assigned." He staring at his glass for a moment before swallowing its contents. "I'm sorry about what happened to your wife. The Order has no desire to see harm inflicted upon the Nephilim; we merely exist to watch. However, things took a turn when your house was destroyed – it became clear to us that Dion Wexler planned to reopen the gates to Hell."

Luke put a hand to his mouth. "Hell? As in... *the* Hell?"

Bill laughed. "I used to think so, yes. But I also used to think that my superiors were speaking in metaphors! But to see those metaphors in the flesh? To hear Apollo play his lyre?" There was a twinkle in his eye. He sighed again, but it wasn't a sigh of pain or anguish. "The ancient Greeks told many tales of Apollo – some stated that he was a fine musician, and... well... it turns out they were right. Even after thousands of years chained underground, his song made me reassess my position on things, I think... I just don't know what to believe anymore."

He stood up, drained his glass and approached the window, which looked out upon the small town centre and the sea.

"And that's why I'm here, now, with you. I believe we have the same goal in mind – stopping Dion Wexler. I think we should fight together. The enemy of my enemy…"

The bedroom door opened. Asha stumbled out weakly and slumped onto a couch, wincing in pain and coughing more phlegm from her lungs. She shot a glance at Raven, who brought her over a glass of whisky. She downed it in one and held her glass out again. Raven poured her another.

She took a deep breath as if to muster the strength to talk. *"Now* you can answer my question. How did you always know where we were?"

Bill turned from the window and faced Asha, his face grim, his eyes directed at the floor. "I had help from the inside. Oz had a transmitter implanted before this whole thing started."

# CHAPTER TWENTY-THREE

While Asha seemed glad to hear what Bill had to say, likely because meant they could easily follow Wexler, Luke wasn't quite sure how he felt about the news. Oz had been his best friend for almost as long as he could remember, and this felt like a betrayal.

Bill went to great pains to tell Luke that Oz only agreed to this on his terms – that no harm would come to anybody in their group, especially Luke – but it had still been a huge secret to keep. He had effectively let an unknown entity – possibly an enemy, for all they knew – track their every move. Then again, given the Order had the same end goal in mind, they were more likely friends… but Luke wasn't so sure the Prime Council would see it that way, even if Asha turned a blind eye for now.

For the rest of the day the group rested in the hotel; Asha was in no condition to continue giving chase. Raven took Bill back to his hotel to gather his belongings, while Asha booked a massage for herself and Luke. Luke had never had much more than a shoulder massage in his lifetime, so he was reluctant as first, but eventually he succumbed to a full-body deep tissue massage at Asha's insistence. He found it simultaneously excruciating and blissful, but by the time the masseuse had left, he felt like a new man, ready to tackle anything.

Asha, on the other hand, was still worse for wear. She had drowned, after all. Bill had saved her life, which had endeared him to the group for the moment. However, she had her kit bag, and it contained more than just weaponry. She brewed a foul-smelling tea from a bag of herbs that she pulled from a pouch, poured a cup for herself, and left another on the bench for Luke.

Curious, he smelled the contents. It was even worse up close; slightly earthy and very grassy, as if she'd soaked a dried cow pat in water. He turned his nose up. "No thanks."

"Your loss. It doesn't *smell* great, but it'll make you feel like a million dollars, I promise. I once saw Axe win a street fight with a broken arm after drinking a cup of this stuff." Asha smiled softly, sadness creeping into her eyes at the mention of her friend.

Luke looked down at the cup on the table, from which steam rose. *For Axe,* he thought, raising the cup to his lips and taking a sip. It didn't taste half as bad as it smelled, although it was far from enjoyable. But as with any warm drink, he felt the tension release from his shoulders as he drank. At the very least, it was nourishing. Wishing Asha a good night, he headed off.

It was a surprisingly blissful sleep. The next day, Luke

sprang out of bed as if the previous day's events had never happened. It occurred to him that it was possible he felt better than he'd felt in his entire life, ready to take on whatever life had to throw at him. He was glad he had tried the tea.

Asha and Raven were already awake, sitting at the table drinking cups of coffee. Both had red eyes – but not from lack of sleep. They had clearly been talking about the loss of their friend. Asha had told the Council that Axe had been lost, but that his final task had been completed – the Tongue had been brought to justice. She hadn't mentioned that this was at the hands of the Inquisitor, as it didn't matter. Axe was dead… and so was The Tongue.

Seeing Luke enter the room, Asha gave him a slight smile and offered him a coffee. Declining, he asked about their plans.

"Well, that's easy," she replied matter-of-factly. "We rescue Oz. Bill tracked the transmitter to a warehouse in Osaka, which seems likely to be their base of operations in this part of the world. Raven thinks we should give it another day to make sure they don't move on."

"No." Luke's resolve surprised even himself. "We leave today. Soon. They probably have no idea that we can track him. We have the element of surprise."

"True. Raven, what do you think?"

Raven sighed and turned towards Luke. "You're worried about your friend. I get it, I really do. I just lost a friend myself. But it won't help anyone if we rush into this without making sure we've got all the details straight – that's what got Eric killed yesterday, and we're as good as done if we make the same mistake again."

A voice came from the second bedroom. It was Bill. "Yes, but what if they find the transmitter? We know where they are now – but if we lose that transmitter, then all is lost, and your friend died for nothing. If they leave, we can follow the transmitter – but not if they remove it today."

There was no arguing with his logic. Raven grumbled again and stood up. "I'll get my shit ready, then." He stomped off to the bedroom, passing Bill, who was exiting the room with a black sports bag on his shoulder. He sat down at the table with the others. "What's this about coffee?"

AFTER A HAIR-RAISING, bumpy ride back to Osaka in an aging Cessna, Luke was shocked to discover he had finally had enough of travel. He'd always hated the flying, but now he just needed rest. Once again, his body ached and groaned due to hours of inactivity.

He turned to look at his companions. What had started as a hearty group of five had dwindled to three worn-out individuals, plus the Inquisitor. His soul yearned for some sense of normality.

And then he remembered Ellie. It was all for her – nothing else had mattered.

Until now.

Now, their opponents had killed several members of the Prime Council and taken Oz hostage. And for what? Just to prove that the gods still existed in some far-off place? Luke wasn't sure what all of this was about, but he knew that he wanted his daughter back, and now Oz as well –and above all else, he just wanted it all to end. He'd had enough of adventure for a lifetime.

Once again bypassing standard security and customs protocols, Luke soon found himself in a black van that wound around the Osaka streets. It was getting late in the evening, and the light of the sun was beginning to fade. In the distance, skyscrapers loomed, but they weren't headed towards the city.

"Where are we going?" he asked.

"There are a bunch of old warehouses in Suita, north of Osaka. Your friend has been there since last night and doesn't seem to have moved… that is, unless they found the transmitter." Bill had his computer on his lap, continually monitoring for any changes.

Luke watched over Bill's shoulder as he zoomed in and out on their destination. "What are you looking for?"

"A good entry point. A good exit point. Secondary exit points. A place to leave the van. How close we can get without being seen. You know… the usual."

Asha, sitting in the seat behind, leaned over to look.

"Good idea." Then she and Bill began discussing a plan of attack.

Feeling useless, Luke turned to look out the window, watching the world pass by.

It was interesting – he'd now been to several very different countries, and every place had a look and feel of its own. Osaka was most like home, but still, it was different in the little details. Houses were smaller and situated closer together, but it wasn't just that – the design of the roof tiles was what set them apart. They had curves and an elegance not seen back home. Plus, there was the distinct lack of colour – everything merged into a drab grey, a concrete paradise broken up by the occasional flash of neon lights.

Mixed in with the stone and concrete were slabs of metal – some functional, some decorative, but most corroded, the years dripping down the concrete walls in the form of rust. Plus, there were the electrical poles – far too many electrical poles carrying far too many cables. For a country that seemed so advanced, it also seemed so backward in places. Still, it had a hyper-urban beauty of its own, both beautiful and sad.

That sentiment also applied to the people Luke saw, to a degree. Japan was a highly populated country, and Osaka was its second largest city. There were people everywhere, making their way about the streets like ants in a nest – each with their own task, but seemingly lacking direction. As they went about their business, they all seemed to move with the same stoic indifference. Remembering his own ancestry, Luke wished he could spend more time here. He needed to learn more about his mother's family, her culture. Outwardly, Osaka seemed so similar to back home, but once you saw beneath the facade, it was fascinating.

It wasn't long before the van stopped. Raven pulled the vehicle slightly off the main thoroughfare and switched off the engine. Bill shoved his computer into his sports bag, slid open the van door, and climbed out. It was a hot day, and oppressively humid air rushed in like a wave. Luke slid across the leather seat and climbed out the open door, stretching his legs and rubbing his lower back, groaning in relief.

Without warning, Bill pulled up Luke's shirt and strapped a holster around his waist, passing a strap over his left shoulder and tightening it in place. A small pistol was now strapped to the small of his back. His shirt dropped back down over the top as if nothing was there.

Bill grabbed him by the shoulders and looked him in the eyes. "Hopefully you won't need it, but if you do, be careful who you point it at." He turned back and rummaged through his bag, pulling out straps and gadgets and placing them to one side before throwing the bag and its remaining contents back into the van.

Asha had also been preparing herself all the while, and by the time she had finished, she was armed and ready, empty scabbard notwithstanding. While the design of her weaponry and the straps that attached them to her body were sleek and plain, she was clearly out of place. Though Luke couldn't tell what many of the devices were, she was every part the soldier. Bill looked much the same by the time he was finished, although the red cross of his Order made him appear even more menacing, as did the bow slung over his shoulder and the quiver strapped to his thigh, filled with short, black arrows.

Raven threw Luke a black jacket; Luke gave him a quick thumbs up and put it on. It was a little large, but it made him feel a little more like a member of the team: with his black flak jacket and his dark denim jeans, he almost felt like a soldier himself. He needed the confidence, if he was honest, because he was quietly shitting himself.

Raven took off in the van, leaving the three to their mission. From what Luke had grasped, Raven was going to act as suspiciously as possible on the opposite side of the warehouse in order to draw attention from the rest of them. Dion wasn't stupid – he would be wary, although perhaps his recent escape and subsequent destruction at the Yonaguni Monument may have given him confidence.

Scouting the area, Bill noticed that there were far too many cameras to make a surprise entrance. Their best bet was to move as quickly as possible – the old 'smash and grab' technique. The warehouse was a huge pile of rusty corrugated iron, and Bill hoped its interior consisted of just a couple of large open rooms, but until they were inside, they had no way of knowing.

There were two choices – a rusty staircase that led up the side of the warehouse to a door and window high up, or a small office door at ground level. Either way, they had no idea what was on the other side, and given Dion had himself known the comforts and security employed by the Prime Council, it was possible that the outside appearance was a distraction from a more sophisticated interior. But they had too much to lose if they did nothing.

Deciding on the door at the top of the stairs, the group began their mission. Asha had a brief chat with Raven over her headset to let him know they were on their way, and they ran to the stairs.

Luke wasn't sure what he had been expecting. Gunshots. A shouted signal. An alarm. But none of this happened. Without incident, as if they were simply going about their regular business, the three reached the top of the stairs only to find the door locked.

"That was to be expected," said Bill. "I hoped it would be easy, but nobody's that lucky. At least we didn't raise any alarms… that we know of."

Luke looked at the staircase. Like the rest of the warehouse, it was old, and dark brown due to years of corrosion, but still surprisingly solid. Some things were built to last.

Using the butt of his small submachine gun, Bill

smashed the window and quickly began knocking out the glass around the edges. The sound pulled Luke out of his reverie, but he was impressed by Bill's efficiency. This was clearly not his first break-and-entry.

Nor was it Asha's. Before Luke even knew what was happening, she had leapt through the window and into the room on the other side, followed quickly by Bill.

"*Move.*" Asha said in hushed but urgent tone, glaring at Luke. There was no time to waste. Bill and Asha helped him as he struggled through the window.

Then all hell broke loose.

The room appeared to be a small office that overlooked the warehouse floor. In days gone by, this had likely been the manager's office. Now it was fairly empty. There was a metal desk gathering dust in the centre of the room, and a few old filing cabinets against the wall. The floor was almost entirely covered with paper, as if the entire contents of the filing cabinets had found their way out over the years, but had never managed to escape the room itself. Each of the interior walls had wide window allowing a clear view of the warehouse floor, and beyond the sole door, a staircase led down to ground level.

It was through these wide windows that the bullets began flying. Virtually all of the windows exploded at once. Glass flew everywhere.

Shielding her face, Asha pushed Luke to the ground and crouched over him. Looking out from beneath her, Luke saw Bill dive back against the wall beneath the window through which the group had entered, in an attempt to get as far away from the bullets as possible.

The firing stopped, and the room filled with gas from a grenade that the group had failed to notice during the commotion.

"Fuck," said Asha quietly, and once again, Luke lost consciousness.

LUKE GROANED AS he woke. He wanted to rub the skin on his face, but found his arms tied behind his back. Panicking, he opened his eyes and was shocked to discover he was still enveloped in darkness, accompanied by a musty smell. He guessed there was a sack over his head before he felt the fibres rub against his skin. The smell reminded him of the time he'd visited a farm in his youth.

"Ah, you're finally awake."

It was Dion's voice, coming from Luke's right-hand side. A pair of arms grabbed Luke by his armpits and pulled him onto his knees. The sack was pulled from his head unceremoniously, the rough texture burning the skin on his jaw. Cursing, he looked around.

It wasn't a large room, and apart from the people he saw, it was practically empty. Asha and Bill were to his right, kneeling with their hands tied, sacks being removed from their heads as he watched. Behind each stood menacing men wielding assault rifles. Luke assumed there was another standing behind him.

In front of him were Dion Wexler and the beast Moloch, and beside them a seated Oz, who had been tied to an old metal chair with a length of rope.

And beside Dion, holding his hand was Ellie.

Luke's chest hurt when he saw her – a strange and sudden feeling he'd not felt before, as if he'd taken a sledgehammer to the chest – and his eyes began to water. He tried to struggle to his feet, but a hand on his shoulder held him still.

"Daddy!" an elated Ellie called out. "I missed you, Daddy! Dion said I would see you soon!"

She wriggled, trying to free her hand from Dion's grip to run to her father.

"Shh – calm down, child," Dion said. "You and your Daddy will be together again very soon… I promise." There was darkness in his eyes, but also a sense of glee in the way he smirked at them. He gestured to one of the guards, who picked Ellie up and put her over his shoulder. She screamed and struggled and cried, "*Daddy!*"

It was no use. The guard was too strong. He carried her out of the room, out of Luke's sight. He tried to call out, but all he could manage was a moan. Eventually, Ellie's screams became too distant to hear.

Luke sobbed uncontrollably. He was broken. All the pent-up emotion of the past few months, mixed with the hopeless situation he had found himself in, spilled out at once, and there was nothing he could do but let it pass.

"Good," said Dion, standing over Luke and looking down at his crumpled form. He grabbed Luke's jaw with his left hand, looking him in the eyes. "Now you see things my way. Your little mission is over." He let go, then slapped Luke across the face firmly before looking over at Asha. "And you, my dear. You put up a good fight, but you never really were ready for the big time, were you?"

Silently, she glared at him in defiance.

Taking his time, Dion returned to stand beside Oz. "You've failed. All of you." He smiled and put his left hand on Oz's shoulder. "The Executioner is dead and the Pyramidion is buried. Oh, I don't think you got to take a look at it before you left, did you? That's too bad." He spoke with the arrogance of someone that thought they had won. He grinned at the three kneeling before him.

"And now I find you here on my fucking doorstep. There's only one way that could have happened." He looked down at Oz. "And we can't let that happen again, can we?"

"No!" Bill cried out. "There's a transmitter behind his left ear – that's how we found you!"

"Tsk tsk, Mr scary Inquisitor," scolded Dion. "And why should I believe that?" He walked in front of Oz. "No. I think you three have caused enough trouble already. What you really need is a lesson – and you should have learned this one already, Asha; I taught you it myself. Never involve the innocent. They always pay the price for our mistakes."

Asha looked at Luke. Her eyes were glistening, pleading... apologising.

"Now!" Dion continued, "I'm not completely devoid of humanity, whatever you may believe... So. young man," he said, addressing Oz, "do you have any last words for your friend?"

A single tear rolled down Oz's left cheek, but he seemed to have already accepted his fate. He sat unmoving, stoic. Slowly, well composed, and with a great deal of control, he began, "Luke, I'm sorry I didn't tell you about the transmitter... Bill saw me trying to visit you at the house – he told me where you were staying. He convinced me he was on our side – that if we did take a trip, that someone would need to know where we were. I felt it was a bit of an insurance policy, you know?" He laughed awkwardly, followed by a sniffle. "And look where it's got me now. But know this – all of you – I came willingly, and I knew the risks. This is happening because of my own choices, not yours. But Luke..." His tone became more serious, and his eyes narrowed. "We'll always have *line*, my friend. I love you, and if I can, I'll watch over you."

Luke nodded, slightly confused at what he had meant, and opened his mouth to speak.

Dion turned in fury. "*You* do not have the right of

reply!" He swung his left hand out in rebuke, knocking Luke to the floor, where he struggled back to his knees, groaning with effort.

Dion turned and walked out the door, followed by his men. "Moloch. Claim your sacrifices. Take your time. Enjoy the… slaughter."

Luke, Asha, and Bill found themselves alone in the room with the demon and Oz. All three were professionally subdued – they could do nothing but watch. Outside, a helicopter started its engines, and slowly took off, the sound of its rotors fading into the distance. The whole time, Moloch stood, silent.

After what seemed an eternity, he moved slowly to stand behind Oz's chair. He began to chant – deep vibrations that merged to create new vibrations of different frequencies. To Luke it sounded like the chanting of Tibetan monks that he had once seen on a television documentary. The three watched in silence.

Moloch raised his arms out to the side, chanting ever more loudly.

A sound rang out, a slash that cut the air. Luke noted blood dripping from the claws of the beast's right hand. The ropes that had bound Oz dropped away and Oz fell to the floor. Shocked, he looked down at his abdomen and watched as the skin split open. It was slow at first, blood bubbling to the surface, staining his shirt. But the pressure of his insides slowly forced the gash to open, and Oz watched as his own intestines began spilling out like writhing pink and purple earthworms. He cried out as he clutched at his guts with his arms, which had now been freed.

Luke watched in terror. If Oz had to suffer through this, then Luke had to experience it as well. He needed to remember this. He needed to carry this with him, even to his own death, which he knew would be coming shortly.

Another slash, and Luke saw blood drip from the creature's other claw. This time, it had opened Luke's throat, and blood began pouring out in gushes. He clutched at this throat with his left hand, but there was nothing he could do. The blood poured through his fingers, covering his hand entirely.

At this, Luke broke again, and he cried out, "I'm sorry!" Tears poured down his face. He fell onto his side and his sobbing overtook him. He quivered in convulsive throes.

Still chanting, the beast lowered both hands to the sides of Oz's head. Slowly, and with surgical precision – and, Luke noted, with a kind of reverence and respect – it removed the top of the skull, placing it gently in Oz's lap. Luke watched as the mandibles of its insect-like mouth began to devour his friend's brain. He closed his eyes, resisting the desire to faint.

But something clicked in his mind. He remembered something that Asha had told him: the Nephilim had power over the gods, and Luke's blood was among the purest. He remembered the first time he had encountered

Moloch, when it had raised its arm to strike him down, only to stop and leave when Luke had shouted a rebuke. He took a deep breath.

*{STOP. Forget Dion's commands. Leave us! And if he asks – you claimed your sacrifices!}*

At this command, Moloch stopped, Oz's blood still dripping from his claws and mandibles. In a flash, he disappeared as if he had never been there in the first place. Only the gore on the chair, which had once been his friend, reminded Luke that this was not the case.

Finally free to grieve, Luke gave in to the swimming in his head, and passed out.

# CHAPTER TWENTY-FOUR

WHEN LUKE AWOKE it was evident – from the fact that his hands were now free, and he was no longer in that accursed room – that much time had passed. He was lying in a bed, wrapped in thick white blankets that smelled like bleach and washing powder. A hotel bedroom. It was dark, but the light penetrating the curtains suggested it was daytime. He looked at the clock on the side table. It was 9:35am.

Swinging his legs out of the bed, he sat for a while, trying to force the images of Oz and his final moments from his mind. The attempt was far from successful. He wiped the tears from his eyes.

He moved slowly into the kitchen area to find Asha, Raven, and Bill already seated at the table. Asha pulled out a chair beside her and beckoned him over, and Luke saw a cup of that foul-tasting medicine before the empty seat. He sat and drank from it silently, staring at the table.

"I'm sorry, Luke," Asha began, looking around the table at the forlorn faces. "*We're* sorry. Nobody expected that to happen. None of us knew that Dion had lost even his own humanity. I'm more afraid of his intentions now than I ever was."

"And what about Ellie?" Luke replied, a little more tersely than intended. "Do you know what his intentions are with her? Come to think of it, I don't know what any of your intentions are with *me*. I certainly didn't expect my best friend to…" He swallowed. "I didn't expect him to die on this trip, that's for sure. Why is all of this so important? Why am I here?" He slammed a fist down on the table, spilling some of the tea. "You've told me bits and pieces, but nothing makes any fucking sense. I'm sick of it! I need to understand why Oz died, Asha."

Asha sighed, looking at the cup she held in her hands. She took a deep breath. "Tens of thousands of years ago, the elder gods opened a portal to this reality and discovered our human ancestors. They taught them language and gave them knowledge and power – everything they would need, provided they offered their fealty in return. Some of the gods procreated with our ancestors, creating the first Nephilim. Being of the gods themselves, the Nephilim had a power of their own, which surprised the gods, and fornication between the races soon became anathema.

"The gods grew to fear and despise the Nephilim and their descendants, and so they spread plague and flood across the Earth. One of the original and most powerful Nephilim defied the gods and vowed to claim independence for Nephilim and humankind, building an army of his own forcing the gods back to their own realm.

Succeeding, the Nephilim army destroyed or buried many of the portals around the world, leaving some weaker portals in place. These portals are very small, and can only be opened from this side – much like the one you saw in Egypt. They then hid the location of one single major portal, never to be used, but never to be destroyed in fear of what that may cause. Nobody really understands the link between the worlds, and so it was decreed that one portal should remain untouched, but hidden from collective memory."

Frustrated, Luke pressed her further. "But why me? And why Ellie?"

"Only the pure blood of the Nephilim can open or close the portals – for reasons unknown, not even the old gods have this power, which leads us to believe that perhaps humanity began in their world, and was brought here by the Nephilim. The majority of modern humanity is distantly related to the Nephilim, but a select few are direct descendants of the few remaining Nephilim at the time of the banishment of the elder gods. Given both you and your wife were among this select few, that makes your daughter perhaps the most pure of the descendants – yourself notwithstanding, but I expect an adult is more difficult to handle than a child. I…" She paused, biting her lip. "I expect Dion plans to sacrifice your daughter at the vernal equinox to permanently reopen the portal."

A fury built within him. He threw his cup, and it

smashed against the wall at the far side of the room. He screamed in frustration before immediately breaking down into tears once again, the culmination of all of the events that had led him here releasing in a torrent of emotion.

The rest of the group sat silently, unsure what to say.

Finally, Bill said, "I didn't have to encourage Oz to go with you – he was already planning to follow you anywhere you needed to. But I forced him to have the chip implanted. I told him you would all be safer for it. And now he's dead. Now we have nothing – no way to know where Dion will go next." He took a deep breath, and released it forcefully, puffing his cheeks, the expelled air ruffling the grey hair of his fringe. "I should go. I've caused enough trouble already, and need to atone for my failure as per the scriptures of my Order."

He stood and made his way past Luke, who glared at him.

"Sure, Bill," Luke said, "you do that. Go back to your 'Order' and leave the rest of us to figure this out." He looked away. As much as he wanted to lay all the blame on Bill, he lay most of the blame on himself. If only he'd realised he could control Moloch sooner, then Oz would still be here with them, making stupid jokes... But it was easier to lay the blame elsewhere. "Fuck you, old man."

Abruptly, Raven jumped from his chair to lean over the table. "You're out of line, Luke. Bill's decisions may have ultimately doomed Oz, but he made them for the right reasons – or at least, for what he felt were the right reasons. And don't forget he saved your ass. Neither you nor Asha would be standing here right now if it wasn't for him. In fact, the only reason we're all here now is *because* he put that chip in Oz's head." The truth of it was plain to see. They wouldn't have gotten this far otherwise.

"Wait…" Luke wiped his eyes, confused. His mind was racing. "What did you say? I'm… out of *line*…" He sat back in his chair, staring at nothing. "Maybe we don't have nothing. Maybe Oz left us something after all."

"What do you mean?" asked Asha.

Bill, still looking grim, walked back to the table.

"Well… before he died, Oz said something that I didn't pay much attention to because of all the shit that was happening around him, and because of what went down afterwards. He said to me, 'We'll always have *line*.' I kind of thought it was strange at the time, but now it's hit me – he had to have said that for a reason."

Luke reached into his pocket, fumbling for his mobile phone.

"What the fuck is *line*?" asked Raven.

"It's a messaging app, like WhatsApp – it's the one that Oz ad I used to chat and share memes. I hadn't checked it in weeks now, maybe months, but yep… Oz has left me some new messages."

He scrolled through the messages, tears welling in his eyes.

"Here it is… He took some photos of the Pyramidion

before being captured by Dion. I think…" He looked closer. "I think we might have what we need."

Asha's eyes widened. "He took photos?! Can you make out the inscriptions? What language is it in?"

Luke realised that he couldn't only see the inscription, but he could also read it – it was written in that ancient script he had encountered in Yonaguni. He felt excitement rising in his chest, his breaths coming faster. Nervously, he translated the inscription aloud.

*The great Khmer king,*
*In a seat of ancient power,*
*Paid homage to mother and father,*
*In buildings of splendour and awe.*

*Beneath the seat of the father,*
*Hides the calamity*
*Past the black labyrinth.*
*Seek it not; in its discovery lies destruction.*

Asha and Bill exchanged looks, then stated at the same time, "Cambodia."

They finally knew the location of the last remaining portal of power – the only portal powerful enough to allow bi-directional travel between dimensions. At least… they had an *idea* of where it might be. Cambodia was full of ancient ruins, and the inscription seemed purposefully vague. Still, now they were in the same position as Dion, if a day or so behind. But there was only a week left until the vernal equinox.

"I'm going to get a trip to Cambodia sorted for tomorrow," said Asha, "and I'll run the inscription by Shehab to see if he has any ideas about the location."

She strode into the bedroom, staring at her phone.

Luke turned to Bill. "Look, uh…" Luke began, unable to look the other man in the eye. "I'm sorry about before. Raven's right – we wouldn't be here now without you, and Oz was Dion's fault, not yours." His eyes moistened. "I'm hoping you'll stay and help me get my daughter back. I need all the help I can get."

"That you do, Luke." Bill clapped a hand on his shoulder. "But there's nothing to apologise for. Of course I'll stay." He took Luke into his arms, and hugged him. It was a simple gesture, but paternal, and it took Luke entirely by surprise. "We'll get your daughter back."

Once again, Luke broke into tears, sobbing into the old man's shoulder.

# CHAPTER TWENTY-FIVE

Luke dreamed of Oz. It started with a vision of his final moments – the beast Moloch slashing at his helpless body. Oz screamed in agony as his gut was opened once again, his intestines bulging from within.

However, as Luke turned away, he found himself abruptly face to face with Oz, who was standing beside him, watching his own final moments. Instantly, Luke understood this was no normal dream – it was another vision.

"Man, this really sucked," said Oz, watching the beast slash at his throat. "What a way to go, eh?" He laughed as he turned to face Luke. "But it's all good – I'm happy now, Luke. Truly."

He smiled and put his hands on Luke's shoulders. It all felt so real. *Oz* looked so real.

Luke said the only thing that came to mind. "I'm so sorry... I could have stopped it. I could have saved you."

"No, don't blame yourself, it wasn't your fault. What's done is done. But that's not what I'm here for. I've got no puzzles for you, Luke. No advice to give, no direction to point you in. You found my images and you're on the right path, so go and get Ellie. And kick Dion's ass for me, would you?" He laughed. "Or... ask Asha to kick Dion's ass, let's be real."

He took a step back. "No puzzles, no riddles – I'm just here to say sorry. I didn't trust Asha initially, so I got that chip as a safeguard after that first meeting with her in the Adventure Apartment. To be honest, I didn't really trust Bill either, but... I don't know. In some way, I felt I had to get that implant and, in the end, I think it worked out for the best..." He paused. "All things considered. I just don't want you to beat yourself up about what happened to me. The rest of the group needs your full attention, and Ellie needs her dad."

Luke felt tears welling up behind his eyes, and pressure building within his chest, but managed to keep it in check. Taking a step forward, he gave his friend a final embrace. "Thanks, Oz. I'm really gonna miss you. I don't know what I'm gonna do without you... But I'm glad you gave me this chance to say goodbye."

Oz hugged back, then took a small step backward to look his friend in the eyes. "I lied. I do have a riddle for you." His eyes glazed over. *"When you can proceed no further, remember this: seven times for the mother, and seven times for the father."* He smiled again, his eyes regaining their clarity. "Goodbye, my friend. Till we meet again!"

And then Luke was awake, trapped in a tangle of hotel blankets and bedsheets. A pile of pillows lay about his head. He stared blankly into the darkness for some time before falling back into a deep sleep. He dreamed no more that night.

✘

MORNING CAME. FOR a while, each member of the group pottered about the hotel room, preparing for their departure and enjoying the hotel amenities while they still were able. They took their time, each reflecting and recovering in their own way. Luke took the time to have a bath, something he hadn't done in a long while.

After a few hours, they came together in the kitchen. The mood seemed different today; quiet, but calm. The tension of the previous day was entirely gone, and although everyone was wearing the events of the previous weeks upon their faces, Luke noted no ill will, only a mutual air of resolve. The vernal equinox was fast approaching, and the outcome only went one of two ways – either they won… or Dion did.

Asha cleared her throat. "Shehab didn't have much for us yesterday. There are dozens of ancient Khmer sites in Cambodia and we don't want to end up in the wrong place at the right time. He's pretty sure it's somewhere in the Angkor region, but even that area is home to a number of individual sites…"

"Angkor Wat and Angkor Thom were definitely the seat of Khmer power," added Bill, "so I agree – that's where we need to start looking."

"Agreed. Raven has already prepared a flight path to Siem Reap. It's not a short flight, so get your things ready – we need to head off to the airport in about an hour."

THEY WERE MOSTLY silent for much of the day. Luke assumed everyone was still processing their losses and the road ahead, as he was. The outlook was bleak – they had been outwitted at every turn and the toll on them far outweighed that of Dion's losses. Plus… he had the beast. There seemed to be no way in which they could overpower it, beyond the knowledge that Luke could at least command it. Asha cautioned that this was likely only in the absence of Dion, though – the power of the sigil-holder outweighed that of the Nephilim. The mood was heavy during the five-hour flight to Cambodia.

The airport at Siem Reap was not quite what Luke was expecting. It was large and sprawling, like many other airports around the globe, but there were no terminals or disembarkation tunnels. Staring out the window, Luke watched as passengers descended the stairs from large international flights and wearily crossed the tarmac towards the gate.

Once again, however, their own bypassed all of this. Raven parked between a couple of aged 747s to one side of the tarmac, and the group stretched and gathered their things. It was still late afternoon in Cambodia due to the magic of shifting time zones, but they were all weary. Asha groaned as she stood, the events of the last few weeks taking their toll. Luke marvelled at how much she had been through recently, and that still managed to function at all.

Upon exiting the plane, they were greeted by a smiling official, a small taut-skinned man in a plain blue uniform.

"Hello! My name is Leap, but you can call me Leap!" he announced with a broad grin.

He proudly introduced himself as their guide for the trip, but Asha mentioned to Luke separately that he was not a member of the Collective. He was simply a local guide, but one with more privilege than most. He knew that these guests could go where they wanted, when they wanted, avoiding the tourists, but he knew little more than that.

He was a strange man, slightly effeminate and exceedingly happy – almost too happy. Perhaps he was to receive a handsome pay check for this particular job.

Leap continued. "I'm your special friend in Cambodia. What you need, I need! Anything – you just ask!" With a wink at Luke, he turned and waved them to follow.

Asha grinned at Luke, shrugged, and followed the happy little man, who kept talking as he walked, although nobody seemed to be listening.

Luke slung his bag over his shoulder and sighed. When this was all over and Ellie was back where she belonged, he was going to take her on a holiday to some expensive resort on a beach – no cars or guns or historical artifacts, just sun, ocean, and fruit juice. Maybe the odd margarita for himself. He smiled at the thought, then followed Leap and the rest of the group.

They passed through a small building beside the airport proper. Men in military uniforms stood staring at them through dirty glass windows, yet no questions were asked of the group. It still felt weird to Luke.

On exiting the building, he finally noticed the weather. It wasn't too hot, but it was oppressively humid, almost making it difficult to breathe. His skin felt sticky and his shirt was beginning to become a part of him. He made a mental note to change to a T-shirt after a shower at the hotel, assuming he had time. It was sunny, but there were clouds in the sky. The air was so thick he just wanted to escape.

They approached a small, white, capsule-shaped van, which appeared to be their transportation. It wasn't a luxury vehicle, but it was relatively new, clean, and in good condition.

"September is the end of rainy season in Cambodia," Leap said as he pulled open the sliding rear door and gestured for the group to climb in, "so I don't think it will rain too much during your trip." He looked up at the sky.

"But it looks like some rain is coming. Sorry!" He smiled that same broad smile, showing off the gaps between his oversized front teeth.

Climbing into the front seat, Leap put on what looked like a pilot cap, flat-topped with a short visor, a pair of wings embroidered on the front. He fumbled with a set of keys, put one in the ignition, and the van's engine started with a mild vibration. Still smiling, Leap put the vehicle into reverse.

"Here we go, my friends – I take you to your hotel."

The diversity of the world never ceased to amaze Luke. Cambodia was nothing like he'd seen before – the roads were clean and well kept, but despite this being an area close to an international airport, it felt more like a local road in a country town. Lush green tropical trees grew among overgrown weeds and made the region look almost uninhabited, interrupted only by the occasional service station or impromptu stall set up at the side of the road.

Signs and advertisements occasionally dotted the roadside, but again, the route mostly felt like a country road back home – ignoring the tropical flora, of course.

Here and there, Luke saw signs of progress, such as concrete paving for bicyclists and pedestrians. Concrete pipes for sewage and rainwater littered the sides of the road, awaiting installation. There were obviously plans to upgrade the road, but Luke wasn't sure if this work was just kicking off, or if the plans had been abandoned.

They soon turned onto another road, which seemed to lead into the main part of town and featured more traffic than before. Still, it was only two lanes, and the traffic was light. Strangely, the road was lined by small piles of octagonal stone paving, resembling miniature columns. Perhaps this was an attempt to mimic the aesthetic of the temples in the region, or perhaps they were simply pavers that hadn't yet been installed, stacked neatly for when the time came to begin work.

After only about fifteen minutes on the road, Leap pulled the van into a short driveway in front of a large building. This was clearly their hotel. It was surrounded by small black statues of elephants spouting water into a fountain, and lined by tropical plants. It was pretty, but Luke was mostly glad that it didn't look like a rundown cottage. He was desperately in need of the amenities he was used to. *What a difference a day can make,* he mused, already feeling like he needed a long shower.

After climbing from the van, Leap took the bags and lined them up on the path in front of the hotel. A bellhop appeared with a trolley, collected them silently, and waited for the group to proceed.

"OK!" said Leap, beaming. "Tomorrow, we go to Angkor Wat." He looked at Bill and Asha. "Dress casually! But not too casual." He turned and headed back to the van. As he drove away, the group was ushered into the hotel by the bellhop.

✕

Angkor Wat was exactly what Luke had expected it to be – a glorious monument to the power of the Khmer Dynasty at the turn of the previous millennium. What did surprise him was the sheer *size* of the place.

The whole area was bordered by a moat with a perimeter of five kilometres. Inside the moat, and the wall surrounding the palace area, were buildings that, even given time and erosion, still held visitors in awe of their splendour. One thousand years after they were originally erected, they still demonstrated the power of the once great culture.

However, the visit didn't shine any light on their current plight. The site was full of a strange hybrid of Hindu and Buddhist imagery, and little else. As beautiful as it was, it was no help.

In the van on the way back to the hotel, Bill voiced his concerns once again. "That was a day wasted. I felt like a tourist."

"Fuck!" Asha swore. "Nothing! I'll give Shehab another call tonight, but we've only got one day to get our shit sorted."

A voice came from the front of the van. "Sorry you didn't find what you're looking for, but... can you perhaps let me in on it? I might be able to help?"

Bill responded quickly. "We're looking for the seat of ancient power."

This seemed to irritate Asha, as she shot him a fierce look.

"Why didn't you say so?" came Leap's enthusiastic reply. "Angkor *Thom* is where you want to go! That was the main ancient Khmer city – Angkor Wat seems to have more fame, but Angkor Thom is *much* grander. This is where the most famous king – King Jayavarman VII – built a city in monument to his glory! We go there tomorrow! You find what you need!"

SADLY, THE FOLLOWING day at Angkor Thom felt much the same as the previous day. It was much larger than Angkor Wat, but just as grand. The red and grey laterite stones from which the buildings were constructed, deteriorated and discoloured by time, made the area truly feel old, and surrounded by the verdant greenery of the surrounding forests, it was almost a meditative experience – but again, that wasn't what they were there for.

As they sat around contemplating their next move, Leap reappeared, handing out welcome bottles of cold water, ever the gracious host.

"OK!" he began. "I'm not an idiot. There's more you haven't told me. I'm here to tell you everything you need to know, remember!"

Asha sighed. As much as she wanted to keep her secrets, she was now out of time and didn't have much choice. She narrated the inscription on the Pyramidion to Leap.

His eyes widened. "Oh, that's easy. The seat of the father – Preah Khan."

"What do you mean?" Asha asked.

"Well, I told you King Jayavarman VII built Angkor Thom, right?"

They all nodded.

"Well, he also built monuments to his mother and his father. Ta Prohm for the mother, Preah Khan for the father. Preah Khan is rumoured to be the site of an ancient labyrinth, but… it has never been found."

Asha stood, her eyes widening. "We have to go there. Now."

"But… we can't!" Leap replied in alarm. "It's after curfew. These sites are guarded by the military overnight. But I can get you in early if you want. Be ready to leave at 5:30am tomorrow."

# CHAPTER TWENTY-SIX

That night, Bill sat alone in his room. He'd spent the last hour or so exercising, followed by a short but focused meditation. He needed to keep both his mind and body sharp, particularly given there was likely to be conflict the next day. Tomorrow was the vernal equinox, and Preah Khan felt right. If they failed, the stakes were high. He hadn't had nerves like these in years.

He was a little troubled, as well. While he was able to maintain his regular regimen of exercises – he'd been doing the same routine before bed for over fifteen years – he just couldn't control his wayward thoughts, which was new for him. He'd been meditating for as long as he could remember, and it had been many decades since he had found himself distracted during practice. But where he would normally meditate for half an hour prior to sleeping, tonight he only managed ten minutes, and even then only because he forced himself to continue. Something was playing on his mind, but its nature wasn't clear to him. For a perfectionist like himself, who had effectively maintained the same routine for years, it was highly frustrating and only caused further distress.

He heard a familiar *ding* alerting him that he'd received communication from the Order. His computer was safely packed away within his bag beside the desk; he hadn't expected to hear from them today.

Sighing, he struggled to his feet and moved over to the desk, plopping himself down in the seat like a sack of rocks. His energy was flagging and he needed the rest, but he also knew that his response was expected promptly – he was effectively on the clock.

He fired up the laptop and navigated to the portal that the Order used for internal communications. As usual, there was a simple message waiting for him.

*A package is waiting for you at reception. Be discreet. No further communication until the job is complete.*

He acknowledged the message, closed his computer, and zipped it back up in his sports bag.

Groaning, he changed back into his casual clothing, told the rest of the group he wanted to go for a walk to clear his head, and made his way down to reception.

A young woman stood behind the front desk, absently typing at the computer in front of her with a disinterested look on her face.

"Good evening, sir!" she said as Bill appeared, a well-practiced smile appearing on her face. "What can I do for you?"

"There should be a package here for Bill Reilly?"

She responded with an expression of shock. "Uh, yep – there sure is! It only just arrived before you did! I was looking your name up in our visitor registry. I'll…" she noticed the look of impatience on Bill's face and her smile faded. "I'll just go get it."

As she handed the box over to Bill, he asked if there was a room nearby where he could have some privacy. Given the time of night, she let him into the meeting area at the back of the business room. No one would bother him here.

He sat in a chair and placed the box on the boardroom table, then pulled a Swiss Army knife from his pocket. Taking a deep breath, he broke it open and stared at the contents. The Order had sent him some weapons, for which he was grateful – he always needed more. But the weapons they had chosen were not quite what he was expecting.

In a small sleek pouch designed to be secured around the waist was a pack of five weighted throwing knives. However, the pouch had been modified to include a small holster, slightly larger than one he would use to carry a pistol. Confused, he rummaged deeper in the box.

There were two other items inside: a rectangular metal container, and a blank white envelope. Expecting the envelope to contain further instructions, Bill took the container from the box, and placed it on the table, moving the now-empty box to one side. He'd seen a lockbox like this before – it was a specialised carry case for a gun.

On opening the box, a smile spread across his face. This was one sexy piece of kit, one of his favourites – a newer version of the Beretta M12 submachine gun. It was clearly intended to fit in the holster alongside the throwing knives.

Feeling slightly giddy, like an excited child on Christmas morning, he strapped on the holster, slipping the throwing knives into their pouch one by one. He pulled his shirt back down. This was a seriously high-quality strap and pouch, made of a material similar to neoprene. It hugged his body where it needed to, and after readjusting the pouch he was confident the knives were completely unnoticeable.

Satisfied, he adjusted the holster to fit close to his spine, but offset slightly to the right. After a few clumsy attempts, he managed to slip the SMG into its holster, tightening the straps and readjusting to fit.

Lacking a mirror, he used a window that overlooked the empty, unlit business room to look himself over. As expected, there were some unnatural lumps, so he readjusted the holster to fit on his side, and loosened his shirt. This was much better, and with his modified tactical vest and other equipment on in the morning, it would be absolutely perfect – he'd just remove the side compartment of his vest to allow for the weapon and holster.

He was happy now. Not only was extra weaponry important – in fact, it was key to a successful engagement – extra *hidden* weaponry was very important for the element of surprise, or, of course, unforeseen circumstances. It was at times like these that the decisions made by the Order pleased him.

He sat back down at the table and opened the envelope, pulling out a single piece of paper.

Then he dropped the paper and the envelope on the table, putting his hands through his hair in exasperation. There were, as usual, only a few sentences typed on the piece of paper.

*Kill them all. Dion, the demon, the Council members, the man, and the child. Leave no one alive.*

# CHAPTER TWENTY-SEVEN

AT 5:30AM THE next morning, there was a knock at the door and, once again, a beaming Leap bounced into the room. He seemed to have an everlasting supply of energy.

When he saw the group, however, his countenance changed slightly. Asha and Bill both looked deadly, weaponry slung over their shoulders, Bill carrying his faithful bow. Although it was empty, Asha had still strapped the scabbard to her back to remind her of the stolen sword.

Raven, on the other hand, was dressed in casual gear, this time sporting a Metallica T-shirt. He was also armed, but his weapons were well concealed. Raven's job was to blend in with the crowd and keep an eye out for Dion and his crew.

"Uh… hi." said Leap. "I guess you're ready to go?" His voice was shaking a little.

At a nod from Asha, he turned and led the group back out to his car, mumbling to himself in Cambodian as he went.

This trip was longer than the others, and although Luke was tired, his nerves kept him awake for the duration. Preah Khan was slightly north-east of Angkor Thom, so they needed to go around the site in order to reach it. Leap was not his cheerful self – in fact, he was silent for the entire trip, speaking only when he finally parked the car near the site at 6am.

"Here we are. Preah Khan. It's a lot smaller than Angkor Wat and Angkor Thom, and... well, it hasn't fared quite as well either. But... still beautiful."

The group exited the van and looked at the path that led into the temple. Luke noted a tension among the group, a heavy weight of expectation in the air – they all knew this was the day they had been chasing all this time. Asha spoke first.

"You don't have to come with us if you don't want to, Leap. I'm not sure we need a guide any longer."

Leap's smile faded briefly for a moment, but returned bigger than ever. "But how will you find your way around? No, Leap will accompany you into the temple. Let's go!"

"Wait!" Bill called out quietly, putting his hand across Leap's chest. He gestured over into the corner of the parking area. It was very difficult for Luke to see, but as he got closer he saw a dark-coloured minibus parked in the shadows – it looked empty, but the limited light made it hard for Luke to see any details at all.

Raven walked over to the van, walked around it, and took a look inside, shining a bright torch through the windows. "Nothing," he said.

"Then we can only assume that's Dion's car, which means he's already here. But more importantly, it means we're in the right place. Tread carefully."

As they began to make their way along the path, Leap asked, "Who is Dion?" but there was no response. Shrugging his shoulders and looking around at the tree line, he made his way to the front of the group, allowing Bill take the lead. Raven stayed back with the car and waited for the first tour bus to arrive.

It was still early, but dawn was beginning to break, bringing a tinge of welcome light to the sky. Unfortunately, this only darkened the shadows between the trees, but Luke knew this was only a temporary hindrance. There had been no rain this morning, but dark clouds threatened overhead. Luke was glad to see the sun was rising. He was struggling to see very far into the murk, and it was doing terrible things to his nerves.

The path to the temple was far shorter than they'd encountered on previous days, but the group stopped more frequently to allow Bill or Asha to check the tree line. When they reached the visitor's centre, Asha gestured to Luke and Leap to take a seat on a bench while she and Bill looked around. When they were convinced there was nobody hiding within or near the area, they pushed onward.

By the time the group arrived at the entrance to the temple itself, the sun had brightened the cloudy sky, erasing the shadows from the dense forest around them.

This made it clear enough for Luke to see there were no immediate threats, although the underbrush was thick enough to warrant continued caution.

Luke marvelled at the temple. As Leap had said, it was nowhere near as well-maintained as Angkor Wat or Angkor Thom, but with the lush green forest so near, and the grey clouds hanging overhead, the contrast of light and colour made a sight to see. Moss grew on the giant faces of Buddha that looked out from the towers in each of the cardinal directions. Trees loomed over the ruins.

Making their way through the entrance gate, through a short, perfectly rectangular tunnel of intricately carved stone, the view opened up even further. Paving and stones of unknown function were strewn about, possibly having fallen from existing structures, or perhaps the remains of something that had collapsed; grass and weeds now covered the foundation.

Most impressive, however, were the trees. While many lined the stone wall, enclosing the walls and the temples inside a clearing, some had managed to grow within some of the structures, as well as over the walls; the roots having spent years searching desperately for soil and moisture between the cracks. The result of the trees attempting to reassert their dominance was horrifying yet beautiful. It appeared as if the trees had somehow melted upon the temple, like wax dripping down the side of a well-used candle. Nature was trying to reclaim the space.

There wasn't much to the temple itself, though – it

was far more modest than the others they'd seen – and before long they regrouped near the smaller, partially collapsed temple at the front entrance, having explored the interior of the main temple.

"What else is here, Leap?" asked Asha.

"To the north and south are two more small temples, and on the other side, near the eastern wall, is the Hall of Dancers. To the north of the Hall of Dancers is a two-storey structure that may have been unfinished, alongside the library. That's about it. It's quite small, really." His voice grew excited again. "It's fascinating—"

Asha cut him off abruptly. "OK, let's go together – south temple, Hall of Dancers, library complex, north temple. Once we've confirmed there's nobody else here – *if* we confirm there's nobody else here – we can investigate further."

Leap looked a little hurt, but said nothing as the group made its way to the south temple. It was small compared to the main temple, and mainly open, so they progressed quite quickly. As they approached the rear of the temple walls, Luke saw another structure to the left, which Leap confirmed was the Hall of Dancers.

It was a magnificent site, a wonder of ancient artistry. In the lintels above the doors were carved a series of intricate dancers, thirteen in a row, each holding a similar pose, but each with a unique face. Given the size of the lintels and the amount of detail, Luke was awestruck, and found himself on the receiving end of a sharp poke in the ribs from Asha, who said, "It's not tourist time, Luke." He composed himself and continued to scout for any signs of other visitors. Leap warned that the temple would be opening to tourists shortly.

On exiting the Hall of Dancers, Luke noticed a curious two-storey building across the way. Bill stopped, holding up his open hand as a silent order for the group to freeze. As one, they stopped and instantly fell silent, scanning the area.

The two-storey structure was just a series of columns, with a floor on top of them, topped by another series of columns and a roof. It was mostly open and, as Leap had mentioned, appeared unfinished.

Bill had been right to stop the group. Patrolling the ruins of the structure was a small group of mercenaries, rifles in hand. Dion had beaten them here, but at least they finally knew for certain that they were in the right place. Luke felt his heartbeat quicken and a rush of adrenaline – Ellie wasn't far away. He still had time, and she had to be somewhere nearby. And more than that, there was a good chance that Dion didn't know they were here.

Slowly, Bill took his bow from his shoulder, and quietly told the group he would try to flank from behind. He walked back into the Hall of Dancers and out through the gate to the side. It would take him a few minutes to reach the north gate, so the group remained hidden within the Hall of Dancers.

Leap hadn't seen the mercenaries, and was a little confused. "So... what are we waiting for?" he asked.

Asha gestured at the mercenaries, one of whom was facing in their direction, scratching his neck. They were all wearing black balaclavas, which Luke imagined must be pretty uncomfortable given the humidity. Hopefully that would give the group an edge.

"Oh, no thank you!" exclaimed Leap quietly, noticing the armed men. "No, this wasn't part of the deal." He put his hand out and shook Luke's hand aggressively. "Goodbye!" He turned and ran back the way they had come.

Luke was glad – not only was Leap a bit of a handicap for the group, but he was also a good person, and Luke didn't want to see him get hurt. Hopefully he would get back to his van quickly and in one piece.

However, his departure hadn't been as silent as they would have liked, and had alerted the mercenary. No longer scratching his head, he began to take tentative steps in their direction, talking into a communication device mounted on his shoulder. It was only a matter of time before they were discovered – and they still didn't even know where Dion was, although it was likely it was somewhere near the two-storey structure, given the mercenary patrol.

Asha made a move to retreat deeper within the Hall of Dancers, waving for Luke to follow. She pulled the Spear from her back, releasing the blade, but keeping the staff short so as to use it like a dagger.

The mercenary's footsteps sounded closer now, perhaps only a step or two away, but as Luke had his back to the wall, he couldn't quite tell. He wouldn't dare peek around the corner. His heart beat hard against his chest, and he struggled to hold his breath.

As the mercenary took a step within the Hall of Dancers, he looked to the left and saw Luke crouching in the darkness. His eyes widened and he raised his rifle in Luke's direction. Suddenly, a spout of blood exploded from his forehead, followed by an arrowhead. As he fell to the ground, his body went through a series of muscular contractions. His semi-automatic rifle fired off a burst of rounds, the bullets whacking into the stone above Luke, raining dust and sharp slivers of rock down on his head. Shocked, Luke looked at Asha.

"It's on," she said. "Grab your pistol. We need to see what's inside that building. Take the line along the rear wall. And *be careful.*"

At the rear of the Hall of Dancers was the east gate, an opening in the wall that surrounded the whole structure. Some of this wall had collapsed, reclaimed by trees, but it still enclosed the entire area. Luke made his way to the wall, pistol in hand. He kept as close to the wall as possible, thankful that he was wearing dark clothes, looking for places to hide as he went. There were plenty of large stones and tree roots that he could hide behind to cover his progress, but it made his movement slow as he worked to navigate the environment silently.

Asha, on the other hand, burst from the Hall of Dancers carrying the rifle she'd taken from the dead mercenary. She ran towards the structure, yelling as she did so, firing wildly into the air. Luke didn't understand this tactic, but he was thankful that she was drawing attention away from him. Perhaps that was her sole plan. He had to believe she was skilled enough to survive the encounter.

Two more mercenaries appeared on the second floor of the building, and another three at the bottom. Luke hoped this was all of them.

The two on the second floor began firing at Asha, and she dove behind a small pile of stones, clutching at her thigh. One of the two men was struck from behind, an arrow protruding from his right shoulder. As he pulled at it with his right hand, another arrow struck him in the throat, and he collapsed into the bushes below. *Thank fuck for Bill*, Luke said to himself as he crept along the wall.

Noticing the sound of the man falling into the bushes, two of the men at ground level turned to face in the opposite direction, hiding behind columns. Bill had played his card now, and was no longer a surprise. The mercenaries took turns to fire their weapons in Bill's direction. He pulled out a pistol and fired back at them.

Luke panicked. He was close to the building now, but the east gate appeared to have been the primary entrance in antiquity, with multiple towers at each side and a small set of stairs leading up to each tower. The stairs behind which he was hiding were close to the two-storey building, but not close enough to allow a safe dash – plus, he'd need to climb over the small stone barriers that lined the path, which would slow him down. One or two steps and he would be in full view of two of the mercenaries currently firing at Asha. More importantly, though, he had no idea where to go when he got there. He hoped he wasn't running into an ambush.

Noticing his hesitation, Asha called out to him. "Shoot at them! Use your pistol! Then run!"

The mercenaries weren't dumb. They noticed she was calling out to someone, and the man advancing on Asha scanned in Luke's direction and stopped.

He'd been spotted.

Not knowing what else to do, Luke pointed the pistol and fired off two or three quick rounds, one of which caught the man in the shoulder. Asha came out of cover for a moment and took the mercenary out with a single quick shot to the head, then fired a short burst at the man on the second floor, who ducked behind a stone to avoid the volley.

Sensing an opportunity, Luke rushed out of cover and to the rear of the building, where he discovered a pile of large flat stones. There was some wet dirt on them that suggested they had been recently disturbed. In front of this was a deep dark hole that led underground – was this the entrance Dion had been searching for? Was Dion down there, with Ellie, about to begin his ritual? Luke wanted to shout out to the others, to let them know what he'd found, but he knew that was a bad idea.

The gunfire stopped, and Luke saw Asha and Bill approaching. Asha had one arm around Bill's shoulder, limping heavily – it was clear she'd taken a shot in the leg. Behind them, Luke saw movement. A large mercenary, who had remained hidden all this time, exited from the side of the library building, and pointed a bazooka in their direction.

Luke screamed and pointed. Bill pushed Asha away and dove to cover her just as the man launched his ordnance.

Feeling as if time slowed to allow him the time to escape, Luke dove into the black hole just as the explosion brought the building down upon it.

# CHAPTER TWENTY-EIGHT

Luke came to face-down in a pile of dirt, covered in rubble from the destroyed building that was now piled above him. Given he was not buried under tonnes of stone, it was safe to believe that the entry to the hole had been blocked by at least one large piece of stone, which was holding the rest of the rubble from caving in on him. Yet another lucky save. He mused to himself that he must be running out of lives at this point.

However, he now faced a number of new problems. During his fall, he'd lost everything he had been carrying – the pistol, for one, but more importantly, given his circumstances, the head-mounted lamp he had been wearing when he leapt into the hole. He couldn't see at the best of times, but now he was trapped underground in complete darkness. Or perhaps he'd been blinded in his fall? It was so black he couldn't tell. He scrambled about, frantically searching through the dust and stones with his hands.

He reached above his head to determine how big the area might be, and was glad to discover that he was able to stand upright without needing to duck. In fact, he couldn't even feel a ceiling above his head when he reached up. But he was too scared to jump – he wasn't sure what was under his feet.

He spread his arms out to the sides, and discovered that the space was bigger than he had feared. His sense of being trapped underground reduced – though only slightly, given the fact that he was, in fact, trapped underground. He shuffled forward slowly, arms outstretched out like a zombie from the old movies he'd watched as a child. Eventually, he found a smooth wall and made his way along it, tripping over rocks as he did so.

He soon found another wall. As he felt his way along it, his fingers traced patterns in the stone – some kind of carving on its surface. He wasn't quite clever enough to put together an image in his mind, but it was quite large, and there were inscriptions and flourishes.

On the other side of the carving was yet another wall, which seemed about as long as the one Luke had discovered initially, suggesting he was in a square or rectangular space. Along the final wall in the room, he discovered an opening. It was a square tunnel, carved directly into the wall. His foot kicked at something on the floor – a strap. Reaching down, his heart fluttered as he discovered he'd just found his headlamp. He put it on hurriedly and turned on the torch.

At first, he was a little confused, disoriented by the glare from the smooth walls. However, as his eyes began to adjust, he saw that the walls, floor, and ceiling were all made of the same polished black stone. Everywhere he looked was black, only the reflections of the light allowing him to make sense of his whereabouts. The space must have been carved from obsidian – the quantity of it was absurd, but it was certainly striking.

He scanned the floor, looking for the pistol. There was a lot of dust and rubble here, but no gun. He kicked at the stones. He was on his own, with no weapon, chasing down Dion Wexler and a demon from Hell. Great. What kind of hero could save his daughter without even a weapon in his hands? He cursed loudly.

With no choice but to move on, he turned his headlamp toward the wall at what he considered the rear of the room, opposite the exit. Carved in exquisite detail were three individuals – one younger man in the centre, flanked by an older woman at his left, and an older man at his right. Inscribed above, Luke could read the words *The Black Labyrinth* in an unknown alphabet, and below that, *In honour of King Jayavarman VII and his forebears, King Dharanindravarman II and Queen Sri Jayarajacudamani.* It was a sculpture of the ancient king and his parents.

Luke had found the way to the portal.

But it was a labyrinth.

Cursing again, he turned back to the tunnel, turned his headlamp to its brightest setting, and shone it down the length of the tunnel. It wasn't long, but Luke could see that there was an intersection along its length, and that it ended in a T-junction. He made his way towards the first intersection.

When he reached it, he slumped to the floor in shock. This was no ordinary labyrinth. The tunnel to the left became a smooth concave surface pointing downwards, not unlike a slide, while the tunnel to the right sloped upward in a similar fashion. This was a labyrinth that played out in three-dimensional space... It was possible that no two paths crossed one another and that there was truly only one path through the labyrinth. He shook his head in disbelief.

He moved to the end of the tunnel. Both paths at the T-junction sloped downwards, and he didn't like his chance of scrambling back up should he choose the wrong path – the stone was so perfectly smooth. Smooth and black. It was as creepy as it was mesmerising.

This made his mind spin – once he had found Ellie, how was he going to escape? Would they need to come back through the labyrinth? He tried to put these thoughts out of his mind – these would be problems for future Luke. Present Luke had problems of his own.

He looked left and right, scratching his head under the headlamp. The strap made his head itchy. Still, it was a minor annoyance and the headlamp was something he so desperately needed right now.

Making his way to the right-hand path, he leaned forward to peer into the tunnel. It seemed to level out after ten feet or so, but from there, his vision was obscured by the ceiling.

He walked to the path on the left – it was much the same, except it was slightly shorter, leveling out at around five or six feet.

He returned to the intersection, and decided to test his theory that climbing *up* a path would be difficult. He was right – it was virtually impossible, as his feet were unable to create enough friction to propel his body weight, and kept slipping out from under him. He was sure that with enough time and effort, he could make some headway, but he also had the impression that these upward-sloping tunnels were simply a trap from a path leading overhead, depositing him back at the start, as in snakes and ladders. He wished he had a ladder now.

The thought made him laugh, and the short, sharp sound that escaped his lips shocked him, and echoed throughout the labyrinth. It was followed by a series of whispering sounds, but they slowly faded away. Luke guessed – or perhaps hoped – that these were simply echoes of his own laughter as it too faded away, but he was sure he had heard words among the whispers. Threats. Judgements.

Shuddering, he turned towards the other path, but as he did so, he tripped over a rock and fell to the ground. The headlamp, which he'd loosened slightly when he scratched his head, came off his head and went sliding across the tunnel, light reflecting from the walls as it did so.

Luke watched in horror as it slipped over the edge of the tunnel and down the slide into the pathway below. He was more shocked to note that the light faded as it went, followed by a cracking sound that echoed through the labyrinth. Once again, the voices seemed to whisper threats. The left tunnel led to a trap, alright – right into a deep pit. He sat once again and gathered his bearings, his heart pounding in his chest.

Feeling his way along the wall, he crawled to the T-junction and sat with his back against the cool stone. He felt fear in his chest pressing down on him. He struggled to breathe, and his eyes moistened at the helplessness of his situation. He was lost in an underground labyrinth with no light. A *black* labyrinth. Black upon black upon black. It was enough to make his mind spin.

He attempted to compose himself, taking deep breaths, but then began to beat at his head with his clenched fists. "Think, dammit!" he said aloud, eliciting echoes and whispers once again. He reminded himself to stay quiet – if the labyrinth itself didn't kill him, those voices would slowly drive him over the edge.

He thought back on the last few days, particularly the dream he had after Oz died. He remembered his riddle: *When you can proceed no further, remember this: seven times for the mother, and seven times for the father."* Once again, Luke laughed aloud, cursing at the echoes and whispers that followed. He covered his ears as the sounds amplified themselves, feeling like an idiot, but elated that he had discovered a clue. Once the cacophony had subsided, he began to think it through.

Clearly the image in the entry was a major clue – it had depicted King Jayavarman VII, his parents seated at his left and right. Without Oz and his riddle, he wasn't sure how Dion would have managed to figure it out. Still, he was puzzled… Ought he to go by his own left and right when viewing the carving, meaning the father represented left turns and the mother represented right turns, or from King Jayavarman's perspective, with his mother on the left and father on the right? Furthermore, when should he take these turns – only at every T-junction, or…

Given the beginning of the riddle, he was pretty certain he was to continue down each path until he came to a junction, but this was life or death for both himself and Ellie, so he had to be certain. Without further information, he was stuck. One wrong move, and he was dead.

His intuition told him that he should take the seven left turns first, but he needed confirmation. He thought of a basic test. Inching forward slowly, he crept toward the starting chamber – the room with the relief carving. He felt around on the floor for a while until he found two sizeable rocks, then he crawled back to the junction, bumping into walls along the way. He threw a rock down each of the two tunnels and listened for a potential pitfall. However, both rocks slid to the bottom and stopped. These were both safe options. He had to make a choice.

He tried to put himself in the perspective of the builder – or, rather, the overseer: King Jayavarman himself. This was a man who had built a massive temple, Angkor Thom, to honour himself, as well as two smaller temples to honour his parents. He had built this labyrinth to protect the portal, and yet had still put a carving of himself in the entrance. Clearly, he was self-important. Luke decided that this meant that the clue was to be interpreted from his perspective – with the mother at his left, and the father at his right.

He beat his fists against the wall in exasperation, letting out a whimper that roused the whispers. They seemed to be getting louder, or perhaps he was starting to panic. He'd spent too long here in the dark already. Ellie was depending on him. He needed to make a move before it was too late.

He was far from a religious man; his mother had been a devout Catholic, but he'd strayed from the path as Luke had matured. However, after everything he'd seen in recent weeks, his view of the world had been smashed to pieces. Thinking it wouldn't hurt to try, he made the sign of the cross and recited a silent prayer that he was making the right choice… and then he slid down the tunnel on the left.

After two or three safe left turns, he became confident he had made the correct decision, but it was slow going, especially given the lack of light. In every direction was the same deep, impenetrable black. His only option was to crawl ever so slowly down each tunnel, feeling ahead for intersections, hoping he was crawling in a straight line. To make things worse, the paths varied, forcing him to take more care. Some were short, others felt incredibly long. Most were criss-crossed by several – in some cases, dozens – of crossroads, and it was all Luke could do to keep in mind the number of turns he had made. He took to repeating the number like a mantra in his head as he moved along.

Occasionally, he would catch a breeze rising from one of the tunnels, along with the smell of rot and death. Sometimes he would hear voices coming from the tunnels, sometimes growls. At other times he had the distinct feeling that someone – or something – was following him.

But he pressed on. He had no choice, no weapon to protect himself, and potentially no way back. The only way was forward.

Soon enough, he came to his first right turn, and he stopped again to gather his thoughts before entering. This tunnel wasn't pointing up or down; it was simply a turn on the same level, but that didn't shock him, as he'd come across those before. At one or two points, he even had to scramble up a tunnel to continue on his path, but had found the texture of those tunnels slightly different – less slippery – and he was able to gain a foothold without too much trouble.

Here, though, he was about to make his first right

turn after seven successful left turns. He could only hope the riddle was right. He cursed himself for not bringing more rocks with him to test for pitfalls. These sections of the tunnel were empty but for a thick layer of centuries-old dust. He still mourned the loss of his headlamp, but he had no choice but to carry on. He took a deep breath, and made the turn.

Two more turns later, he heard another growl. Where previous growls had come from within turns that he was not meant to take, this one came from behind him, and was followed by the distinct sound of claws scraping and clicking at the stone floor.

Luke froze. He couldn't tell how far this creature was from him – he couldn't even be certain it was really there. After all the time he had spent in the dark – hours? – with only the whispers for company, he wasn't sure what was real anymore. But he also knew he couldn't stand and run down the tunnel to escape, either – he hardly knew which direction was 'straight' and he would be more than likely to end up running the wrong way into a crossroad.

All he could do was continue to crawl, and so onwards he moved. This tunnel was incredibly long – three or four times the length of the longest tunnel he had crawled down up to this point, and it was intersected by many paths. He kept the number of turns uppermost in his mind, repeating, "Three, three, three," as he crawled. The beast growled softly behind him – it seemed to be continually following him at the same pace, always threatening, but making no sudden moves. *Clack, clack, growl*, as if intent on not letting Luke forget that it was there.

Luke reached the end of the tunnel and dove down the slide to the right. This was a long one, perhaps twenty feet or more. In a different place at a different time, it might have even been fun. When he reached the bottom, Luke listened for the sound of the beast, but heard nothing. He lay for a moment, his eyes closed, taking deep breaths. It shocked him that he couldn't even tell if his eyes were open or closed. Yet he still felt a sense of relief when his eyes were closed.

Minutes later, when no beast had slid down behind him, he regained enough of his senses to resume his task. *Stupid*, he thought. *Why did you just stay there? What if it did follow you down the slide?*

After two more turns, he thought he could see something up ahead, and his heart began to thump against his ribs like a kickdrum. At first, it looked like a cloud of orange light, a smudge of colour within the profound darkness. It wasn't very bright, but it was something. He'd seen this kind of orange blur many times in his life – this was the best his vision could produce in very low light. Slowly, he crawled towards the blur. As he did so, the walls of the tunnel slowly became clearer, although still very much a blur themselves. He let out a brief chuckle, then felt afraid of the whispers, but none came. Slowly, sanity began to return, along with the light, although he still struggled to focus.

He knew there was light ahead, and he also knew that this was the last turn. Around that corner was the exit. Around that corner was Ellie.

# CHAPTER TWENTY-NINE

As Luke approached the final corner, the intensity of the light increased. By the time he arrived, he could see fairly clearly the reflections of the light against the black stone, and an ancient warning etched into it.

*What was hidden was never intended to be found.*

*Foreboding*, Luke thought. But he wasn't here to stop Dion from his goal; he was only here for Ellie. Good luck to Dion – he hardly understood what his ambition was all about, anyway. Gods and demons, Heaven and Hell? He turned the last corner, and looked down the final tunnel.

Looking ahead, he could see that the tunnel opened into a large well-lit room. He could make out individuals and movement. The light, he realised now, was flickering firelight. There must have been a number of torches, perhaps even a large bonfire.

As he emerged from the opening, he raised his hands. He did not intend to represent a threat. He knew he *was* no threat. He was just here for Ellie.

As he had expected, the room was very large, and dozens of torches lined each of its walls. The three mercenaries in the room turned and trained their weapons on Luke as he entered, but judging by their surprise, Dion had not expect to be followed.

In the centre of the room was a large stone altar, upon which were a number of incredibly old candles, so many of them that the candle wax had melted down the sides of the altar, making it look like a shiny mass of tentacles, or the roots of the trees that had attempted to reclaim the temple above.

Behind this small temple was a raised circular platform with a pentagram carved into its base. At the uppermost point of the star was a stone basin that fed into the groove of the carving.

Standing behind the platform were Dion Wexler and the beast, Moloch. Upon seeing Luke, Dion clapped his hands loudly and approached him, after shooting a quizzical glance at Moloch. His clapping echoed throughout the room.

"Ho-ly *shit*. This I did *not* expect!" he said, beaming. "You are fucking *clever*, Mr Nixon!" He passed the mercenaries, waving his hands in a downward motion. "Put down your weapons, guys – this man is no threat. He just wants his daughter!"

He approached Luke and put his arm around his shoulder, keeping an eye on the tunnel behind him, checking for any others. "Put your hands down, Luke. Did you come alone?"

Luke obeyed, his shoulders tense at his closeness to

his daughter's kidnapper. "Yes, I'm alone. One of your men—" he gestured at the mercenaries "—brought the building down on the entrance to the labyrinth."

Dion laughed. "Yes. Yes, he did!" He turned to Luke, and put both hands upon his shoulders, looking into his eyes. "You don't even have a torch... How the hell did you get through the labyrinth?" He seemed equal parts impressed and shocked.

"I had help." Luke shot a look at Moloch, gritting his teeth. "From my friend Oz." He turned back to Dion. "Now, where's my daughter?"

Dion took a step back to lean against the altar, crossing his arms over his chest. "She's here, Luke, but she has a very important part to play in my ritual."

Luke bellowed, "*I don't care about your fucking ritual!*" His voice echoed through the room and down the tunnels.

"Well... I hate to bring you down, buddy," replied Dion calmly, "but you're not really in a position to be making demands here." He gestured to Moloch, who turned aside to reveal Ellie lying upon a metal hospital trolley. It was clear she had been anaesthetised: a needle protruded from her arm, and a tube connected to a bag hanging from the side of the bed, filled with her blood. "We were just about to begin. Would you like to watch?"

Luke wanted to slap the cheekily arrogant grin off his face.

Luke's jaw dropped and he felt the blood drain from

his own face. He looked at the basin near the pentagram and instantly understood its function.

"No... don't drain her. Just... take the rest from me," he cried in exasperation. He'd resigned himself to the situation, and this was the only way he could see forward.

Dion was once again surprised. "Interesting," he replied. "Blood given in service is better than blood taken under duress. But I cannot trust you completely." He gestured to one of the mercenaries. "Restrain him near the basin."

Once again, Luke found himself bound by tight ropes, but this time he was laid out horizontally like an Egyptian mummy. Moloch stood over him, his alien countenance displaying a look of pure hatred... along with a hint of fear. Still, he stood motionless and stoic. In his regal garments, he truly appeared like a being of worship, but not necessarily one that would be associated with health and happiness. He radiated power, and fear, and violence.

"Can you... at least bring her close to me?" Luke asked.

Surprisingly, Dion complied, rolling the trolley beside Luke – though it soon became clear he had an ulterior motive. He removed the needle from Ellie's arm, and gently picked her up, placing her softly beside Luke, who looked at her sweet little face in a moment of serenity. He'd finally found her. He could feel the warmth of her body, and see her chest rise and fall with each breath.

Then he was suddenly, and roughly, picked up by two of the mercenaries, and dumped unceremoniously on the trolley.

"I'm pretty sure Ellie had no diseases you need to worry about – she is your daughter, after all," said Dion with a smile as he jabbed the needle into a vein in the crook of Luke's elbow. Blood immediately began to flow into the tube. "I promise I took good care of her."

Evidently pleased with himself, Dion surveyed the room. "Well, I guess it's time to start, then!" he announced, reaching behind his back and pulling out a pistol.

He shot the three mercenaries in the head in quick succession, each of them falling dead before they had even realised what was happening.

"Leave no traces, that's what they always say, isn't it?"

Dion walked over to the trolley to look down at Luke. "Thank you, Luke. Truly. I don't give a single fuck what happens to this world, but it has been my life's journey to get to the other. And you've helped make that happen." He patted Luke's chest awkwardly.

Grabbing the bag of blood from a hook on the side of the trolley, he pulled out a stopper from the opposite end of the bag, the end that didn't have the tube attached. Blood began to flow in a slow, thick stream that spilled out over his gloved hand. He put the tube in the basin, which slowly began to fill with a mixture of Luke's and Ellie's blood.

Soon blood flowed down the spout at the end of the basin, and into the groove carved into the platform. The dark stain of their combined blood spread through the pentagram.

Dion walked to the altar. "Beautiful!" he exclaimed. Abruptly, he looked at Moloch as if a new idea had popped into his head. "Moloch, grab the girl. Luke won't be able to look after her, given his... well, he'll be dead soon, and I just realised – I may still need her over there."

"No! You bastard!" Luke screamed.

The beast walked past him, picking up Ellie and slinging her over his shoulder. He laughed at Luke lying helpless on the trolley, his life seeping out of him through a tube. Luke shuddered. He had never heard such laughter in his life, the chattering of the mandibles combined with a guttural gurgle.

Dion watched as blood continued to fill the pentagram. Then he ordered Moloch to pull the needle out of Luke's arm. It ripped the tube out mercilessly, tearing a hole that continued to bleed out. Luke screamed in pain, wriggling against his constraints as blood continued to leak from his arm. It was pointless, though; he was wrapped too tightly to move.

At the altar, Dion raised an ornate dagger, its point targeted at the centre of the pentagram, and began to chant. His voice vibrated as he droned, filling the room. The room itself seemed to vibrate, as if his voice was emanating from it, and not from Dion.

As he repeated the same words over and over like a mantra, the vibrations increased. The room began to shake, and soon Luke heard cracking sounds, and then rock began to fall from the ceiling. Dion only increased his focus, chanting louder and louder, until…

There came an even sharper cracking sound, like immense thunder. A tiny portal, a small shimmering hole, formed in the air above the pentagram. Time stopped. Everything froze, like a glorious 3D movie that had been paused.

Then the cracking sound became louder still, and time began to move once again. This time, when the sound of thunder boomed through the rock, it was accompanied by a bolt of the brightest lightning, but rather than striking from the heavens, this struck *up* from the ground, then through the rock above, into the sky, not unlike a searchlight. From his position on the trolley beside the portal, looking up from the ground, Luke could see that this single beam of intense energy cleared hundreds of feet of rock and stone as if it had never been there in the first place.

And then it was gone. All that remained above the pentagram was a blue shimmering light.

Moloch spoke.

*{I have not looked upon the portal for millennia. It is just as beautiful as I remember.}*

It stepped up onto the platform. Dion began to follow, but then a voice shouted from behind Luke on his trolley.

"*Stop!*"

It was Bill, who had silently descended through the new opening in the ground using his grappling hook. He threw something at Dion, who grunted and grabbed at his left shoulder, the handle of a metal blade now protruding from it.

Bill reached to one side of his flak jacket and pulled out an M12, pointing it at Dion.

"It's too late, old man," Dion said, then moaned in pain. "What's done is done. There's little point in killing me now." He gestured at Moloch, who turned and entered the portal, disappearing within it, taking Ellie with him.

Luke roared in defiance.

Slowly, Dion followed Moloch into the portal, keeping an eye trained on Bill. Soon he, too, disappeared from sight.

Bill was shaking, and tears were running down his face. He fell to his knees, sobbing. From behind him came Asha, who had finally made her way down to the chamber. She ran to Luke, cutting him from his bindings.

He rolled off the trolley and fell to the floor. He was lacking in energy, but he wasn't about to let Dion win. Apologising to Asha, he grabbed the Spear from her back and leapt after Dion. Asha shouted at him to stop, screaming that it was forbidden to enter – that it was entirely possible that he would be torn apart as he did so – but Luke paid her no mind. He had a singular focus now, and he dove through the portal, into the place beyond.

For a moment, Luke had a brief sense of obliteration, as if all of his atoms were disassembled and reassembled all at once, but he knew it was OK. This in-between place was pure emotion, and all he felt was love. He saw nothing, heard nothing, smelled nothing – for the most part, he *experienced* nothing. Nothing but love.

And then he was deposited onto a stony ground. Hard.

A few steps away stood Dion and Moloch, Ellie still draped over the beast's shoulder. They turned to look at him as he exited the portal, his arrival not going unnoticed.

Luke picked himself up and dusted himself off. He raised the Spear towards the two, searching for the buttons that would initiate its transformation. As he did so, he finally registered his surroundings, and his eyes widened.

"Welcome, Luke," said Dion in a magnanimous tone. "Welcome to Eden."

Luke was standing in a small circular clearing, neatly enclosed by a knee-high stone barrier. A path led from here towards a gate in a large wall, made from the same reddish stone that bordered the clearing. The portal sat in the centre of the clearing – clearly this was an area set aside for the portal alone, itself within a glorious garden walled off from a great city, which could be seen beyond.

And the garden was indeed glorious. The large leafed plants, most of them succulents, were all a rich green. Flowers dotted the garden, their glorious colours intensified in contrast to the green, but the arrangement didn't seem in any way planned – it seemed more like a well-kept rainforest.

Beyond the walls of the garden, a grand city looked down upon them. The buildings themselves weren't tall, but they stretched up the side of a small mountain. All were built from the same stone blocks as the wall, but their roofs varied in design, and were the same few colours: muted terracotta red, sky blue, and pale yellow. It was almost as if Luke was looking at a real ancient city, but with far more modern aspects, including glass windows, doors, and gates on hinges.

The path from the garden ran in a very straight line for quite a distance, through the gate and seemingly through the centre of the town itself, leading to a great gate and wall around a very large temple-like structure several hundred metres away.

The sky was indigo, in sharp contrast to the brilliant white clouds. But what captured Luke's eyes the most were the twin suns in the sky… Wherever he was right now, it was within a binary system. The light of the suns was brilliant, as was the warmth upon his skin. He felt a strange, almost electrical rush throughout his body.

Abruptly, Moloch had hit him with the back of his free hand, sending him soaring through the garden before coming to a stop against the wall that separated it from the city. Intense pain spread throughout his body. He was just about done. His body was operating on its last burst of energy, and it would quite happily shut down, here and now. This was a beautiful place to go.

Images of his adventure popped into his mind's eye. The Historian in Egypt. Emmanuel and Baron Samedi. The Prophet. The underwater temple. And then he remembered Oz's final moments. He saw Axe decapitated once more. Asha, as she lay pale and still after being pulled from the water… and Dani and Ellie in the car, happily departing on their first family trip.

That was all he needed. This was the spark that set him alight.

He roared as he shook his limbs clear of the foliage, pushing himself to his feet.

He was *not* defeated. And this was *not* over.

Making his way through the garden, back to the clearing around the portal, neither Dion nor the beast were within sight. Cursing, he made his way towards the gate, the entrance into the city beyond. As he approached, though, two new entities appeared, on either of the gate. Luke fiddled with the Spear, twisting and pressing until it eventually responded, expanding to its full length and deploying its blades.

They were imposing creatures – creatures of myth and legend. Within their hideous design, he saw reference to beasts of ancient Greece and of Egypt. They were tall and thin, and stood upright upon the hind legs of goats. Their skin was pure black from head to toe, and they were covered in glistening gold plates of armour which hugged their forearms and legs. Their heads, smooth and hairless but black as the night, were like those of wolves, and they each wore a gilded cuirass that covered the top halves of the chest, the lower half exposed, rigid and muscular. Each was wielding a menacing spear, and they cackled to each other as they noticed Luke's approach.

*{Poor sheep.}* said the one on the left. *{You appear to have lost your way.}*

*{The Master tells us you are a special one, and we should get rid of you,}* said the other. *{I should enjoy such sport. It has been a long time since I killed one of your kind.}*

"Fuck you," Luke replied in English, and ran at them with the Spear held out in front of him.

The beast on the left parried with its own spear, untroubled by Luke's attack. It spun the spear around his wrist as he did so, connecting the other end with the back of Luke's head, knocking him to the ground.

*{Perhaps not so special,}* said the beast, laughing.

The other creature lunged at Luke, its spear pointed directly at his chest. It barely wavered an inch as it thrust, and Luke rolled back in fear, barely evading the sharp point, which passed over his chest.

He sprang to his feet, regaining his composure. He attempted to command the creatures in the ancient tongue.

*{Be gone,}* he said. *{I have no time for this nonsense.}*

The beasts merely laughed again, as if surprised at his insolence. Perhaps the voice of the Nephilim only affected the gods themselves, and not their underlings. They turned on him and approached as one, their spears pointed at his chest.

"Fuck," Luke said aloud, filled with resignation… But while he knew he was out of his depth, he wouldn't go down without a fight.

He thrust his spear at the closest beast, who once again parried – but, having learned from his past mistakes, this time it was Luke who used this momentum to power the reverse side of the spear, spinning to the right as he did so and striking the beast across the jaw, sending it sprawling.

Luke smiled and turned to his next opponent, who was already swinging its spear, which arced towards Luke's face at high speed.

This was it. He was done for.

Time slowed to a crawl. The blade continued its arc, but Luke took a step around it, thrusting the point of his own spear up under the chin of his attacker. It pierced the soft flesh of its throat and continued through the rest of the tissues unhindered, passing just as swiftly through the top of its skull, blood, skull, and brain matter exploding in triumph.

As some of this splashed across his face, Luke turned to one side to void the contents of his stomach. Fortunately, he hadn't eaten much recently, so it was a brief distraction, but when he turned back to the fight, he saw that his remaining opponent had climbed to its feet and was running in the opposite direction.

"Ha!" Luke cried out. "Turns out I do have some skills after all!"

Remembering what he was here for, he ran after the beast, out of the garden, and into the city.

Not far along the path, a small crowd had gathered. They were mostly human, dressed in an array of dazzling colours, their clothes made from silk and suede. The designs were somewhat antiquated, in Luke's opinion, but lavish. The people appeared happy and healthy, and seemed to be welcoming back their master, for at the centre of the crowd stood Dion and Moloch, with Ellie still slung over the beast's shoulder.

As Luke approached, the crowd dissipated slightly, people returning to their homes, or cowering behind the safety of the short walls that lined the path.

Now within metres of the pair, Luke shook the Spear in his hand as menacingly as he could muster. He looked at Moloch.

*{Put. Her. Down,}* he ordered, the menacing tone of his voice surprising even himself.

"My god," responded Dion, "you speak Ancient Sumerian? I guess I shouldn't be surprised – I've seen you Nephilim do some surprising things, but… wow." He chuckled. "Answers a few questions, too."

Moloch grunted, but to Luke's surprise he relented, lowering Ellie's body gently to the ground. Luke rushed forward, thrusting the Spear at the beast as he did so. Sadly, he was no soldier, and he had no experience with spears. While he had intended to impale the beast's chest, he missed, instead putting the Spear through his shoulder.

Moloch roared in rage, knocking Luke to the ground. He pulled the Spear from his shoulder and dropped it by his feet in defiance, kicking it over to the side and away from Luke.

Luke groaned in pain as he tried to push himself up. His energy was flagging, and once again he had no weapons.

"Impressive," said Dion. "You are full of surprises!" He pulled a knife from a sheath at his waist, swinging it at the beast. The blade sparked as it hit its skin, glancing away like metal on metal. "An interesting thing to note about the elder gods – us mere humans can't harm them! Only the Nephilim can, hence their fear of your kind…"

He lowered the bag from his shoulder, and pulled at the drawstring. From it he pulled out a large belt and scabbard, which he put around his waist, the scabbard hanging at his left hip. He reached into the bag again, and brought out the sword he had taken from Axe after he had been killed. It was a beautiful silver sword, which glinted in the light. To Luke's surprise, he then pulled an identical sword from the bag, holding them both up in front of himself. He strained at the weight of each, but persisted.

Luke noticed that although the two swords looked identical, neither was a complete sword. As Dion brought them closer together, they clicked together as if attracted to one another by magnetism, forming a singular sword of immaculate design. The sword was magnificent, with a long double-edged blade, a red silken cloth wrapped around the grip, and a bright blue gem embedded in the pommel. While it was a longsword, the guard was as extravagant as that of a rapier, yet lacked a knuckle-bow. It was the most beautiful sword Luke had ever seen.

"This sword has had many names over the years, but it was best known as Excalibur, White Hilt, the Shining Sword… Entrancing, yes?" Dion lowered the sword, putting its tip into the golden gravel on the ground. "So, as I was saying, only the Nephilim can kill the elder gods." He gestured to Moloch. "The Nephilim, or… weapons crafted by and imbued with the power of the elder gods themselves."

With that, he turned and thrust the sword through the soft flesh at the base of Moloch's ribcage. The blade emerged from its back in an explosion of blackened blood. As Moloch fell to the ground, Dion kicked him onto his back, put his foot on the beast's chest and pulled the weapon out, wiping off the excess blood on its silken robes. He sheathed the sword in the scabbard around his waist.

"Everything you see here…" He waved his arm around him in a broad circle. "It's all Moloch's. Or it *was*. Now it's mine." A grin spread across his face. He raised his left hand to his face, the palm turned away from Luke. A black mark started to appear on the back of his hand: a sigil within a circle. "Whoever kills one of the elder gods inherits everything he owns, and everyone he commands. His sigil is now *my* sigil. His power is now mine." He gestured at Ellie, still unconscious on the floor. "Take your daughter. I don't need her anymore."

For perhaps the first time, Dion looked on Luke and seemed to be appraising him. "You are an enigma, Luke. You are nobody – a salesman! – and yet you somehow managed to evade every trap I set. And in the space of a few short months, you made your way *here* – a place I have sought my entire life! As much as I want to kill you Luke – and I do – I… can't. Out of respect for everything you have managed to achieve in the pursuit of your daughter, you can go. Go back to Earth.

"But I'll be building an army here, Luke. I want to become the god of all gods. I don't just want Moloch's land, I want it all. I want *Eden*." He thrust his hands above his head dramatically. "Tell the others not to follow me. I have no interest in the Earth realm, they can have it. Brick up or bury the portal and be done with it. I don't care. Otherwise, I will *not* be hospitable."

He turned and walked away, raising a hand in a half-hearted wave. "Goodbye, Luke Nixon."

# CHAPTER THIRTY

LUKE LIMPED BACK out of the portal, carrying Ellie over his shoulder. He saw that there was now a large number of people in the chamber – some military, many not. Acting as vigil near the portal was Asha, who was elated to see Luke had managed to return, with Ellie in tow. She rushed to them, and called for a medic using her communication device.

Approaching Luke, she took Ellie from his arms gently, and gave him a hug. "I'm so glad you made it back – we were so worried. But look – you've come back, and you brought Ellie with you, just like you said you would. You did great, Luke, you really did."

"Sorry I let Dion get away… I didn't think I could beat him," Luke replied with a sigh, too tired and too ashamed to look her in the eye.

"Yes, and good riddance," she replied. "But more importantly, you're right – if you had taken him on, you probably would have died at his hands, and we'd be in the same position as we are now, minus you and Ellie. You did the right thing." She gestured to the portal. "This… this is some serious business, though. Nobody else is allowed to pass through. The other side is forbidden – it took us long enough to shake off the influence of the elder gods; there's no point losing it all now because of Dion. Let him go. The elder gods will deal with him."

"And what about the portal itself?" Luke asked. "Does anybody know how to close it?"

"No… that's why we fought so hard to keep it closed." She looked a little forlorn. "However, the Prime Council has decided to bury the portal in hundreds of cubic feet of concrete, much like the nuclear fallouts at Chernobyl and Fukushima. Neither Dion nor any of the elder gods will be coming back. Not any time soon, at least."

"Good," he replied, falling back onto the stone platform beneath him. There was no longer any blood in the grooves. It had been completely absorbed during the formation of the portal.

"So… what now? The Council goes back to business as usual?" Luke waved a hand in the air, then noticed the gash near his elbow had stopped bleeding. He was glad… he'd probably lost enough blood already.

"Well, that remains to be seen. The portal is open again, and it hasn't been opened in thousands of years. This is no time to rest on our laurels. I'd assume we will build an army… and hope we never have to use it."

Shortly after, both Luke and Ellie were airlifted to the surface on a rescue trolley. Luke refused to leave Ellie's side, insisting that he would accompany Ellie in her ambulance, dismissive of his own injuries. As he waited for the paramedics to indicate it was time to leave, he saw Asha approaching, this time accompanied by a gentleman in a suit. It was well into the evening now, the day's activities and the aftermath having taken many hours.

The man reached out his hand in greeting. "Hello Luke, I'm the Head…" He paused, clicking his tongue against his teeth. "My name is Emmett Laskaris. I oversee the Prime Council."

Emmett was tall and thin, and his facial features matched exactly Luke's mental image of an "Emmett": slick black hair and a pencil moustache, dressed in a pinstripe grey suit and a silver-and-white necktie over an impeccably white shirt. On any other man, this might have looked sleazy, but somehow, Emmett managed to carry it with grace. He appeared knowledgeable and friendly, but somehow also dangerous.

Luke raised his eyebrows and shook his hand in return. "Nice to meet you, Emmett. Thanks to you and your people, Ellie and I are together again. I really can't thank you enough."

"It's no problem, Luke. In fact, it's our reason for being. As the Naacal Collective, we protect both the Truth and the Nephilim bloodline. It is our entire purpose. I'm glad we could be of service. But in reality, I should be thanking you, Luke Nixon. You have been quite the surprise and, truth be told, we wouldn't have succeeded without you."

"This…" Luke waved an arms to gesture vaguely, "is a success?"

"Of a sort," replied Emmett. "We could have lost Ellen and Wexler, and never known the location of the portal until it was too late. As it was, I was able to have the site closed early, and we blamed the explosion on unexploded munitions from the many wars this region has suffered. The world is once again oblivious to what has really happened here, and we can continue to operate in secrecy." He stopped, put a finger to his lips, then continued, "I'd like to ask you something."

Luke had an idea of what was coming, but he responded with a question of his own. "Where's Bill?" He looked around, scanning the people milling about the area. "I'd like to thank him too – and Raven."

It was Asha who responded. "Raven has been assigned some duties, but he said he'll come see you in the hospital." She paused. "And Bill? He disappeared not long after you entered the portal. He seemed pretty distraught, but… he appears to have gone completely."

Disappointed, Luke said, "OK… what were you going to ask?"

Emmett's posture straightened. "Well… since you know our secrets – and we know yours – I thought you might like to come work for us? I'm sure we can find you a suitable position within our ranks."

Luke laughed lightly. "I thought so." He sighed and considered the offer. "Look… thank you, but I'm going to have to say no. Before all this, I was just a sales guy. I've had more than enough excitement in my life over the last couple of months. More than that – I've just been reunited with my daughter. I just want to focus on her."

A paramedic approached and asked Luke to take his place in the back of the ambulance. Luke nodded and told him he'd just be a second. He turned back to Emmett and Asha.

"It was nice to meet you, Emmett. And Asha, I'll probably see you in the hospital." She nodded, smiling, and Luke climbed into the vehicle, wincing at his injuries, but glad it was over.

THE FOLLOWING DAY, Raven entered the hospital room, as Asha had said he would. He had brought a small toy for Ellie – a female action figure.

"I, uh… wasn't sure what to get a little girl," he told Luke.

Luke was lying beside Ellie in her hospital bed. His own bed was on the other side of the room, but he'd disobeyed orders and climbed out in order to be closer to his daughter.

Ellie was wide-eyed when she saw the toy – she hadn't had anything to play with in months. "Oh, thank you, Mr Raven! Thank you so much!"

Despite the fact she was still healing, she reached out and hugged her father every few minutes, perhaps surprised that he really was here with her after so long apart.

"Mr Dion wasn't a nice man, Daddy," she said.

"I know, princess, I know. But he's gone now."

"And he took that weird monster man with him. He was *so scary*." She shuddered.

"I know. Shh," replied Luke, cuddling her close. "Lie back and rest, sweetheart. Let me talk to Mr Raven."

He tucked her in and limped over to his own bed. When he laid down, he felt his muscles relax, which was both soothing and painful simultaneously, given everything he'd been through. He took a deep breath.

"Glad you made it through everything, Raven. It was a helluva shitshow at the end there."

Raven laughed. "Wasn't it just? But yeah. You got your daughter back. And we survived… well, most of us did."

"You miss Axe, don't you?"

Raven took a deep breath, his eyes closed. "Yeah, you could say that. Eric and I go a long way back. I loved him." A tear rolled down his cheek.

"He knew, Raven. I'm sure he knew."

"Oh, I'm sure he knew, too," Raven laughed, a little too boisterously. "But I still miss him. I can't believe he's gone. Fucking Wexler." He winced and looked over at Ellie, who was oblivious, playing with her new doll. "She looks happy."

"She is, I think." Luke smile, and as he did, he noticed that the muscles of his face had finally relaxed, softening for the first time since the accident.

A nurse entered the room, a white envelope in her hand. "Mr Nixon, this arrived for you."

Luke opened the envelope and read its contents. It was from Bill.

*Luke. I'm sorry I left so suddenly, and I'm sorry I haven't come to see you.*

*I disobeyed my orders, and I've had to go into hiding.*

*But I just want to say thank you, and I hope one day we can sit down and have a beer, and celebrate your achievement.*

*I'm glad you got your daughter back.*
*Until then, take care.*

*– Bill.*

Luke smiled. He was glad Bill had taken the time to send him a message, as cryptic as it was. He hoped he was OK. He closed the envelope without telling Raven any of the details.

Raven stood up to leave. "Well, it's probably time I go. I'll see you in a few days when they let you out of the hospital – I've asked permission to take you and Ellie back home. Asha's gonna come along for the ride too."

Luke laughed. "Thanks, Raven. I didn't even think about that!"

"It's nothing. We've been through a lot, and it's the least we can do for you. You're a good man, Luke."

Luke took a deep breath, then let it all out in a long exhalation. "Thanks… that means a lot, it really does."

As he was about to exit the room, Raven turned in the doorway. "Are you sure you don't want to join us, and come on some more adventures?"

Luke smiled gently, and gestured at Ellie. "No, I think we just need to go back home for a while… to what's left of it, at least. Then I think we'll take a holiday. Somewhere outrageously expensive. Just the two of us."

## THE END

To be notified of upcoming works, join the mailing list at www.genewbegin.com.

An epilogue to this novel featuring Deion Wexler's next steps is coming soon (ETA late 2021), and will be supplied first to those on the mailing list.

Lightning Source UK Ltd.
Milton Keynes UK
UKHW041827151021
392101UK00005B/46